INTOXICATION

Anne looked at Deveraux with apprehension. He had drunk too much—and Deveraux drunk was even more dangerous than Deveraux sober.

"Alas, my flask is empty, or else we'd share it," he told her.

"I should decline," she said. "The last wine I had from my cousin was drugged."

"Drugged wine?" he said. "Fordyce displayed a shocking lack of address. I have never had to resort to such measures to seduce a female." A smile played at the corners of his mouth. "Never."

"Really, sir, but this is most improper," Anne protested.

"I told you—I'm not a very proper fellow, Miss Morland," Deveraux said, meeting her eyes with a gaze more potent than the strongest liquor . . . .

ANITA MILLS resides on a small acreage in rural Missouri with her husband Larry, eight cats, and two dogs. A former teacher of history and English, she has turned a lifelong passion for both into a writing career.

THE ROGUE'S RETURN

Anita Mills

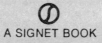

A SIGNET BOOK

SIGNET
Published by the Penguin Group
Penguin Books USA Inc., 375 Hudson Street,
New York, New York, 10014, U.S.A.
Penguin Books Ltd, 27 Wrights Lane, London W8 5TZ, England
Penguin Books Australia Ltd, Ringwood, Victoria, Australia
Penguin Books Canada Ltd, 10 Alcorn Avenue, Toronto, Ontario, Canada M4V 3B2
Penguin Books (N.Z.) Ltd, 182-190 Wairau Road,
Auckland 10, New Zealand

Penguin Books Ltd, Registered Offices:
Harmondsworth, Middlesex, England

First published by Signet, an imprint of New American Library,
a division of Penguin Books USA Inc.

First Printing, June, 1992

10 9 8 7 6 5 4 3 2 1

*This book is
dedicated to my friend
Sue Hughes*

1

Throbbing consciousness returned slowly, painfully at first, then with it came the memory of her abduction. Lying very still upon the wrinkled, mildewed bedcover, Anne Morland tried to think. Judging by the raucous sounds coming from what was apparently a taproom below, Quentin Fordyce had brought her to an inn of the worst sort, and as the distinct briny, fish odor of the room nearly overwhelmed her, she guessed it must surely be wharfside. Did he mean to carry her out of the country? And why? Not for even a moment did she believe his protestations of undying devotion to her. The foul taste of the drug rose in her mouth, forcing her to swallow.

Suppressing a groan from the ache in her head, she opened her eyes cautiously, just enough to escape notice, and looked through the veil of her lashes. The room was dimly lit by a cresset lamp that smoked badly, adding to the tawdriness of stained, cracked plaster walls. Above her the rain pelted the roof, and water seeped from the ceiling, dripping onto the bed beside her. A flash of lightning illuminated the figure of a man sprawled in a chair, a glass in his hand. As the clap of thunder followed, he set it down and rose impatiently to stand over her.

"Curst rain," he muttered. "I'd thought to be aboard ere now, but there's no sailing in this." For a moment he stared downward, then reached to touch her shoulder, stroking it. "Passably pretty—give you that. Ain't going to mind this by half."

To her horror, he sank down onto the bed beside her and leaned to whisper thickly above her ear, "No need to wait for the fun, is there? Marry you in France anyway."

Stale wine soured his breath, nearly gagging her, and yet she was afraid to move, to betray that she was awake. But as his hand slipped lower to the small buttons at the nape of her neck, she stiffened, then rolled for the side of the bed. As he grabbed awkwardly for her, she managed to gain her feet and back away. Pain shot through her head, and the room reeled about her. For an instant she feared she would retch violently. She wiped her mouth as she retreated from her drunken cousin.

"No need to be missish, Anne, for I mean to wed you," he coaxed thickly, following her.

"You drugged me, Quentin!" she spat at him. "You knew I would not come otherwise! You never intended to take me to my grandfather's!"

"Will," he promised. "When we get back. Wedding trip to France first, then go beard the old man. Come back as Mrs. Quentin Fordyce, and he'll want to see you." As he spoke, he moved closer. "You'll like it—you'll see."

"I'd as lief marry a toad!" she shouted defiantly. Her heart thumping with the fear she tried to hide, she cast about for the means to escape and saw none. He was between her and the door. "You'll let me go, else I shall scream for someone to fetch the constable—do you hear me, Quentin? I shall scream loudly enough to bring this rackety roof down! I have no intention of going to France or anywhere else with you—not now, not ever!"

Despite her angry words, he smiled smugly. "Ain't nowhere to go, Miss Morland. For one thing, Mrs. Philbrook won't welcome you back—ruined, don't you know? And for another, you'd best hold your tongue, for there ain't anybody downstairs as you'd want to encounter, I can tell you. Ought to be grateful, I mean to marry you."

"You ought to be clapped up in Bedlam!"

Again he narrowed the distance between them. "Show you I ain't half bad as a husband—be nice to me, and we'll trip along tolerably well. Make the old man happy even."

"To think I trusted you—to think I welcomed you as my cousin," she muttered bitterly, backing up against the rough stone of the empty fireplace. "You, sir, are the blackest scoundrel of my acquaintance!"

"Told you—my intentions are honorable enough," he protested, cornering her. "Ain't as if you was likely to get another offer anyway, is it? And when you are married to me, your grandpapa ain't going to cavil about your mama anymore. Make him forget she was an opera dancer."

"Opera *singer*," she said, shrinking away from him. "Mama was the toast of the Continent before she met Papa. And her family was as respectable as the Morlands, if you want the truth of it."

"Didn't come to talk about any of 'em," he murmured, leaning into her. "Pretty Annie Morland. I ain't going to repine," he added.

"Touch me, and I'll—"

Her words died as he caught her and bent her head back, forcing his kiss on her lips. She struggled, pushing at him as his insistent tongue darted between her teeth. Furious, she bit down hard, tasting salt. His hand caught in her hair, pulling it, but he raised his head to howl in pain.

"Ow! You little witch! What'd you do that for? Serve you right if I didn't wed you!" With his free hand he wiped his mouth. For a moment he stared at the blood on it. "Damned vixen—that's what you are."

"Mr. Fordyce—Quentin—if you do not unhand me this instant, I'll have you arrested. You cannot abduct a female in England!"

"Told you, this ain't the kind of place where anybody'd care if I was to throttle you," he reminded her sarcastically. "Come on, be a good girl. When the deed's done, when the knot's tied all right and tight—teach you to like it."

Once again he bent his face to hers, and the wine on his breath nearly overwhelmed her. As his wet lips touched her mouth, she sagged in his arms. He staggered from the sudden shift of her weight, and she was able to feel for the iron poker behind her. Her fingers closed over it, and she brought it up, prong end out against the inside of his leg. He jumped back, releasing her, and she darted, poker in hand, for the door, but not quickly enough.

He caught her viciously, pulling her by the sleeve of her gown, growling, "Try that again and I *will* throttle you— half a mind to do it anyway—d'you hear me? Now . . ." The cloth of her gown gave way, baring her shoulder and the zona beneath. As she turned toward him, he leered at the swell of her breasts. His free hand reached to touch the zona. "I'm going to like taming you. I'm—"

She raised the poker and brought it down with as much force as she could muster, striking a glancing blow against his neck. His ardor forgotten, he jerked her around furiously, shaking her, shouting, "Drop it, damn you, drop it!"

For answer, she twisted free beneath his arms, and struck again, this time catching him squarely on the temple. His eyes widened in surprise, then his body seemed to fold like a marionette, and he fell at her feet, hitting his forehead against a chair leg. She stood over him, poker raised, waiting for him to rise. He did not move. For a time she waited, thinking he perhaps feigned unconsciousness, but his face was ashen in the faint, flickering light. Another bolt of lightning lit the room briefly, followed by a crash of thunder that shook the floor beneath him, and still he lay there.

Gingerly she bent down and touched him with her free hand. "Mr. Fordyce . . . Quentin . . ." Getting no response she pinched his cheek hard. He did not even flinch. She dropped to the floor and leaned over him, listening for his breath, hearing nothing. Panicked, she stared at his inert body. Had she killed him? She began pummeling him, hoping for some sign of life, until it became apparent that he would not respond; then she sank back on her haunches. She had to get help—she had to get help. But where? How?

Would any believe that she'd been defending her honor? She glanced at her torn gown, seeking reassurance, then considered how it must appear to a magistrate—opera singer's daughter murders peer's son, claiming he intended ravishment. When she told that he'd attempted to force her into marriage, a jury would laugh in her face—before they convicted her of killing him. For who would believe that he

had abducted an unwilling indigent female? And Mrs. Philbrook would be certain to say that he'd called but twice,
probably out of curiosity, and then only to claim he was her
cousin on the side of the family that denied her very
existence. No, she'd be branded a scheming adventuress, and
there'd be none to defend her.

The wind and rain came down harder, rattling the window,
and the water dripped steadily from several places in the
ceiling. A sense of utter helplessless descended over her. She
was alone in some wharfside pigsty, she knew not where,
and when discovered, she would be charged with Quentin
Fordyce's murder. Unless someone had seen him carry her
in. Unless someone could swear she'd been drugged.

She heard the stairs creak and the floorboards groan as
someone came down the hallway outside. She rose and
hurried to crack the door, then drew back. A lantern's yellow
light caught the face of a reeling fellow she'd not want to
meet anywhere, and then another door opened close by.

"Wishful fer a tumble, air ye, dearie?" a female voice
asked him. "Ain't a fit night ter be alone, is it?"

No, she could expect no aid there. Instead, she listened
as the man and woman haggled briefly before he disappeared
inside. Dispirited, Anne stood there considering whether to
throw herself on the mercy of the innkeeper. But if what she'd
just seen was indicative of his custom, she feared the
constable was the lesser threat. She would give Quentin
Fordyce a little longer and hope he revived somehow. But
if he did not regain consciousness, she would have to do
something. She returned to kneel over her cousin's body,
listening again for some sign that he lived, but the raging
storm drowned out everything except the pounding of her
own heart. Finally she prayed.

In the taproom below, a solitary gentleman sat hunched
over his rum-laced wine punch, apparently oblivious of the
noise or the curious, speculative stares sent his way. As the
wind hurled a spray of water against the thick, distorted glass
panes behind him, he silently cursed himself for his folly.
Even the weather seemed to mock him, offering scant

welcome to the returned profiligate, thwarting him instead. After a harrowing, storm-tossed crossing, he could discover neither a horse nor a rig to hire before morning.

His eyes focused on the reflection of the guttering candle's flame in the cheap glass in his hand. The wine beckoned him seductively, promising the comfort of temporary oblivion. He drank deeply, then stared into the dark-flecked dregs as though they would give soothing answer to the doubts that plagued him. Ever since his cousin Trent's messenger had reached him in the comparative safety of Lyons, he'd been either in the saddle or on shipboard, daring to reenter England, escaping the notice of authorities seeking his arrest. But now that he'd managed to arrive undetected, now that he'd come to this miserable, mean place, he had to admit a greater fear, not for his safety, but rather for his welcome.

If his mother yet lived, if she'd not already succumbed to the brain fever Trent had described, would she even care that he risked life and limb to come to her? Or would she turn from him, saying that her only son had died in the war?

Plagued by doubt now, he wondered if perhaps the greater mercy for them both would lie in his turning back to France before he caused either of them more pain.

As always, the wine gave him no answers. And this night, it was even a deuced poor balm. No, at dawn he would put this fleeting cowardice aside and heave his weary, aching body into a saddle and ride northward. And he would leave it to the vagaries of that most faithless of mistresses, Fate, to decide if he had been right to come.

Around him, there were those whose interest in him was more than perfunctory. Despite the drabness of his sodden cloak, despite the plainness of his coat beneath, he drew more than his share of decided measuring glances from several cutpurses come in to prey on the unwary. He was, to put it bluntly, the best prospect in the place.

"I dunno," muttered one. "Mebbe. Big'un, though."

"Gentry," another observed succinctly. "Got clean hands."

"Aye, a gentry cove," a third agreed low. "But that don't say he's got a full purse."

"Looks like a rum customer to me," the first fellow ventured nervously. "Ain't much ter pick from."

"We got ter eat, ain't we? And there ain't a tuppence to spare 'twixt the rest, I'd say," their companion asserted.

Behind them the door opened, admitting a cold gust of rain-laden wind, and a slender young man entered. Unlike the gentleman at the table, this one was obviously plump in the pockets, for everything from his caped greatcoat to his spattered Hessians bespoke Quality. As his eyes darted over the ill-washed assemblage, he hesitated as though deciding whether to enter. Outside, a bolt of lightning illuminated the sheeting rain briefly, then the thunder crashed with such force that those within jumped. Reluctantly the young man turned to close the door as those who'd been but moments before appraising the seated gentleman exchanged smug glances. He was, one of them whispered, a "blooming gift o' Providence."

Briefly Albert Bascombe considered fleeing again into the storm, but another, even louder clap of thunder, followed by the fearful neighing of his horses outside, decided him. Settling his shoulders manfully, he approached the slatternly woman whose ample stomach was covered with a soiled apron.

"Good dame, I'd bespeak a private parlor for supper," he said with as much authority as he could muster.

"Ain't no private parlors here," she retorted. " 'Tis the common room or none."

Tired of wallowing in the morass of his self-pity, Dominick Devereaux had started to rise, but had sunk back when the door opened. He tensed warily, then eased back into the shadows to watch the newcomer with faintly amused interest, now noting the half-score and more assorted pickpockets and cutpurses who came to attention. The poor pink was, he considered dispassionately, a pigeon about to be plucked.

As a particularly ugly customer vacated a chair at the next table, Dominick appropriated it, pulling it toward him easily with a booted foot. Resting his leg across it, he continued to observe the newcomer until recognition dawned. He groaned inwardly. It was Haverstoke's dim-witted heir,

Albert Bascombe—called Bertie or Birdie, depending on one's opinion of his brain. An amiable bubble, Brummell had once labeled him. The notorious Viscount Westover's empty-lofted but over-loyal friend.

Resolutely, the object of his scrutiny shook water from the greatcoat, then removed his soaked beaver hat to reveal disordered red-gold locks, and all the while his eyes darted about the room, seeking a friendly face. Even for Albert Bascombe, it took no great powers of perception to know he'd delivered himself into a den of thieves. The steamy bodies that occupied the room reminded him of the unwashed who circulated amongst the theater pits picking pockets. He felt the stiff points of his collar tighten, and he considered that he ought to have insisted on Cribbs and Davies coming in with him rather than ordering them to sleep in his carriage to protect it.

His gaze discovering Dominick, he brightened visibly, and he hurried forward gratefully. Despite the plainness of the cloak, there was no mistaking that the solitary drinker bore the look of a gentleman, and that was a comfort to him. He was not entirely alone in this foresaken place. As he approached, his expression took on the amiable appeal of a pup expecting to be welcomed.

Dominick slouched in his seat, pulling his hat further and turning his face away from the candle too late. He could only hope that Bascombe was as dim as reputed and somehow would not recognize him. Or that he would hold his tongue if he did. But even as those thoughts crossed his mind, he doubted both possibilities. From all he'd ever heard of Haverstoke's heir, the fool was a complete muddler. Schooling his face into utter indifference, Dominick appeared bored as the younger man approached.

Bertie peeled off his kid gloves and peered through the smoky, steam-filled semi-darkness, observing hopefully, "Devilish bad out tonight, ain't it? Collect the weather drove you in also, eh?" His eyes moving contemptuously to the cracked, soot-streaked walls, he complained, "Call it the Blue Bull on the sign, but it ought to be the Dead Ox, by the looks of it."

"The place suits me," Dominick muttered.

"Eh? Heh-heh. Collect you are funning, ain't you?" Even as he spoke, he cast about for an empty chair, then settled on the one beneath Dominick's boot. "Mind if I was to join you? Name's Bascombe—Albert Bascombe, by the by."

"I do."

Thinking he'd not heard aright, Bertie reached for the chair, and as he leaned forward, he was afforded a better glimpse of the shadowed face. "Egad—Deveraux!"

Dominick started to deny it, but his unwanted intruder rattled on, "Trent's cousin, ain't you? Heard you was out of the country! Beresford died, you know." As the blue eyes hardened, Bertie was taken aback by the sudden coldness in them. "That is, I . . . well, dash it, ain't you supposed to be in France somewhere?" he demanded aggrievedly, then lowered his voice. "Heard they were looking for you—Patrick said Beresford's papa was offering money to see you swing on the Nubbing Cheat."

Abruptly Dominick kicked the chair toward him. "Sit down," he ordered brusquely. "And put a clamp on your tongue, for I cannot abide a fool." Leaning forward, he added so softly that Bertie could scarce hear him above the taproom noise, "Beresford was a fool."

"Eh?" There was no mistaking the warning in the bigger man's eyes. "Oh . . . collect you don't want it known," the younger man decided as he sank into the chair. "Well, I ain't saying nothing—didn't like the fellow myself, in fact. If anybody ever deserved to cock up his toes, 'twas him. Bad *ton*, you know—even m'father said there was no loss there." He paused, then leaned across the small table. "But I heard they were pursuing the matter and saying it was . . ." He stopped short of uttering the word "murder," choosing instead to finish lamely, " . . . well, it don't signify. Guess you wouldn't be here if the matter wasn't settled all right and tight, would you? Good thing, too, since it don't seem right to put money on a gentleman's head."

"No." Dominick looked down at a bead of condensation on his glass, then flattened it with a fingertip casually. "I believe the amount is still one thousand pounds." When he raised his eyes, he looked straight into Bertie's. "All you have to do is deliver me to the nearest constable, Bascombe," he said softly.

"Do I look like a curst rum to you?" Bertie asked plaintively. "Dash it, but I ain't that sort! Ain't my business if you was to plant a dozen fellows! Besides, I told you, I never liked Beresford myself."

"Bascombe!" Dominick's voice rose sharply in warning.

"Oh." Bertie straightened, whispering loudly, "If any was to ask me, I ain't seen you. Stood by Westover, you know. But Patrick wasn't a coward about his business—he stayed for the inquest. Coroner's jury ruled Bridlington fired too soon. Sorry—didn't mean you was a coward—daresay circumstances was different, after all."

"Very." Turning the conversation to safer ground Dominick inquired politely, "And what of the lovely Miss Canfield? I heard you were to be leg-shackled. Surely you have not left your bride so soon?"

"You *have* been away, ain't you?" Bertie grinned smugly. "Near thing, it was, but she wed Rotherfield instead. Thought I was off the harridan's hook then, but . . ." His expression sobered suddenly. "Thing was, got m'father to thinking about my future," he recalled glumly. "Thinks I ought to get a wife. Since I escaped Miss Canfield, he's paraded a whole string of 'em at me—some long-toothed, some even still in the schoolroom—short, fat, skinny, spotted ones—it don't seem to matter to him. Says I got to choose one of 'em or he's goin' to talk to Miss Brideport's father. Guess he don't think I'm much of an heir, and he hopes I'll give him a better one ere he's planted." He fell morosely silent for a moment, then recovered. "Running," he uttered succinctly. "Got to—Miss Brideport's got one of them high voices I can't abide. Going to France when the weather clears. Hope m'father forgets, but ain't got much expectation of that. I ain't in the petticoat line, you know, but he don't listen to me."

"I own I *had* suspected," Dominick murmured dryly.

"Never liked Rotherfield until the Juliana thing," Bertie mused, wandering backward briefly. "Cold. Like your cousin Trent. Sorry—didn't mean anything by that either. Don't know Trent but by rep, but I hear he ain't the sort as one would want to cross." When the other man said nothing, he sighed. "Regular prattlebox sometimes, ain't I? Don't mean no harm, I hope you know."

"Yes." Abruptly Dominick rose. "Your servant, Bascombe. As I doubt I will see you on the morrow, I'll wish you a good journey now."

"Wait—don't suppose you are wishful of sharing your chamber?" Bertie asked hopefully.

"No." With a straight face Dominick added, "I am inclined to snore."

"You? But . . . well, daresay a little noise wouldn't bother me."

"Good night, Bascombe," he said definitely.

Unable to stand it any longer, Anne again cracked the door and was about to inch into the deserted hall, when she heard heavy bootsteps on the stairs. Shrinking back into the shadows, she waited for this man to pass also. From below, she could hear someone calling up, "I say—wait for me! Dash it, but they ain't got no other rooms!"

The man stopped a scarce five feet from her, and turned back just as a flash of lightning struck something outside, affording her the briefest glimpse of a gentleman; then all was dark again. The crash of thunder shook the walls with such force that an empty sconce fell, breaking beside her door. Startled, she gasped audibly, drawing his attention.

"What the deuce?"

Dominick spun around, his body suddenly tense, his mind wary, and he saw her. As dark as it was, he could scarce make out much beyond her disheveled hair and the faint gleam of a bared shoulder. His mouth curved cynically, and he was about to tell her that there was a greener man coming up the stairs after him, when she stepped out to face him. As another flash of lightning illuminated the bleak hall, she swallowed visibly.

She hesitated, for the man before her suddenly seemed as forbidding as Lucifer. Wiping wet palms against the skirt of her gown, she dared to blurt out, "I am Anne Morland—Miss Morland, sir—and I have been abducted!" Despite the darkness, she thought one black eyebrow rose in disbelief, and she added baldly, "I think I have killed Mr. Fordyce."

Hackles rose on the nape of Dominick's neck, warning him that it could be a ruse to rob him. And yet there was no sign of anyone else there. His hand crept beneath his still-damp cloak to grasp the reassuring butt of his pistol. Behind him there were more steps on the stairs.

"Deveraux?" Bascombe called out tentatively. "They ain't got an extra room. If you was to share, I'd sport the blunt. I say, Deveraux, but this ain't the number—" Bertie stopped when he saw the shadowy figure of a girl. "Oh . . . sorry to intrude," he mumbled. "Your pardon. Didn't know."

He started to back up apologetically, caught his foot in the frayed edge of the rug, tripped, spun around several times, and fell forward through the open door. For a moment he lay there regaining his breath, before he rolled to sit. Then he saw the body. He blinked a couple of times as though he doubted his eyes, but the cresset lamp above told him otherwise.

"Oh, lud, you didn't . . . " He looked up reproachfully at Dominick Deveraux.

"Of course I didn't! For one thing, I don't even know who he is!" the other man snapped.

Bertie turned his attention to the body before him, leaning to peer cautiously into the still face. "Can't see . . . Dressed like a gentleman . . . Who . . . ?"

"He is . . . or he *was* Quentin Fordyce," Anne answered with a calmness she did not feel. "He abducted me, and when he threatened my virtue, I hit him with the poker."

"Fordyce," Bertie murmured. "Shocking bad *ton,* if you was to ask me—fellow's run off his legs. But even *he* ain't sunk to a place like this, I can tell you. What was he thinking of, bringing a female here?"

"Ravishment, apparently—if Miss Morland can be believed." Dominick bent over to feel along Fordyce's jawline. "He's still warm, but there's a nasty lump—the skull's probably fractured. Can't tell if—"

His observations were lost in the pounding on the front door below. "Open up! Open up! 'Tis the law!"

Bertie clambered awkwardly to his feet, his face suddenly stricken. "Egad! Deveraux, you don't think I—"

"The law? Oh, dear!" For a moment Anne was at a loss; then she sucked in her breath and let it out slowly. "Well, I shall just have to face them, I suppose," she decided, squaring one shoulder while holding her torn dress against the other. "But who could have known . . . ?"

"It ain't you—daresay 'tis Deveraux they want," Bertie told her. "But I didn't tell 'em—I swear it!"

"It was probably someone who heard you downstairs," Dominick muttered dryly, adding a curse under his breath.

"Got to get you out of here. My fault—my accursed tongue—devilish sorry for it, you know." The younger man ran his hand through his hair as though it would help him think. "Can't be found with another body—hang for sure. Got to escape ere you are taken."

"*Another* body?" Anne echoed faintly. "But . . . *oh, dear!*" She looked at Bertie. "Before they come up, sir, do *you* think you could tell if he . . . ? Her eyes dropped to Fordyce's still-inert form.

"Don't know—and don't want to know neither," he answered, shuddering. "More to the point, you got to run now."

"The window—does it open?" Dominick demanded.

"I don't know," she answered truthfully. "I just awakened here."

Even as she spoke, he was already working at the window. "Damn! Water's swelled the wood. Stand back." He picked up the chair and swung it against the rotted frame, hitting the panes with such force that the wood splintered and the glass shattered. A hail of rain pelted the frayed carpet. "Which carriage is yours, Bascombe?"

"I say, but . . . No! Can't . . . Dash it, but I don't want anything to do with this!"

"Don't be a fool, Bascombe! Do you want to be caught with a body?"

Bertie wavered. "But what about Miss Morland? It don't look like she can stay here either. Tell you what—the two of you run, and I'll go to France."

For the briefest moment Dominick looked to where Anne stood watching him curiously. "Come on. We can quarrel amongst ourselves later."

"Me?" she responded faintly. "But I—"

"Do you want to hang?" he asked brutally. "If he doesn't come round . . ." His voice trailed off meaningfully.

She could hear the landlord below disputing loudly that he ran a respectable place, an assertion that was greeted roundly by guffaws and derisive shouts. And above the din someone shouted they'd come for a fugitive, that the rest could go back to their drinking.

"We'll have to jump for it," Dominick decided.

"Dash it, but it's the second story!" Bertie protested. "Got to be a back way out." But already there were running footsteps coming up. He hastily pushed the door closed and turned the key in the lock, hoping for time.

Dominick had grasped Anne's arm, and when she pulled back, he snapped, "Miss Morland, there's no time for vapors now. Either you go or you face them."

Someone rapped loudly at a door, and in the next room a woman complained vociferously that they had no right to interfere in a girl's living. Anne hesitated, and the tall man's eyes seemed to mock her as he held back the worn curtain from the jagged panes. He was right—she could stay and face a magistrate, or she could flee with strangers. It really was not much of a choice. White-faced, she nodded.

"We're fronting the roof over the taproom," Dominick told Bertie. "You go first, and I'll hand the girl to you."

"*Me?* But I ain't . . . Dash it, but I don't like heights!"

"Open up! 'Tis the law! In the name of His Majesty, I command you to answer!"

The door banged against the jamb with the force of the pounding. Swallowing hard, Bertie managed to step through the broken window, scattering pieces of wood and glass. A sheet of rain hit his face. Shivering as much from fear as from cold, he turned to reach for Anne Morland, and as his

weight shifted, he lost his footing on the slippery roof.
Grasping wildly, he caught at the gutter to break his fall,
then went over the side, to hang several feet above the
ground. Terrified, he looked downward. His scream seemed
to catch in his constricted throat as he lost his grip and fell
to the muddy alley below.

Anne had no time to protest before she was thrust through
the window. For an awful moment she wanted to close her
eyes, but the man behind her steadied her, and the tightness
of his grip was reassuring. He slid his other arm about her
waist, then edged toward the gutter where the other fellow
had disappeared. When she looked down, the slender man
was struggling to rise.

"Try to land on him," Deveraux advised against her ear.
Then, before she could stop him, he dropped her, and she
fell, to lie in a tangle of Bascombe's flailing arms and her
sodden clothes.

Above them Dominick Deveraux spread his cloak like bat
wings and jumped. His feet hit the ground in a heavy thud,
and his knees bent from the force.

"You might have warned me you was giving her the
heave," Bertie muttered, standing to lend Anne a hand.
"You all right, Miss Morland?" Then, before she could
answer, he looked down at the mud on his clothes. "Dash
it, Deveraux, but you've ruined a good coat!"

"And my gown!" Anne looked down, and felt hot tears
sting her eyes. The dress that had cost her four months'
wages, the one she'd wanted to wear to her grandfather's,
was now torn from hem to knee and soiled beyond repair.
" 'Tis my best!"

"Get a new one," Dominick advised brutally. "Which
coach, Bascombe?" But even as he asked, he caught Anne's
arm and started to run, pulling her after him. Rain swirled
around Bertie as he broke into a trot to keep up. "The bays,
but they ain't—" The wind seemed to carry his words away.

Hazarding on the largest conveyance in the innyard,
Dominick headed for it. Hearing the clamor of men coming
out of the inn, Bertie lunged to wrench open the door, and
his driver rose up sleepily to protest. Seeing his master,

Davies kicked the sleeping coachy awake, and Cribbs righted himself sheepishly. "Sommat the matter, sir?"

"Get inside," Dominick ordered Anne.

Before she could find the step with her muddy slipper, he'd lifted her, tossing her roughly into the interior. She sank against dark velvet squabs and tried to breathe. Through the sheet of water on the pane she saw shouting men carrying lanterns. Bascombe grasped the doorframe and hurled his slender body past her, falling into her lap.

"Sorry," he mumbled, righting himself. "Clumsy."

" 'Tis all right," she managed, rubbing her cold, wet arms.

Dominick Deveraux swung up onto the box and grasped the coach whip from its holder. Cracking it, he caught a fellow who tried to grab the lead harness. The four bays sprang to life, surging forward. Inside the passenger compartment, the occupants were thrown back against the seats. As Anne looked out, another foolhardy fellow ran alongside for about a hundred feet, then fell, rolling away from the pounding hooves. Beside her Bascombe wailed, "My cattle—he'll ruin 'em! Dash it, but I've got a packet to catch, come morning! Can't go racketing about the country! And what's m'father to say? I'd as lief face the constable as him!"

But the carriage already careened wildly through rain-slicked city streets, the loud spray of water from its wheels hitting the underside of it like birdshot. Lantern lights emerged from the darkness, hurling themselves into view, then disappeared again with shocking speed. Several times the coach tilted precariously taking corners, then righted itself as dark, silent buildings blurred. The driver and coachman exchanged uneasy glances, while Anne held tightly to the pull strap, forgetting modesty for survival. Lightning zigzagged through sheets of rain, illuminating Bascombe's pale, frightened face. The thought crossed Anne's mind that if she survived it, it was a ride she'd never forget.

Streetlights faded to the occasional twinkle from scattered houses, then to nothing, and the coach still plunged headlong into a black oblivion punctuated by brief flashes of lightning. The only sound beyond the pounding hooves and

rattling carriage was the steady rumble of thunder. To Anne
it was as though Thor's fury had dissipated to mere
grumbling, and she eased her grip on the strap long enough
to rub her icy, aching fingers. The carriage finally slowed
to a steady pace, and the rhythmic beat of the wheels against
macadamized road kept time to the rain.

His hands shaking, one of the men across from her tried
to spark the wick of the inside lamp. A tiny red speck took
hold, then grew to a yellow flame, bathing the dim interior
with a flickering, almost eerie light. His companion rubbed
at the stubble on his face as though to reassure himself he
was whole before casting reproachful eyes at Bascombe.

"Oo's got me ribbons?" he wanted to know.

Whether it was actually so, or whether it was the yellow-
orange glow from the carriage lamp, the color appeared to
be returning to Bascombe's face. He took a deep breath, then
sank back into the squabs before answering, "It don't signify,
Davies."

"Don't signify?" the driver howled. "Been lookin' into
the pits o' hell, and it don't signify?" His voice rose indignantly. "When we stop, I'm-a-gettin' on the box—else I'm-
a-givin' me notice!"

As if the Almighty heard him, the coach pulled to the side
of the road, stopped, and Deveraux jumped down. Opening
the carriage door beside Anne, he stuck his head inside.
Water ran in rivulets from his soaked hair and dripped onto
the skirt of her ruined gown.

"There's none following now," he announced as though
there might have been the possibility. "Everybody all right?"

"Demned fortunate we ain't dead," the coachy muttered
under his breath.

Deveraux's eyes flicked over Anne impersonally. "Miss
Morland?"

"I am fine, sir." She did not think she'd ever be warm
again, but otherwise she meant it.

His gaze returned to her face, and he favored her with a
faint smile. "Not even a mild case of the vapors?"

"No."

"My compliments, then, Miss Morland."

"Well, I ain't all right," Bertie announced with feeling. "What was you thinking of, Deveraux? You dashed well could have killed us!"

The smile broadened boyishly. "But I didn't—drove to an inch, in fact. Good cattle, Bascombe—I own they surprised me."

"If yer lor'ship was ter move, I'd get inter the box," Davies offered, pushing his way out.

Dominick Deveraux nodded. "At Alton, take the road to Reading, then continue north toward Nottingham. Do you know the way?"

"Aye."

Cribbs looked at the steady rain for a moment, sighed, then followed his superior. "Demned poor night fer drivin', Mr. Davies, if ye was to ask me," he complained.

As the two men climbed up onto the driver's seat, Dominick pulled off his soaked cloak and heaved himself up into the passenger compartment, taking the place across from Anne and Bascombe. Settling in, he extended his boots between them.

"I ain't going to Nottingham," Bertie declared. "Hire you a carriage at Reading."

"Too risky. I might be recognized."

With one hand holding the seam of her rent skirt together and the other pressing her torn bodice against her shoulder, Anne spoke up. "Sir, I should like to return to London forthwith. As it is, 'twill be difficult explaining to my employer where I have been. And I must contact the authorities about Mr. Fordyce, though I am sure I do not know what Mrs. Philbrook will have to say on that head." Looking downward at her ruined gown, she sighed. "She's overgiven to censure anyway."

"No! Damme if I'm going back to London, Miss Morland. Got to go abroad," Bertie maintained stoutly. "Put you down at a posting house. As for Deveraux, they ain't going to be looking for him on the common stage. Me—I got to go to France ere m'father finds me."

"I assure you Miss Morland will be noted in that gown— every man jack between here and London will be ogling what isn't covered." Dominick reached beneath his sodden cloak and drew out his pistol. Laying it across his knee, he looked at Bertie. "Now, I believe I said Nottingham, did I not?" he asked with deceptive softness. As the other man recoiled visibly, he turned his attention to Anne. "Quite fetching, my dear, but were I you, I'd cover myself with a carriage rug ere I enlivened Bascombe's amatory instincts." Leaning back, he closed his eyes, murmuring, "And I shouldn't advise any movement this direction, Bascombe, for I sleep rather lightly."

"Really, sir . . ." Anne began stiffly. "If we had not left so precipitately, I should have brought my shawl."

"It's all right," Bertie interrupted her. "I ain't going to do nothing foolish—and I ain't got any amatory instincts. Ain't in the petticoat line," he added, as though that explained everything. Leaning down, he retrieved a rug from beneath his seat, then straightened to hand it to her. Casting a significant look toward the other man, he murmured low, "Dominick Deveraux is the one with the rep for the females, Miss Morland. He's the one you got to watch. Not me. I got no address."

"You give him too much credit, I am sure," she retorted, "for if he has any, I've not yet seen it."

One blue eye opened briefly. "How very unappreciative you are, my dear. At least you are not on your way to jail."

The image of Quentin Fordyce lying pale and still rose in her mind, stifling any answer. For a long moment she felt again the panic; then she managed to master it. When she looked up again, Dominick Deveraux appeared asleep. She pulled the carriage rug close about her and tried not to think beyond the present.

2

The storm had abated, replaced by an enveloping mist that beaded rather than trickled. Inside the carriage, the windows were steamed over, obscuring the graying dawn. Anne Morland shifted her weight uncomfortably, seeking ease for her cramped limbs, and wondered where they were. Taking a corner of the carriage rug, she wiped at the window, but there was naught to see outside. Her gaze moved to Dominick Deveraux, then to Albert Bascombe, and she asked herself dispiritedly how they could sleep, for she certainly could not. Not with the awful pounding in her head.

A scant twenty-four hours ago she'd been snug in her bed at Mrs. Philbrook's, blissfully unaware of what was to befall her. Quentin Fordyce, her newly discovered cousin, was yet to come for the promised visit to her grandfather. He had not yet revealed himself as the unprincipled blackguard that he was.

How could she have been so deceived? Had her eagerness for acceptance by her father's family made her foolish? Mentally she reviewed her brief acquaintance with Mr. Fordyce, wondering if she'd somehow missed something, some clue that ought to have warned her. But he'd seemed so kind, so interested in righting an old wrong. And she, seeking escape from the intolerable burden of Mrs. Philbrook's grudging charity, had been taken in by his dashing, elegant manners. She could not have known he would turn into a lecherous fiend, she consoled herself. But he had.

Once inside his carriage, he'd shared a basket of sinfully rich pastries from Gunther's, something she'd only heard of but had never tasted before. And then he'd plied her with a bottle of expensive wine, all the while paying lavish compliments to her face, her form, her hat, and her dress, until she'd begged him to be serious. But he'd pronounced himself smitten from the first, saying despite the brevity of their acquaintance, it was his hope to make her his wife. As his hands had possessed hers, she'd begun to feel quite odd, as though the carriage were spinning, separating her mind from her body. She remembered accusing him, hearing herself say, "You never intended to take me to Oakhill, did you?" But if he'd answered her, 'twas after she'd sunk into a drugged oblivion.

The next thing she could recall was her painful awakening in that miserable inn. And Quentin Fordyce's amorous advances. She closed her eyes briefly, seeing for perhaps the hundredth time his inert form upon the shabby carpet. And the awful fear that he was dead, that she'd killed a man, once again assailed her, knotting her stomach. She swallowed hard, thinking she ought to have stayed to face the authorities, to have explained she'd done it to save herself. But she'd panicked, allowing a stranger to persuade her to flee. A stranger whose own past was apparently utterly notorious. A stranger who'd killed someone also.

And now she was in another carriage with him, bound for Nottingham, a place utterly unfamiliar to her, with little hope of getting back to London before Mrs. Philbrook turned her off. Not that she really wished to return to her elderly employer, for even if she somehow were exonerated in the matter of Mr. Fordyce, if she somehow managed to keep her position, she'd be certain to hear of her folly long and often.

"Humph!" the old woman had snorted when Quentin had come calling. "Cousin indeed! Mark my words, missy—a man of any substance don't waste his time on a penniless female. Plain as the nose on your face—he thinks you no better than your mother! And this faradiddle about your grandpapa wanting to see you—why, 'tis utter nonsense! The Morlands is too high in the instep for the likes of an opera singer's daughter!"

"Mama was as much a lady as you!" she'd wanted to shout

back, but somehow she'd held her tongue. Now she wished she hadn't. Just once she'd like to speak her mind to the woman without fear of the consequences.

Instead, it would be she listening to her employer's smug crowing. Mrs. Philbrook would be sure to linger over her paid companion's foolishness, sniffing yet again that she ought to have known better than to waste her money by dressing above her station. And after cataloging Anne's follies, the old woman would discharge her, then wait for her to beg to stay. And, in the absence of any other opportunity, Anne would have to do it.

She did feel utterly foolish. She'd squandered the awesome sum of ten guineas on a dress length of expensive green silk nankeen, then spent more than a week sewing herself her first new dress in two years. And there was another four guineas wasted on the rest of her toilette, including her missing paisley shawl and now-water-soaked kid slippers. Her hand crept to her newly cropped hair, feeling the flat curls, wishing she'd not done that either. What was it Burns had said about the best-laid plans? That they gave grief and pain for promised joy?

But she hadn't wanted to arrive on her grandfather's doorstep looking utterly poor and out of fashion. Perhaps it was merely a matter of pride, but she'd not wanted to give him any reason to pity her, to think she meant to hang on his sleeve. All she'd wanted was to meet him, to discover the family that had refused to acknowledge her mother's existence. But Quentin Fordyce had lied to her. Her grandfather hadn't wanted to see her after all.

She looked down again at her dress, seeing the torn fabric and the mud, and she wanted to weep as she thought of the expense of it. And she'd not even counted the ten shillings she'd paid Clara Smith, a neighbor's dresser, for the miserable haircut. She had to stop thinking on that also, she decided wearily, else she'd drown in her own self-pity.

Beside her, Mr. Bascombe turned in his sleep, and his head slipped once more to rest against her shoulder. For at least the tenth time she pushed him gently away, then pulled the carriage rug up again.

''Sorry,'' he mumbled without actually waking. His head again fell back against the padded top of the seat, stretching his neck, and he resumed snoring softly. For a moment she studied him, wondering how he came to be with the one called Deveraux. Despite his apparent wealth, he was physically and socially clumsy, and even on short acquaintance it was obvious he lacked the intelligence and the daring of the other man. How very different they were in appearance also, Bascombe pale, slender, fair-haired, and amiable, Deveraux dark in more ways than his looks.

When she looked up, she thought she detected a faint, slightly derisive smile on Mr. Deveraux's face. It was, she supposed enviously, that he dreamed.

To take her mind from the ache in her head and her plummeting spirits, she dared to consider his face openly, studying the incredible handsomeness of it—the thick black hair that waved slightly where it lay against his forehead, the black lashes that fringed above the strong planes of his cheeks, the straight, well-chiseled nose that reminded her of one on a Greek bust. Unlike so many of his class, his chin was defined and the line of his jaw strong, solid. If he had a flaw, 'twas that the rather sensuous mouth curved downward, giving him the appearance of a cynic much of the time. When he was awake, he seemed to have a wry, derisive quality, a devil-take-you attitude that set him apart from other gentlemen.

But if he possessed none of that, she still would have been struck by the size of him. She judged him to be six or seven inches taller than herself, well-muscled and quite solid for a gentleman. She closed her arms beneath the carriage rug, remembering the strength of his grip when he held her on the roof. No doubt he was the sort who patronized Jackson's boxing saloon—when he was in the country.

Still, he was a fugitive crossing England, and she could not help wondering precisely why the authorities sought him. What had Mr. Bascombe said to him? *Can't be found with another body—got to escape ere you are taken.* . . . The awful thought went through her mind that she'd possibly jumped from the proverbial frying pan into the fire. But just now, as she watched him sleep, he did not seem so very dangerous.

Dominick Deveraux. She racked her aching brain, trying to place where she'd heard the name Deveraux before, and it came to her. The notorious Marquess of Trent was a Deveraux. Of course. But surely this man was not Trent, for the scandals of that lord had ended with his *ton*-stunning marriage to a nobody. No, this Deveraux was not the marquess, she decided. A relative perhaps. An equally wild relative. A younger relative, for despite the cynicism, just now he did not appear to be much over twenty-five or twenty-six. When awake, he'd looked to be past thirty, but perhaps that was weariness rather than age.

Her gaze dropped to the pistol that still lay against his knee, and for a moment she considered taking it while he slept. Once it was in her hands, she could demand they turn for London. She stretched to reach for it.

"I wouldn't, Miss Morland," he said softly.

Startled, she looked up again, and his blue eyes met hers across the small space. The reflection of the dying coach-lamp flame in them mocked her. She recoiled guiltily.

"Really, sir—"

"I sleep rather lightly."

"More likely you were shamming it, sir," she retorted. "You could scarce be awakened by a glance."

" 'Tis a sense that keeps me whole." He straightened in the seat, shrugging his shoulders, settling them. One of his hands brushed back an unruly lock of black hair, then moved to rub at the dark stubble along his jaw. "Wine," he muttered more to himself than to her, "tastes devilish bad the morning after." He squeezed his eyes shut, then opened them as though he could somehow clear his mind. "I haven't had a head like this since my salad days."

"Perhaps you shouldn't drink so much."

His gaze raked her bare shoulder where the rug had slipped again, and one of his eyebrows shot up as a corner of his mouth turned down. "My, how prim you are this morning, my dear. But fetching."

Her hand reached to tug at the offending blanket as her face reddened. "A gentleman does not note such things, sir," she managed stiffly.

"Ah, but I am not often a gentleman, Miss Morland." He leaned forward slightly and enunciated clearly, "I am a Deveraux, you see."

She felt out of reason cross, and his manner did nothing to lighten her mood. "I think you are still foxed," she muttered.

"Fortunately, there aren't many of us," he added, ignoring the accusation. "And the world isn't repining over the lack, I assure you."

"Not knowing any of the Deveraux, I am afraid I can neither confirm nor deny that."

"Up in the bough this morning, eh? You know, you are in a deuced bad temper yourself," he chided.

She looked out the streaked window for a long moment and sighed heavily. "If you would have the truth of it, sir, my head aches also. I suspect it was the drugged wine."

"Weasel-bit?" he asked more sympathetically. "What you need is a hair of the old dog." It was his turn to sigh. "Alas, but my flask is empty, else we'd share it."

"Thank you, but I should decline. I doubt I will ever drink anything stronger than ratafia again," she responded with feeling.

"Drugged wine, eh?" He leaned back and surveyed her lazily. "'Twould seem Fordyce displayed a shocking lack of address. For all my faults, I have never had to resort to such measures to seduce a female." The faint smile played again at the corners of his mouth. "Never."

"Really, sir, but this is most improper. I cannot think—"

"I told you, I'm not a very proper fellow, Miss Morland. I have never been invited to Almack's," he added significantly. "Nor do I wish to go there."

"Do you always declare yourself a rake to females upon acquaintance?" she inquired curiously.

"Not a rake, Miss Morland—a rogue. There is a difference." His smile faded. "Women are but one of my faults."

"You are a gamester," she hazarded.

"No more than any other." Briefly his voice betrayed a trace of regret; then his jawline hardened, and the planes of his face seemed suddenly harsher. "I have a devilish temper, Miss Morland, and it oft leads me where I would not go." He picked up the pistol, hefted it in the palm of his hand, then slid it beneath the cloak that lay beside him. When he looked across at her again, he noted brusquely, "You ought to sleep—'tis a long way to Notthingham."

They lapsed into silence, and for a time there was only Bertie Bascombe's rhythmic breathing, which seemed to keep time to the roll of the wheels. Finally Anne could stand it no longer.

"If you are a Deveraux, sir, you must be relation to the Marquess of Trent," she blurted out.

"He is my cousin," was all he said.

His answer did not invite further conversation. As he retreated into silence, there was naught for her to do but return once more to her own thoughts, to the need to confess the killing of Quentin Fordyce. She almost dreaded the thought of going to London, of facing the magistrate. For a brief moment, hope flared. What if her cousin were not truly dead? The hope flagged immediately, and she sighed. To think he could have survived was no more than wishful thinking, and she knew it.

No doubt she'd made matters worse, compounding the situation by fleeing, for there would be those who would declare that proof of her guilt. So she was a fugitive without so much as a tuppence, utterly dependent on a rogue and a slowtop. Viewed in that light, her predicament made the matter of Mrs. Philbrook seem rather inconsequential. She did not need to worry about employment when she was headed for Newgate.

He leaned back to scrutinize her from beneath lowered lids, speculating on the truth of her story. Assessing her person dispassionately, he cataloged the obvious: she was considerably taller than the ordinary, with good straight features accentuated by warm brown eyes. Unfortunately, any claim to looks was marred by unfashionably brown hair that, having been soaked, had dried flat against her head, giving her the appearance of a drowned Brutus. Her gown, or what was left of it, clung to a less-than-voluptuous figure. She reminded him somewhat of those unfortunate females who sat undiscovered through a Season on the Marriage Mart. In appearance he decided she was relatively unremarkable. But, beauty or not, she had his grudging admiration—on the roof of the inn, and later during the wild ride, she had shown herself to be pluck to the bone, a rare quality in a female.

He was drawn to the faraway, almost stricken expression in her brown eyes. She was in a devil of a coil, and he could not help pitying her for it. If Fordyce had any family of note, she could expect little justice from a system more bent on protecting the sensibilities of the wealthy than in discovering the truth.

And yet something was wrong with her tale. Albert Bascombe had said Fordyce was run off his legs, which made Anne Morland's tale suspect. A man already in dun territory did not steer his barque toward a penniless female. Perhaps Miss Morland had led Fordyce on, hoping for an honorable offer, and when she discovered marriage wasn't on his mind, she parted his skull with the poker. But that didn't ring true either. In spite of the circumstances of their encounter, Dominick was ready to wager that she was one of those shabby-genteel respectable females.

"Tell me, Miss Morland," he asked suddenly, "what is it about you that prompted Fordyce to abduct you?"

His voice cut into her reverie, and for a moment she was not sure she'd heard him correctly. "I beg your pardon?"

"What is it about you that prompted Fordyce to abduct you?" he repeated.

"I have not the slightest idea."

"While your face is passable enough, it scarce seems sufficient to provoke desperate, unbridled passion," he mused aloud. "And if you are worried about your employer, you obviously have no money," he added with crushing candor.

"I told you—I don't know," she retorted, irritated. "He knew my situation, I assure you."

"While you are a trifle tall and a bit too slender for my tastes, I suppose it could have been your form that enticed the fellow," he hazarded. "But I would doubt it."

"I daresay one man's beauty is another man's sow," she managed stiffly. "But you, sir, are utterly lacking in address."

He inclined his head slightly, and the faint smile returned. "Being a Deveraux, I am not expected to have any."

"How unfortunate you were to have been born into a family where apparently even a modicum of manners was not required."

"High ropes again, Miss Morland?" he quizzed her.

Thinking he merely amused himself at her expense, she sought to give him a solid set-down. "Well, whatever my attraction for Mr. Fordyce, it is not really your affair, is it? If I don't have the least intimation, why should you? Besides, a gentleman does not pry."

He inclined his head slightly, acknowledging the barb, before answering, "Curiosity, Miss Morland. As profligate as I myself have been, I cannot say I have ever before encountered a female over a man's body.." One corner of his mouth twitched as he amended, "At least, not over a seemingly dead one." When she made no reply, he put his fingertips together and continued to consider her. "Morland. Where have I heard the name, I wonder . . . ?"

"I wouldn't know that either. Obviously I do not travel in your circle of acquaintances."

"But you have relations, surely. Even I am encumbered with a few."

"My father's father is General Morland, but I have never met him. He cut the connection when Papa married Mama."

"Ah, the *mésalliance.*"

"Papa didn't think so." She stopped, wondering why she felt it incumbent to justify anything to him. "But you cannot possibly be interested in my family," she added coldly.

"On the contrary, Miss Morland. As we are now fugitives

together, I'd know from whence you are come." Once again
the faint smile played at his mouth. "I collect your mother
must have trodded the boards—or something equally unsuitable."

Her chin shot up, and her eyes flashed momentarily. "My
mother was one of the finest opera singers of her genera-
tion, Mr. Deveraux," she declared, daring him to dispute
it. "You have perhaps heard of Eliana Antonini?" She had
the satisfaction of seeing his eyebrows lift in surprise.
"Despite hundreds of admirers, she was never anyone's
ladybird, and there was never the slightest hint of scandal."

"How unusual."

She thought he mocked her, and she bristled. "Her papa
engaged guards to protect her from the importunities of
licentious lords like yourself, in fact. It was merely by
accident that she met Papa at all."

"Acquit me, Miss Morland. Unlike Trent, I told no title—
nor do I have a taste for Italian singers."

"My point, sir, is that my mother was as much a lady as
yours."

The smile vanished, and he looked to the rising sun beyond
the window. When he spoke again, his voice was distant.
"My mother would dispute that. She has long thought the
Deveraux were not good enough for her."

"Mama's family was respectable—the Antoninis go back
centuries. If she sang, 'twas because she had the gift, and
they were proud of her."

"And where are the esteemed Antoninis now—when you
would seem to be in need of them?" he countered, turning
back to her.

"They approved of Papa no more than the Morlands
approved of Mama," she answered simply. "And it is a very
long way to Milan. Even if I would seek them out, which
I would not, I have not the money for the journey. Besides,
I'd not hang on anyone's charity, sir."

"Very affecting, Miss Morland, but Eliana Antonini made
a fortune with her voice."

Her hands clenched over the folds of the rug in her lap.
"Like most English gentlemen," she said evenly, "Papa was

a gamester, and when he died there were debts to be paid. I count it a credit to Mama that she discharged every one of them ere she fell ill herself.'' She met his gaze as she added pointedly, ''But I expect you would not understand that, Mr. Deveraux, for gentlemen do not seem overly given to paying for anything.''

''You may acquit me of that also, Miss Morland. I settle every quarter-day with the tradesmen—and I never play where I do not win.''

He seemed incapable of being set down. Frustrated, she lashed out at him. ''If you are neither a rake nor a gamester, Mr. Deveraux, how is it that by your own account you are a rogue?'' she demanded acidly. ''A disagreeable temper seems insufficient reason for a bad reputation.''

Bertie Bascombe opened his eyes at that, and struggled to sit. ''Tell that to Beresford—or to Templeton and Whitfield, Miss Morland. He ain't bad—he's downright deadly! Crack shot—them that provokes him gets planted,'' he added meaningfully. ''It ain't just temper, it's Deveraux temper. Only a fool would duel with him. He's just like Trent!''

''Bascombe—''

''And you ain't quarreling with me, Dominick Deveraux, 'cause I won't meet you. I ain't bleeding for nobody.''

Anne stared at the man across from her. ''You've killed *three* men?''

''Daresay they all deserved it, Miss Morland,'' Bertie hastened to admit. ''Bad fellows. Like Fordyce. Don't say they abducted females or anything like that, but . . . well, ain't too many as misses 'em, I can tell you. Thing is, Beresford's papa is saying—''

''Quit rattling, Bascombe!''

''Mr. Deveraux—''

''It don't matter,'' Bertie assured her. Raising his arm, he wiped at the window with his sleeve and peered outside. ''More to the point is where we are.''

''We are for Notthingham,'' Dominick reminded him.

''Dash it, but there ain't anything in Nottingham! I got to go to France! And if you was thinking of your skin, you'd be going with me. What if you are caught? More'n likely they'll charge me and Miss Morland with aiding you, don't you know?'' When Dominick didn't answer, he threw up his hands in disgust. ''What the deuce is in Nottingham, anyway?''

''Penance.''

''*What*? Well, if that don't beat the Frogs! You hear that, Miss Morland? He don't have to drag us halfway across England for that, does he? There's churches everywhere!''

Dominick fixed his gaze on his own window for a long moment, then exhaled heavily. ''I had word of Trent that my mother is very ill.'' His mouth twisted briefly; then he managed to murmur, ''Fool that I am, I'd go home again.''

There was no mistaking the pain in his voice. His earlier gibes forgotten, Anne leaned across the seat to touch his arm. ''I am sorry,'' she said softly.

He continued to stare out the window. ''Save your pity for yourself, Miss Morland. You have the greater need of it.''

An awkward silence filled the carriage. ''Well,'' Bertie conceded finally, ''I don't suppose m'father's going to look for me in Nottingham. Never been known to frequent the place before, after all. Daresay when we get there we can get Miss Morland a dress and put her on the mail coach bound for London.'' He hesitated, then asked her, ''That all right with you? If you ain't got the blunt, I'll frank you.''

''It will have to be, won't it?'' She sighed. ''I suppose one more day is not like to make any difference . . .'' Her voice trailed off, and she settled her shoulders. ''Well, I shall have to tell the authorities, and then I suppose nothing will make any difference.''

''Can't do it in Nottingham,'' Bertie decided. ''Won't fadge at all—more'n likely 'twould make 'em look for Deveraux. Wait until London,'' he advised. ''Better yet, forget the whole thing—world's better off without Fordyce. Havey-cavey fellow anyway. Be like Dominick here—he don't repine, 'cause he knows he had the right of the quarrels—ain't that so, Deveraux?'' Not waiting for an answer, he rattled on, ''Besides, we don't *know* he's dead, do we? What if he was to wake up, I ask you? It don't do him any credit to have the tale told, you know.''

"Even if I could do it, which I cannot, Mrs. Philbrook knows I left London with my cousin, sir. And I very much doubt he survives.''

"Well, think on it—no need for haste, now, is there?''

"Mr. Bascombe, I have scarce thought of anything else.''

Abruptly Dominick Deveraux roused and straightened in his seat. His blue eyes were distant, his manner almost brusque as he apologized, "Your pardon, Miss Morland. My pride ofttimes causes me as much difficulty as my temper.''

3

The carriage, which had slowed to a snail's pace, rolled to a halt, and Cribbs hopped from the box. Albert Bascombe, who'd been dozing, came awake as the coachy wrenched open the door to announce, "Team's tired, sir—the lead pair's about ter drop. We got ter stop ere they are lamed—or worse."

"Where are we?"

" 'Bout a quarter-mile ter the Red Hart, Davies says."

"Which is where?" Bertie demanded querulously. "The Red Hart don't mean nothing to me."

"Between Reading and Northampton—closer to Northampton," Dominick answered for the coachy. "I'd say we are about halfway to Nottingham."

"Davies says we got ter change horses," Cribbs spoke up. "Says the bays ain't going to make it without a full day's rest on oats."

Anne's gaze dropped to where the carriage rug covered her shoulders. "I cannot go into an inn like this."

" 'Course you can't!" Bertie looked to Dominick. "Demned if I know why I came—ought to be in Bedlam for it," he muttered with feeling. "Cannot go on 'cause the horses is tired, and cannot stop 'cause Miss Morland ain't got enough left of her dress to go into a respectable place. All right, you tell me—what's to do now?"

Nearly too bone-weary to think, Dominick passed a hand over sore, burning eyes, then rubbed the dark stubble of beard on his cheek as though he could somehow clear the cobwebs from his brain. It did not seem as though he'd slept in days, and he felt the lack acutely now. As much as he wanted to say they'd go on, he knew it was impossible. The horses had traveled more than a hundred miles from the coast in nearly eleven hours, and neither the driver nor the coachman had had any sleep since they'd left the Blue Bull. He reached into his coat, drew out his watch, and blinked to focus on the dial.

"Half-past ten," he muttered.

"And we ain't eaten," Bertie remembered, adding to his grievances. "Dash it, but I didn't even sup last night!"

Realizing she was the sticking point, Anne exhaled before offering, "If you would but send one of the men out with food, I'd stay in the carriage."

"No." Dominick turned his bloodshot eyes to her, and for a long moment he studied her speculatively. "You are nearly as tall as Bascombe," he decided. "Wear his greatcoat in, and once a chamber is bespoken, put on his clothes."

"I say, Deveraux, what the deuce . . . ? I ain't . . . No!" Bertie fairly howled. Then, perceiving that the other man was serious, he argued, "Dash it, but she's a female! Can't go racketing about in breeches!"

But Dominick continued to consider her. "The hair's nearly short enough, and the form is slight enough to pass," he mused aloud. "I think Bascombe could claim you for his nephew perhaps. Are you a game one, Miss Morland?"

"Well, I—"

"I can tell you she don't like the idea! Respectable female, ain't you, Miss Morland? What was you thinking of, Deveraux? Dash it, but it ain't done!"

"I don't know about you, Bascombe, but I could use a shave, a meal, and a decent bed for a few hours. Besides, who's to know?" Dominick countered softly.

"Anybody who looks at her, for one," Bertie retorted.

"I don't think so. We bundle Miss Morland into the greatcoat, tell the innkeeper your nephew's too carriage-sick to go on, and we help her up to a chamber. There she changes into a coat and breeches ere she is seen, and then, apparently feeling better, she joins us for a nuncheon in a private parlor," he explained patiently. "We rest the horses, get some sleep, and pronounce Miss Morland better ere nightfall. Before dusk, we press on for Nottingham."

"Really, I do not mind staying in the carriage, sir," Anne

said. "Perhaps one of you could borrow a needle and thread of the proprietor's wife, and I could restitch my dress whilst you are gone inside."

"No. 'Twould cause too much comment. Besides, if Cribbs and Davies elect to remain with the carriage, they'll need to sleep on the seats. If not, you are open to the importunities of any who might discover you."

"Still—"

Dominick turned to Bertie again. "I presume you did not intend to go to France without clothes, did you, Bascombe?"

"No, but dash it, I—"

"Then 'tis settled. I am quite certain Miss Morland would welcome a bed as much as you or I, for she looks positively hagged."

Between fending off Albert Bascombe's head from her shoulder and contemplating the awful fate that surely awaited her in Newgate, Anne had slept very little also. The appeal of a bed was almost too great to deny. And her stomach had been rumbling uncomfortably for hours. "But I have no money, sir—not even a shilling."

"He'll frank you—won't you, Bascombe? He's got deep pockets—earl of Haverstoke's heir, after all."

"Don't mind the money," Bertie conceded, "but I dashed well don't like the idea of lending her m'clothes! Took Stultz a month to get the coats right, don't you know?"

"Stultz?" Dominick's eyebrow rose. "My dear fellow—"

"Oh, I tried Weston, but he was wanting to pad m'shoulders too much to get the fit," Bertie remembered in disgust. Then, recalling the matter at hand, he argued, "She still don't look like a fellow to me. For one thing . . ." He reddened uncomfortably. "Well, for one thing, the front of her . . . well, you know, she's . . ." His hands gestured to his chest. "Dash it, but you ain't blind— look at her!"

"She can move her zona up and tighten it. There's not too much to flatten."

Anne stiffened at the perceived criticism of her person. "Sir, but you are—"

"Offending your sensibilities?" Dominick supplied for

her. " 'Tis the truth, after all. Let us face the facts of the matter, Miss Morland—for at least another twenty-four hours we are fugitives together, are we not? We are speaking of survival rather than sensibility."

"See, she don't want to do it!" Bertie crowed triumphantly.

Ignoring the younger man, Dominick went on, "Now, when we reach the Red Hart, Bascombe will go in and procure a private parlor and bedchambers for us, saying you cannot travel further, for you have cast up your accounts all the way from . . ." He paused to consider a likely place, then finished with, " . . . St. Albans."

"I am never carriage-sick, sir."

He favored her with a decidedly pained expression. "Today you are, my dear—desperately so, in fact." Leaning toward her, he ran his fingers through her hair, trying to rearrange it. " 'Tis a trifle too long for a decent Brutus, but perhaps 'twill not be noted," he decided. Sitting back, he surveyed his handiwork and sighed. "Not a very fashionable cut, I'm afraid."

"Not even a bed and a meal could prompt me to cut it again," she managed evenly. "And there is no need to insult me, is there?"

"Decent-looking female," Bertie hastened to assure her. "He don't mean you ain't—just thinks you don't look much like my nevvy, that's all."

"Bascombe, when I am in need of interpretation, I will ask for it. Now, Miss Morland, once you are in your chamber, Bascombe will bring you a change of clothing and hand it through the door. You will answer only when he knocks twice."

"But she don't even know how to tie a cravat, I'll be bound!"

"Being a schoolboy, she'll be forgiven. But if it worries you, tie it for her."

"A schoolboy in Stultz's best," Bertie muttered. Nonetheless, he sighed his resignation. "I ain't registering in my name, you know. And I ain't tying her cravat."

"What about shoes?" Anne looked down at her ruined slippers.

"Stuff something in the toes of Bascombe's."

"No! Dash it, but the coat is enough! You ain't a-giving her m'boots! Let her wear yours! Hoby—"

"Mine are far too large for her."

Cribbs, who had been listening, bemused by it all, spoke up. "Beggin' yer honor's pardon, sir, but what'm I ter tell Davies?"

"Tell Mr. Davies we are to stop at the Red Hart," Dominick answered. "And tell him that if anyone asks, we are come from St. Albans." He looked to Bertie and Anne. "And for the time being, you are both employed by Mr. . . . er . . . Wrexham—Thaddeus Wrexham and his nephew . . . Oliver, I think. And I am the boy's tutor, Mr. Bendell."

"I'd rather be a Smith," Bertie grumbled.

"Ordinary names tend to arouse suspicion, Bascombe."

"How the deuce am I supposed to sign that? I don't—"

"W-r-e-x-h-a-m."

"Well, I ain't putting anything more'n a T for the other one, I can tell you."

But Dominick's attention had returned to Anne. "Miss Morland, while we are stopped, I suggest you get down and wrap yourself in his greatcoat. And when you arrive, you will lean on me and pretend to be sick. Cover your mouth in such a way as to obscure your face. Bascombe, give Miss Morland something for her feet."

"Deuced cold fish about this, ain't you?" For a long moment Bertie eyed Dominick Deveraux with dislike; then he sighed. "Cribbs, get the top boots." Turning away, he mumbled under his breath, "Knew I ought to have brought m'valet—he wouldn't have stood for this."

But as Anne stepped down from the coach and reached for the heavy coat, she heard him repeating softly, "W-r-e-x-h-a-m" over and over.

"Oh, the poor lad," the innkeeper's wife clucked over Anne's wan face. "Had me one like that meself—couldn't ride in the farmer's cart e'en. Well, you bring him on in.''

"Need a cold collation in a parlor," Bertie ordered importantly. "And beds for the day." As the woman's eyebrows lifted, he amended, "And perhaps the night, if m'nevvy ain't able to travel."

She nodded. "I'll give ye a chamber of yer own, sir, and have Hannah show them up t'the other. 'Tis two guineas apiece fer the rooms, and extra fer the meals."

"No!" Anne choked.

"Eh?"

Dominick's arm tightened about her waist in warning; then he spoke up. "Actually, I should prefer a separate chamber myself. Oliver is given to nightmares, I'm afraid, and he tosses and moans when he sleeps."

"Ye don't say!" The woman peered more closely at Anne, who quickly covered her mouth as though she were about to retch. "Hannah!" she bawled. "Come help! Now! Oh, lawks—not on my clean floor! Hannah! First door on yer right at the top o' the stairs, sir—you go on. Aye, and ye can have the one next to it."

As Dominick Deveraux helped her up the steps, Anne could hear the woman telling Albert Bascombe, "Mrs. Grendell's boy was like that, sir—they couldn't sleep a wink fer his thrashin' about. Mr. Marsh said 'twas worms that did it. A sprinkle o' gunpowder and five draps of kerosene o'er a lump of sugar put an end to it, ye know."

Bertie shuddered. "A wonder it didn't put an end to him."

"Now, I could fix ye some, and ye could give it her him ere he eats, ye know. Best to use it whilst the stomach is empty. It don't work otherwise, Dr. Marsh says."

"Makes me queasy to think on it."

"Sometimes, Mr. Wrexham, ye got ter do what's right fer the boy."

At that moment Anne's stomach rumbled audibly. Dominick dropped her arm and leaned against the hallway wall, his shoulders shaking. "What, pray tell, is so terribly amusing?" she hissed at him.

"Nothing, Miss Morland—nothing at all." He regained his composure and moved to open the chamber door.

The room was small but clean, furnished rather sparsely with a bed, a chair, and a washstand. While she surveyed it, he walked to the single window and looked down into the innyard below. "If you stand to the left, behind the curtain, you cannot be seen from here," he decided. Swinging around to face her, he added, "You will not, of course, leave your chamber unescorted. After Bascombe brings the clothes to you, you are to dress, then knock on the wall. One of us will tie your neckcloth for you. Then we will go down to eat together."

"I am not swallowing gunpowder and kerosene to satisfy that woman. Nightmares indeed—never in my life have I heard such a faradiddle, Mr. Deveraux."

"Bendell," he corrected her, starting to leave. "Mr. Bendell. Now, if you will excuse me, I'd best get down and help Bascombe spell 'Wrexham' for the book. Besides, I need to be certain of his discretion."

"Is this elaborate scheme truly necessary?"

He stopped and turned back, and his mouth curved into the faint wry smile. "Yes. Yes, it is my dear. A few ill-advised words from you or Bascombe, and we are fleeing again." His eyes met hers, and his expression sobered. "I do not mean to be taken ere I reach Nottingham. I have not come all the way from Lyons for naught, Miss Morland."

Torn between hunger and a desire to sleep, she sank onto the chair after he left, and she waited for Mr. Bascombe to bring her his clothes. Massaging her aching neck with both hands, she wished wearily that she could wake up in her bed at Mrs. Philbrook's, that somehow she was only dreaming that this was happening to her. But her torn and muddied dress was real, as were the two sharp raps at the door.

"Feeling more the ticket, Oliver?" Albert Bascombe called out, his voice booming too loudly.

"Coming, Uncle." She rose to let him in.

"Here." He thrust the neatly folded garments into her arms quickly, then leaned closer to whisper, "Have a care for m'coat, will you? I ain't easy to fit."

"I will."

Backing out the door, he raised his voice again. "Daresay you'll be fine as a fiddle once you eat."

He was gone as quickly as he'd come, leaving her to sort through the clothes curiously. He'd included everything down to his smalls, but she was by no means certain that she could wear all of it. The underclothing and the breeches appeared decidedly little, while the shirt, coat, and vest looked as though they might possibly fit. The snowy starched cravat was another matter entirely. There was no way she could make anything out of a flat, stiff piece of cloth.

"Well, she'd come this far, she told herself, and she'd not have Deveraux mock her for being a coward. She carried the clothing to the bed and removed her ruined gown. Laying it lovingly upon the coverlet, she fingered the neat, careful stitches she'd taken, and she wanted to cry. No matter what Dominick Deveraux thought of it, she knew she'd never have anything nearly so fine again.

Well, she had not the time to linger over broken dreams and torn dresses, she reminded herself, not if she would eat. She stepped from her petticoat and picked up Bascombe's smalls resolutely, then sat to draw them on. They were almost too tight for comfort, but she was loathe to go without them. The breeches proved only a slightly better fit, a challenge when it came to buttoning the front of them.

She started to discard the zona, then remembered Deveraux's telling her to flatten herself with it. The man had no shame, none at all, even to speak of such a thing to her. And he did not seem to care. Or perhaps, given the circumstance of their brief acquaintance, he'd marked her for some sort of doxy. It did not matter what he thought her, she reminded herself, for after the morrow, she'd never see him again.

Struggling to turn the boned band around to the front, she found the laces and loosened them, then pulled it up over her breasts. She was in the process of drawing it tight when she heard the tap at the door.

"I am not ready," she answered. "I have not knocked on the wall yet."

Sucking in her breath, she started at the top, tugging each cross of tape until the whalebone cut into her ribs. No matter what Deveraux said, she knew it was not going to work.

"You are not as flat as I thought," he observed, coming into the room.

Color flooded her face. "Have you no decency?" she gasped. "I said I was not ready!" As the air filled her lungs, the laces eased. "Get out of here!"

"I assure you, Miss Morland, that seduction is the last thing on my mind," he murmured, moving closer. "Besides, you are covered. Here . . ." Shifting a white cloth onto his arm, he reached for the tapes. "Hold still."

Outraged, she stiffened. "Really, sir, but this is beyond the bounds—I am not that sort of female!"

"I repeat, Miss Morland, that I have no designs on your person." As he spoke, he reached around her with one hand, pulling the zona higher in the back, then returned to straighten the laces in front. His touch was impersonal, his manner brisk. "Suck in your chest, and I'll have you done in a trice." His fingers moved quickly down the opening; then he tied the tapes at the bottom. "There. Can you breathe?"

It was not until he stepped back that she dared to look at him. "Barely." Her cheeks were hot with embarrassment. "One would think you did this sort of thing frequently," she muttered peevishly.

"*Au contraire*, my dear." His usual cynical smile broadened, warming his eyes briefly. "I cannot say I have ever put a female *in* one before. I am a much better hand at undoing them." Turning around, he asked, "Where's the shirt? Never mind—I see it."

"I can dress myself, sir."

"But can you manage to look like a boy?" he countered, carrying the shirt back to her. He held it out. "Button the front, then I'll see what I can do with it. I brought another neckcloth, thinking it would be easier to manage than the one he gave you," he added conversationally. "I thought it unlikely that you are a dandy at your age."

Feeling utterly foolish, she hurried through the buttons. "How old am I?"

He cocked his head for a moment. "As Oliver or Miss Morland?"

"Oliver. I am aware of my own age."

"I'd say fifteen or sixteen. Now, as Miss Morland, I should guess five-and-twenty. On the shelf, but not yet an ape-leader."

"I am two-and-twenty, sir," she retorted stiffly. "And *must* you keep insulting me?"

" 'Twas an assessment, not an insult. I daresay with your hair dressed and your person properly gowned, you could appear somewhat younger." He draped the triangle around her neck, then looped the ends, pulling them down. "Not the best," he murmured, "but 'tis the more difficult task to tie one on someone else." His fingers tugged at the collar points, straightening them above the neckcloth. "Now, put on the coat and boots, if you will."

"There is not even a mirror here," she complained, shrugging into Albert Bascombe's coat.

"I am your mirror, Miss Morland."

"How very lowering, Mr. Deveraux."

"I am accounted to have a very good eye."

"For the wrong sort of females, apparently."

The smile disappeared entirely. "I am not at all certain there is a right sort. On the one hand, there is the so-called lady—usually a ninnyhammer whose breeding invariably is matched by her family's avarice, and on the other, there is the lightskirt—a woman whose greed is entirely her own. While it amuses me to pursue them, neither is very admirable in the end." He pulled her coat snug and smoothed the shoulders. "I suspect there are as few honorable females as there are honorable gentlemen, if the truth were told."

"I consider myself neither sort, sir."

One black eyebrow quirked upward, and one corner of his mouth turned down. "If you are advancing yourself as a candidate for my hand, Miss Morland, you are wide of the mark. I have no intention of making an unfortunate female a difficult husband."

"Certainly not. For one thing, I have positively no expectations and am therefore quite ineligible myself. For another, you appear more than a trifle old for me," she added sweetly.

"A flush hit," he acknowledged. "Actually, I am but seven-and-twenty myself."

"No doubt a life of dissipation ages one."

" 'Tis the lack of sleep, my dear. Usually I show to better advantage." He walked around her, inspecting her critically. "Well, the breeches are a bit tight, aren't they? But the coat fits nicely. Perhaps you are but a growing lad. Go on—put on the boots. I'm getting deuced hungry, you know."

"I am quite sure that the advantage is greatly lessened once you speak, sir. Most of us prefer a more polite discourse than you offer."

He inclined his head slightly. "Another flush hit, Miss Morland. Did none ever complain of your own tongue?"

"Being a paid companion, I seldom get to use it." She sat in the chair and picked up one of Bascombe's boots. Drawing it on, she wriggled her toes in the empty space at the end. "I'll have a blister, but there's no help for it, I suppose."

"Stuff the ends with your handkerchief."

"I'm afraid I haven't one."

"Then filch a napkin from the table downstairs."

"I have never filched anything in my life. Nor do I have the least intention of traveling in Mr. Bascombe's clothes. I cannot breathe, nor can I sit comfortably. Besides, I can scarce take the stage from Nottingham to London dressed like this."

"Bascombe's going to buy you a gown ere we put you on the mail coach. Until then—"

"Until then I shall repair my dress as best I can and wear it."

"Bendell! Is my nevvy ready yet?" Bertie Bascombe shouted outside the door. "Food's ready!"

Dominick shook his head and sighed expressively. "If he persists, I'm afraid we're going to have to give it out that he's more than half-deaf."

"I daresay he cannot help it. He seems to be the sort that means well, after all."

"Alas, but Haverstoke already has his eye on a bride for

his heir. A pity, though—all that money, and an amiable albeit slow-witted husband in the bargain. You could do far worse, I suppose.''

"I am not casting out lures to either of you," she managed through gritted teeth. "I'd rather lead the proverbial apes in hell. Otherwise, I should have taken Mr. Fordyce, who at least professed himself smitten by my charms.''

He already had his hand on the door, but he paused and half-turned back to her. "Miss Morland, are you quite certain you have no expectations?''

"I live on the princely sum of forty pounds per year.''

"Which makes Fordyce's behavior exceedingly odd, don't you think?''

Goaded, she snapped, "Do you have no manners at all, Mr. Deveraux? You know, for a handsome man, you behave most unhandsomely.''

"Very few," he admitted. "I believe in plain speaking. I told you, I am not a particularly proper person.''

"Few manners, few morals, and an utter contempt for your fellowman—I own I *had* noticed your lack of character," she said acidly. "However, I do wish that you would keep your rather unflattering opinion of me to yourself.''

"My dear, if I were as black as you seek to paint me, I would have left you to fend for yourself at the Blue Bull.''

"And I am not your 'dear' either.''

He held the door for her. "A manner of speaking merely. After you, Master Oliver. While we are down, I sincerely hope you will remember to address your elders with proper respect.''

"Mr. Deveraux—''

"Bendell," he corrected her.

Once again the faintly derisive smile played at the corners of his mouth, and she realized she was merely affording him amusement. Swallowing a caustic set-down, she ducked beneath his arm into the hall. It was impossible to win verbally against a man who refused to be wounded.

4

Tap. Tap. Tap.

She was dreaming the wild, disordered dreams of the overweary. The opulently appointed opera house was crowded, its glittering patrons seated in gilded boxes, their jewels reflecting the thousand candles that blazed from sconces on the walls. Center stage, a dark-haired soprano sang, her rich and vibrant voice rising to the dramatic conclusion of the aria so spectacularly that the assemblage seemed to hold a collective breath. And then there was the applause, rolling, thunderous applause, mingled with shouted huzzahs, as the woman took the first of many curtsies. Coaxed, she sang again. And again.

Tap. Tap. Tap.

There was Mrs. Philbrook leaning into her face, her thin lips drawn tight with disapproval. *Your mother was naught but an opera dancer, missy, and we all know what they āre, don't we?*

Not Mama—not Mama! Mama was a lady!

You've got designs beyond your station, missy . . . designs beyond your station . . . designs beyond your station . . .

Quentin Fordyce bowed low over her hand, then smiled at her. I believe we are relations, Miss Morland. I am come from the general. . . . Your grandpapa is wishful of seeing you. . . . She was lying down. He was bending over her, shaking her. A scream rose in her throat. His hand closed over her mouth, stifling her cry.

"Don't be a fool, Miss Morland."

Her eyes flew open, and she stared into Dominick Deveraux's face. For a moment she did not comprehend; then she began to struggle.

There was no mistaking the fear in her eyes. "I am not

given to rapine, my dear," he murmured. "Hold your tongue and listen." He released her and stepped back. "We've got to go, I'm afraid. Thankfully, you slept in the shirt and breeches."

She blinked blankly, her mind not following his meaning at first; then she looked about her in sleepy stupor. Go? It was not even getting dark yet.

"But it cannot be time, surely. I mean—"

" 'Tis a quarter before four."

"I've had no sleep. I—"

"There is not the time to argue with you, Miss Morland. Our Bertie has discovered his money gone, and the looby promised to settle at dinner."

"Gone! But where . . . ?" With an effort, she rolled to sit on the edge of the bed. Already he was handing her Bascombe's coat, but she was too groggy to take it. "But we cannot leave without paying. Surely you—"

"Apparently someone appropriated his purse at the Blue Bull." He lifted her arm and thrust her hand into the sleeve. "And I have not the blunt to spare."

She pulled away, then struggled into the coat herself. "We cannot repay kindness with theft," she protested.

"New custom is arriving already, and we can possibly get out undetected down the back stairs." His gaze dropped to where her breasts were outlined beneath the clothes, and he realized she'd removed the confining zona. He looked about, then spied Albert Bascombe's caped greatcoat. "Here, wrap this around you. If anyone asks, we are going for a walk in the air before we sup."

" 'Tis not right, Mr. Deveraux—'tis not right."

"There's nothing I can do about it this instant—come on." He caught her hand and started for the door, but she pulled away. "Miss Morland . . ." He enunciated the words with exaggerated patience. "I left Lyons rather abruptly, carrying only what I expected to need for myself, and I cannot draw a bank draft without giving my presence in England away."

"No, I suppose not, but—"

"However, my little Puritan, once I am safe, the Red Hart will be paid. 'Tis not my custom to beat the tradesmen, I promise you. Satisfied?'' Not waiting for an answer, he slipped into the hallway, then motioned her to follow. "All's clear."

"Mr. Bascombe's boots . . . I have no shoes . . ." She turned back and groped beneath the bed, retrieving the top boots. Balancing herself against the wall, she managed to pull them on. When she looked up, Deveraux had already disappeared. Tired beyond enduring, cross beyond reason, she stumbled after him.

"*Will* you wait for me?'' she demanded peevishly when she caught up with him.

He grasped her elbow and propelled her down the deserted hall. "Between you and Bascombe, you are determined to have me taken,'' he muttered.

Bertie was standing nervously on the steps. "Got her?'' he asked as Dominick rounded the top of the stairwell. "Don't know why we couldn't eat ere we run,'' he said under his breath. "Deuced inconvenient to flee, if you was to ask me.''

"Cannot chance it—'tis better to leave as others come in.''

"But—''

"Do you want to be clapped up in jail for theft of service?'' Dominick countered.

"No, but . . . well, dash it, I'm going to get hungry!''

"Send the coachman into a pub for something later. Come on.''

"I ain't got any money to eat!''

"I'll sport the blunt for food, Bascombe.'' He caught Anne's hand and pulled her after him down the steep, narrow stairs. Her borrowed boots slipped on the treads, and she tripped, falling into him. "There are times, Miss Morland, when I wish I'd left you at the Blue Bull,'' he told her. Nonetheless, he circled her waist with his arm and supported her the rest of the way down. At the bottom, he released her. "Damn!''

The innkeeper's wife emerged from a side door, her arms laden with linen. "Mr. Wrexham! Why ever are ye back here?''

Discovered, Bertie turned red. "Uh—''

"I'm afraid Oliver's stomach is upset again," Dominick answered smoothly, shouldering Anne, who quickly covered her mouth. "Didn't want to overset your other custom, did we, Wrexham?"

"Eh?" Bertie blinked momentarily, his mind groping for something to say.

"Oliver needs air," Dominick prompted.

"Yes, definitely. Couldn't have m'nevvy castin' up his accounts in the front hall, after all."

"Mr. Wrexham, there's a chamber pot."

"Actually, walking him in the air seems to help."

She eyed Dominick suspiciously for a moment, then looked to Anne, and her expression softened. "Feeling poorly, eh? Ye look like ye been sleepin'."

"Woke up sick," Bertie insisted. "Food didn't set right in his stomach."

"Mr. Wrexham, naught's wrong with *my* food," the woman retorted indignantly. "If ye was to ask me, he's in bad need o' physickin'. I got salts in the cabinet, if ye was to want 'em."

"We'll get them ere he retires," Dominick promised. "At this point, we are not averse to trying anything."

"I could summon Dr. Marsh for ye."

"Perhaps later." His hand pressed into Anne's back, and on cue, she coughed as though she were gagging. "You are all right, Oliver," he uttered bracingly.

"Got to get him outside . . . servant, ma'am," Bertie said hurriedly. "Bendell, go on."

"But it's near to rainin'—ye'd best not keep the lad out o'erlong!" she called after them. "I collect ye are a'stayin' over, ain't ye?"

Once outside, they ran for the carriage, scrambling into it. "Got to give 'em the double, Davies," Bertie declared breathlessly. "My purse is gone!"

Rousted again, Cribbs gave Mr. Davies a look of patent long suffering. Nonetheless, both men hastened into the stable, then emerged with two ostlers, each leading a prized bay. Davies grinned at Bertie.

"Told 'em as how ye was a-racin' ter York, Mr. Wrexham."

"York? Eh? Oh . . . just so. Got to make all haste."

Dominick reached beneath his cloak and retrieved two-pence. When the harness was secured, the two ostlers released the lead pair's heads. "All right an tight, sor!" one yelled. Dominick leaned to toss the coins at them, while Davies flicked the coach whip over the team.

It was not until the carriage began to move that Anne remembered her gown. "I've got to go back!" she cried, reaching for the door.

Deveraux grasped her from behind and pulled her back. "The devil you do."

"No, no, you don't understand! My dress!"

"Buy you another one," Bertie reminded her.

"With *what*?"

Reddening, the younger man turned to Deveraux. "Got a point—got no blunt, you know. Must've lost m'purse when I was bumped at the Blue Bull. You got enough for a gown?"

"Yes," Dominick snapped. "Miss Morland, there is no time." When she appeared to sit back, he relaxed his grip on her. "Before we get to Nottingham, we'll manage something for you to wear on the mail coach. Until then, you'll have to remain a boy, I'm afraid."

But she slipped Bascombe's boots from her feet, then bolted again, managing to open the door and jump. Muttering a curse, Dominick threw himself after her. As the carriage gained speed, Bertie leaned precariously to pull the handle closed.

This time, when Dominick caught her, he jerked her shoulder angrily. "You little fool!" he shouted. "The dress is ruined!"

She whirled around, shaking free of him. "It's mine!" Two tears trickled down her face, streaking it. "I don't want to leave it!"

"Damn!" He lifted his hand, and for a moment she feared he meant to strike her. Instead, he stared hard, then backed away, dropping his arm. "I ought to leave you here, Miss Morland,'' he managed through clenched teeth.

Her chin came up defiantly. "Leave me, then. If you run, you can still catch Mr. Bascombe.''

He looked up and saw the carraige disappear around the corner. When his gaze returned to her, it was murderous. "What now, Miss Morland?'' he asked with deceptive softness. Even as he spoke, the first drops of cold rain spotted his cloak.

She swallowed. "I could not leave my gown, sir. 'Tis the finest thing I have.''

" 'Tis ruined,'' he reminded her brutally. "Utterly ruined. 'Tis not worth tenpence now.''

"I know.'' She looked up at him, her expression stricken. "Perhaps you can take the stage to Nottingham. You can leave me here, and I won't reveal your identity, I swear it.'' She wiped at her wet cheeks with the back of her hand, an unconscious gesture more moving than the tears.

Despite Bascombe's expensive clothes, her disordered hair gave her the appearance of a street urchin. And yet for all that he was vexed with her, he realized what it cost her to make the offer. He felt his anger dissipate, leaving resignation. He started back toward the inn.

"Where are you going?''

"To get your damned dress, Miss Morland.'' He stopped and glanced significantly at her bare feet. "And your slippers.'' His mouth twisted wryly. "Try to hide yourself between the conveyances until I come back, will you?''

The cobbled yard was cold and slippery underfoot. And now the sky poured, soaking everything. The smell of wet wool rose from the capes of Bascombe's greatcoat, disheartening her completely. Through her folly, she and Dominick Deveraux had nowhere to stay and nowhere to go. He couldn't get on the stage with her, not while she was dressed like this. And he couldn't get on the stage with her in her torn and mud-stained gown either. He would have to go on without her. Her stomach knotted at the thought.

"Here, now, oo's snoopin'?''

She came face-to-face with a toothless coachman. He eyed her suspiciously, his gaze traveling from her wet hair, over the fashionable greatcoat, and down to her bare feet.

"Oliver—Oliver Wrexham," she answered. "And I wasn't snooping—I was merely walking."

"Why?" he demanded bluntly. "Ain't naught here fer ye. Where's yer boots?"

"Inside."

"Inside, eh?"

"When there's none to see, I like to get my feet wet," she lied. "Actually, I like the mud between my toes, but I'm afraid my uncle would thrash me for it, so I can only stay on the stones today."

"Well, ye'd best move, fer Mr. Kenneth don't like anybody a-touching his coach."

As she moved away, she could hear him muttering about "the queer starts o' the Quality." She made one more pass between the carriages, taking care to avoid the coachy, then emerged at the end.

"Here."

She jumped, then realized it was Dominick Deveraux. He thrust her bundled gown into her arms, and as she took it, her petticoat and zona came loose, and her slippers fell onto the paving stones. Embarrassed, she tried to roll her undergarments back into the dress. She bent to slide a slipper onto her wet foot.

"Watch out!"

A carriage barreled around the corner, heading straight for them. As Deveraux pushed her to the ground, the coach door opened and Bertie Bascombe leaned out. "Come on!" he shouted. " 'Tis a long way to Nottingham!"

For a moment she lay beneath her protector, the caped greatcoat tangled between her legs, and then he rolled off her. Standing, he pulled her up as unceremoniously as he'd thrown her down; then, before she could retrieve any of her things, he picked her up and heaved her into Bascombe's lap.

"My coat . . . my clothes! Dash it, but they are ruined!" Bertie wailed.

Grasping the pull strap, she managed to crawl to the seat next to him. "Couldn't help it," she gasped.

Deveraux tossed her bundled clothes and the other wet

slipper inside, then followed them. "Your cowhanded driver came within an ace of putting our lights out," he muttered, dropping onto the velvet-covered bench across from Bertie. Reaching to close the door, he discovered the handle had caught in the lacing of the zona. Wrenching the undergarment free, he flung it across the seat to Anne. "Yours, I believe. I wouldn't want to leave anything of value behind, Miss Morland."

Her face flamed as she hastily tucked it beneath Bascombe's muddy greatcoat. "There is no need for sarcasm, Mr. Deveraux. You could have left me."

He wiped mud from his cheek with the back of his hand, then leaned back against the squabs. He regarded her wearily and sighed. "Unfortunately, Miss Morland, a Deveraux always finishes what he begins."

Stung, she retorted, "Perhaps if you had finished a bit less, you would not have to sneak back into this country, sir." As soon as the words had escaped her mouth, she wished she had them back. But they seemed to hang suspended in the air. His blue eyes went hard, his face turned to stone. Ashamed, she reached to touch his hand. "Your pardon, sir. Not knowing the precise circumstance of your difficulties, I had no right to say such a thing."

His gaze dropped to where her fingers lay against his; then he drew away. "There's naught to pardon, Miss Morland. The truth, however unpleasant, is still the truth."

"Still—"

"Spare me a surfeit of conscience, my dear."

"Dash it, Miss Morland, but I knew Beresford—aye, and the others also. Ain't a one of 'em as wasn't a bloody blackguard, if the truth was known. Don't fault Deveraux—there's them as would decorate him, if they were to find him."

"Bascombe—"

"Well, she ought to know!"

"Whether she believes me right or wrong is of no moment," Dominick said abruptly. "After the morrow, 'tis enough that she forgets she ever saw me."

"Nonetheless, I ought not to have said it." Shaking her

head ruefully, she managed a wry smile. "I'm afraid that in the space of a day, my civility has deserted me. I pray you will forgive me."

"I repeat: there is nothing to forgive, Miss Morland."

5

They were stopped before a small village pub whose sign read "Two Ducks, since 1660." Albert Bascombe eyed it doubtfully. "Do you think they'd have anything as a lady or a gentleman would eat?"

"We've not seen much else, have we?" Dominick Deveraux reached beneath his cloak to draw out a decidedly flat leather folder. Opening it, he retrieved a banknote. "Send Cribbs in with this," he said, passing it across.

"I thought the Deveraux were all plump in the pocket," Bertie muttered. "Ain't much to feed five."

"Plump enough—until one has to bribe one's way into the country. And," he added dryly, "this is scarce the Pulteney."

"What do yer want me ter buy?" the coachy asked.

"Whatever you can get—feed yourself and Davies also." Turning to Anne, Dominick inquired, "What would you have, my dear? Your pardon . . ." He inclined his head slightly. "I forgot—you are not anyone's dear, are you?"

"I will eat whatever you buy, sir."

As they waited, Anne gazed down the narrow street. The rain had stopped, but a fog was settling, giving an air of unreality to everything outside. The lights from a dozen small buildings appeared as hazy yellow circles about to be swallowed into an eerie nothingness. It was as though the world had shrunk to little more than the carriage, as though the only people left in it were Bascombe, Deveraux, and herself. For the moment there was no Mrs. Philbrook, no body on the floor at the Blue Bull. But tomorrow . . . She did not want to think of tomorrow.

It did not take Cribbs long to return, bringing two paper-wrapped bundles and an armful of bottles. Shifting the latter, he gave the larger package to his master. The savory smell of meat, onions, and pastry filled the passenger compartment as Bascombe unwrapped it to reveal an assortment of folded pies.

"Egad! All of this?"

"Ain't fancy, I'll be bound," the coachy replied, "but me and Davies like 'em." He passed three bottles in, adding, "Wasn't enough fer the hock, so I brung port ter yer. The pies is marked—pigeon, pork, and kidney." Drawing his head back, he closed the door, and climbed up to share the rest with the driver.

"Well, daresay it ain't what you are used to, Miss Morland, but the pick is yours," Bertie said. "Don't know whether 'tis the big P or the little one on top as means pigeon or pork, but it don't matter."

"I should prefer pork, I think."

"Bite into it—if 'tis pigeon, I'll eat it," he offered. When she hesitated, he chose one with a K and stuffed a large portion of it into his mouth. "Ain't bad," he assured her. "Ain't half-bad."

She'd thought she was too tired to eat, but as she watched him devour the pasty with relish, she realized she was truly famished. Taking one from the papers, she nibbled a corner, fearing the worst. She'd never liked eating pigeon, always seeing the plump birds that begged in the parks, but this night she told herself she was beyond caring. Thankfully, she realized she'd chosen pork.

"Which P is which?" Bascombe asked, his mouth so full that crumbs spilled out.

"The larger letter must mean pigeon."

Dominick reached for a bottle of wine, and using his thumbnail to break the thin coat of wax over the neck, he observed, "Rebottled and cheap." Turning away from them, he took the cork in his teeth and pulled. It squeaked; then there was a dull pop. He held the bottle out to Anne. "Miss Morland?"

"I don't have a glass."

"Neither do we. Have a pull and pass it," Bertie said. When he saw she did not take the wine, he encouraged her.

"Go on—ain't any of us got rotten teeth." Taking the bottle, he lifted it and swigged hugely. When he lowered it, there were crumbs floating in the dark red liquid. He started to hand it back.

"Keep it. Miss Morland and I will share our own, I think," Dominick murmured.

"Really, I am not thirsty."

"As you wish." He opened another bottle, then leaned back to drink.

When she looked across again, he was watching her, his faint smile seeming to mock her. She wondered irritably if everything about her was a jest to him. Determined to appear the proper lady despite all that had befallen her, she tried to eat daintily, taking small bites. Ladies, she reminded herself fiercely, did not gorge themselves even when starving.

The pasty was good, but salty. Long before she finished it, she wished she'd not declined the wine. But it was vastly improper to drink with two men. And she could still remember the pain from whatever Quentin Fordyce had given her. Still, she could not help eyeing the bottle of port with regret.

"Another pie, Miss Morland?" Bertie asked. "Got plenty."

Another one and she'd need a gallon of something to wash it down. Still hungry, she forced herself to shake her head. "No, thank you."

"Don't be a ninnyhammer, Miss Morland," Deveraux advised her shortly. "Surely by now you can acquit Bascombe and me of any designs on your person. Neither of us is a Quentin Fordyce, after all."

"Egad, no," Bertie managed between mouthfuls. "It don't make any difference even if you was to drink a little wine. Ruined, anyway." Then, perceiving what he'd said, he hastened to add, "Well, you would be if 'twas known you been with us, but daresay it ain't going to get out. I ain't telling anybody. Promise."

She knew she was ruined, but it was lowering to hear it, particularly since the situation had not been of her making.

She had no position, no money, and no place to go now—
except Newgate. And she ought not to care what an amiable
fool and a self-styled rogue thought of her. Not at all. She
had nothing to lose but her virtue, and they were apparently
uninterested in that. She wavered, then told herself that it
was all of a piece anyway. Whether she drank with them
or not, if the story were ever told, there would be those who
would suspect her of considerably more than that.

Dominick watched her face, seeing the momentary fear,
then the resignation betrayed in the brown eyes, and despite
his earlier words, he did feel for her. Unlike him, she'd not
been totally alone in the world before. For a female, that
must be devastating. "Blue-deviled, my dear?" he asked with
uncharacteristic gentleness.

Used to his gibes, she was unprepared for the kindness
in his voice. Her throat constricted painfully. Swallowing,
she nodded. "Yes, Mr. Deveraux, I am," she managed to
answer finally. "But I shall survive."

"Shouldn't wonder at it!" Bertie said forcefully. "Got
reason, after all, and it ain't right! Serve Fordyce right if
he was to be dead."

"Bascombe—"

"Very good sort of a girl, I can tell. And if I was in the
petticoat line, which I ain't, I'd as lief offer for you as for
Miss Brideport."

"Thank you, Mr. Bascombe, but I fear I'd decline."

"You would?" Bertie brightened visibly. "I say, but you
are a brick, Miss Morland! Most of the females don't care
how they get a fellow into parson's mousetrap, you know."

"I would consider it very lowering to wed a man I did
not love, sir."

"The romantic Miss Morland," Dominick murmured.

"Is everything a jest to you?" she retorted, stung.

"On the contrary, my dear—I salute you. I would that my
mother had felt the same. Here . . ." He handed her the
half-empty bottle. "Bascombe's right, you know—neither
of us will tell. Besides, 'twas so cheap, 'tis probably
watered."

She sighed and took it. "I daresay it would not matter if you did tell. Ruined is ruined, after all." Lifting the bottle, she took a sip of the wine. It was surprisingly sweet. She wiped the opening and held it out to Deveraux. "Thank you, sir."

"Keep it. You'll need it if you are to choke down another pasty. Besides, there is still this one." As he spoke, he held up the third bottle of port.

That settled, they ate and drank freely, polishing off the meat pies with relish. By the end of her third one, Anne was no longer sipping her wine daintily, but had taken to drinking it with as much gusto as the men. Despite the chilly fog and the darkness outside, the passenger compartment of Albert Bascombe's carriage seemed warm, rosy, and intimate. She was, she supposed, more than a trifle grogged, but this night she did not care. For now, the soft flickering light of the interior lanterns chased the blue devils, and the companionship of the two men comforted her. She allowed herself to forget Quentin Fordyce, Mrs. Philbrook, and her ruined dress. Her stomach was full, her mind mellow, and she was safe. Bone-weary, she fought sleep to savor these last hours of security.

Albert Bascombe hiccuped loudly, then took yet another swig from his bottle. Fixing his rather wine-befuddled gaze on Dominick Deveraux, he announced, "Been thinkin'—too much formality in the world. Deuced nuisance—man cannot say what he thinks for the demned rules. It don't make sense."

Dominick's lips twitched. "Observant of you to note it, Bascombe."

"Bertie—m'friends call me Bertie. Think I'm a slowtop, don'tcha? Well, I ain't, precisely. Just don't think fast, that's all." Turning to Anne, he asked, "You don't mind callin' me Bertie, do you?"

"Well, I—"

"Get tired of being the Honorable Albert Bascombe. Get deuced tired of being Haverstoke's heir too. Don't even want to be an earl." He hiccuped. "Sorry. Ain't got anybody but m'friend Patrick—ain't got no female friends at all,'' he confided. ''But I like you—you ain't like most of 'em.'' His pale eyes met hers earnestly. ''You know what, Miss Morland? You got sense—lots of it. Most females I know, they'd a been waterin' pots the whole way, but—''

''Another bottle of wine, and he would offer for you, Miss Morland,'' Dominick observed dryly.

''Asking her to call me Bertie, that's all. You too.''

''Well, as we have already dispensed with proper discourse between us, I cannot see that it matters anyway. I see no harm—''

''Not Albert—Bertie. Hate Albert—m'father calls me that when I've vexed him.''

She nodded. ''Then Bertie it is. And you may call me Annie.''

''Friends?''

''Yes.''

''What about you, Deveraux? You ain't answered.''

''The name is Dominick, and I cannot say I care very much for it either. But . . .'' He straightened in his seat. ''You may use it, if it pleases you.''

Bertie grinned happily. Lifting his own nearly empty bottle, he proposed. ''To friends—to Dominick and Annie.''

''To Bertie,'' Anne answered, clinking her bottle against his.

''To three souls together,'' Dominick murmured.

''If you are saying we are foxed, I ain't,'' Bertie declared. ''Don't think Annie is either.''

''Positively bosky,'' Anne contradicted him. ''And I am beyond caring.''

''Hold the devil away until morning, eh?'' Dominick asked softly.

''Yes.''

''It does not work, you know. I've tried.''

''Sometimes, Mr. Deveraux, I get tired of thinking on the morrow.''

''Dominick.'' Once again the faint smile played at the corners of his mouth. ''Dominick,'' he repeated.

"I thought you did not like the name."

"I like it as well as Mr. Deveraux."

Giving the lie to his earlier words, Bertie Bascombe's empty bottle slid to the floor, and he cradled his head against a seat corner. His soft, rhythmic snoring seemed to blend with the beat of the horses' hooves against the hard-surfaced road. Anne reached for the carriage rug and laid it over his shoulder. Slowtop or not, one could scarce help liking him, for beneath his frivolous appearance he was far kinder than most of his class.

Settling back, she pulled Bascombe's greatcoat close around her, then looked across to Dominick Deveraux. His smile had faded, and he was regarding her almost soberly.

"What *are* you going to do?" he asked suddenly.

She drew in a deep breath, then exhaled fully. She didn't want to think about that, but she answered, "As soon as I obtain a dress, I shall seek accommodations on the mail coach bound for London."

"And then?"

"Once there, I shall return to Mrs. Philbrook's, where I shall be denounced rather roundly ere I am turned off. But I shall collect my things, then visit the constable."

"What if Fordyce survived?"

" 'Tis most unlikely—he was out for rather a long time, sir."

"Dominick," he reminded her. "But if he did—there is no possibility that this Philbrook woman would keep you?"

"If I am properly chastened, perhaps. Really, sir— Dominick—I'd rather not—"

"Are you quite certain the Morlands will not aid you?"

"I should perish ere I asked them."

"If only for family pride, I cannot think General Morland would wish his granddaughter in jail."

"Perhaps not, but—"

"Which brings me back to my first question, Annie—what will you do? For the moment, let us assume Fordyce lives."

"Well, if I am not in jail, I shall seek employment, of course. Without a character, 'twill be difficult, but not entirely impossible. I shall consult an agency and hope to be referred to an elderly female of better disposition than Mrs. Philbrook.''

''What—not the opera? Considering your mother's fame, I should think you'd have entrée there.''

''Alas, but I cannot sing, I'm afraid—my voice is rather flat. However, I speak creditable Italian.'' She took another deep drink of the wine. ''But 'tis not your concern, is it?''

''No.''

Emboldened by the port and by the intimacy of the small space between them, she cocked her head to study him. ''And you—what will you do? Your case seems quite as desperate as mine, you know.''

''I shall either see or bury my mother. In any event, I mean to go back to France.''

''Did you never think to turn yourself in?''

It was as though his face closed, and for a time he did not answer. He stared into the blackness, then finally sighed. ''I cannot. My mother would never forgive me the scandal. 'Twould be the final sin in her eyes, I'm afraid.''

''You do not appear the murderer to me.''

''Dueling is illegal, my dear.''

Having no answer for that, she leaned back, and as the sudden silence was broken only by Bascombe's snoring, she took refuge in what was left of her port. Why had he asked about the morrow? Why had he forced her to think on the future she did not have? On the morrow she would part from Dominick Deveraux and Bertie Bascombe, and she would be alone. And despite the wine, her spirits plummeted. She blinked back hot tears of self-pity and lifted he bottle to her lips. Just this once, she'd drown her fears in what was left of the port. She'd have a miserable head on the morrow, but she no longer cared.

6

"Miss Morland . . . Annie . . ." Dominick leaned forward to shake Anne.

She shifted her body, raising her arm to cover her eyes, and turned to lay her head on Albert Bascombe's shoulder. Rousing, he straightened up to push her toward her corner.

"Ruinin' m'coat," he mumbled sleepily. He passed his hand over his face and forced his eyes open. "Where the devil are we?"

"The last village ere Nottingham." Dominick touched Anne again. "Miss Morland . . ."

Her head nodded, and she slid down in the seat, leaning once again into her seatmate. "Dash it, but I ain't a pillow," he complained. He looked down, seeing the tousled hair against his arm, and sighed. "S'pose the coat's ruined anyway, ain't it?" Raising his eyes to Dominick, he muttered, "Don't seem right to abandon her, does it? Look at her—plumb fagged out."

"Weasel-bit."

Bertie shook his head to clear it, then winced visibly. "Dreamt you said I could call you Dominick."

"I don't care what you call me. Miss Morland—"

"Call her Annie—said you could—remember that." Bertie squeezed his eyes shut against the light, then gingerly opened them again. "Village don't tell me nothing."

"I sent Cribbs for coffee, and Davies is seeing to the horses, I believe." This time Dominick shook Anne's shoulder more forcefully. "Come on, Annie girl—got to rise."

"Unnnnhhhhh?"

"We've got to find you something to wear."

"Too tired. Go away." She turned her head into Bertie's coat, muffling her voice. "So sleepy."

"I don't know, Dev . . . Dominick, maybe we ought to let her sleep. Ain't hurting anything but m'coat, and the dashed thing's beyond redeeming anyway."

"We haven't the time. Annie . . ." Dominick slipped his hands under her arms and pulled her to sit up. "We are nearly there."

"Where?" she demanded querulously, opening her eyes.

As the stream of sunlight from the window struck her face, she groaned and leaned forward to hold her forehead. Her tongue felt thick, her ears rang, and her head seemed to reverberate to the sound. And she felt queasy. "I cannot even think—where are we?"

"I already asked," Bertie answered, "and 'tis just some village." He twisted his head to look out his window. "Says 'Bennett's Pur . . . '—well, something of 'Drinks of Virtue.' "

"I believe the word is 'purveyor,' " Dominick murmured.

"I don't feel virtuous just now," Anne muttered, covering her mouth. "I think I'm going to be ill."

"Egad." Moving swiftly, the bigger man pushed open the carriage door and thrust Anne's head down. "You'll feel better when 'tis over," he promised, holding her from behind.

"Watch out for m'coat!" Bertie cried. "And the floor!"

She gagged, then retched violently, bringing up soured wine into the street. Her whole body was cold and clammy as wave after wave of nausea washed over her. Finally there was nothing left in her stomach.

"Your handkerchief, Bascombe," Dominick ordered brusquely, his arm still around Anne's waist.

" 'Tis trimmed with Venice lace, dash it, but . . ." Even as he complained, the younger man produced the lawn square. "Thought you was a-going to call me Bertie," he added peevishly.

"Later. Feeling more the thing, Annie?" Dominick asked sympathetically. "Here, wipe your face. I daresay the worst is over."

She pulled herself back weakly and sank against the squabs, closing her eyes. "I feel awful."

"Ain't the first to shoot the cat after a night of tippling," Bertie assured her. "Done it more times than I can count. Got a devil of a head myself, if you was to know the truth of it."

"Where are we?" she repeated, pressing the folded cloth against her aching forehead.

"Cribbs is procuring coffee from Bennett's, and then you are going into Miss Porter's to seek a gown." Satisfied that she was not going to be sick again, Dominick sat back also. Drawing out the thin folded leather case, he opened it and selected several banknotes. " 'Tis the best I can do just now," he murmured apologetically, pressing them into her hand.

She looked down, and for a moment she nearly forgot the throbbing in her head. "Thirty pounds! Oh, but I cannot . . . that is, well, I could not . . . 'Tis too much!"

"Thirty pounds ain't nothing—m'sisters spend more'n that on gloves. I say, Dominick, but it ain't enough," Bertie protested. "Dash it, but she ain't got nothing!"

"This is scarce Madame Cecile's," Dominick reminded him dryly. Turning his attention to Anne, he explained, "If we are fortunate, Miss Porter will have something that you can bargain for on display. If not, I'll find you something at the Haven."

"I cannot go into an establishment like this. Look at me: I've no comb . . . I'm dirty . . . I look like a grubby school-boy in Mr. Bascombe's clothes." She held out the soiled handkerchief for proof. "I am in sore need of a bath."

"Alas, but that I cannot provide on the instant, Annie."

"Mr. Bascombe, you tell him, I—"

"Told you—you can call me Bertie also."

"Is there room for only one maggot in your brain, Bascombe?" Dominick demanded irritably. As the younger man lapsed into a wounded silence, he felt goaded. "Look, I've a devil of a head myself, Bertie, and 'tis not like to improve. If you would be helpful, you would go in with her, for she seems inclined to turn missish this morning."

"*Me?* But I ain't . . . Dash it, I told you: I ain't in the petticoat line! Wouldn't even know what she was to wear! And I got room for lots of maggots in m'brain, if I was to want 'em!" Then, realizing what he'd said, he amended, "But I ain't got any. I may be more'n a trifle foggy this morning, but I know when I am insulted," he finished with feeling.

Dominick exhaled, then nodded. "Your pardon, Bertie,—I am easily tried."

"And we are tired beyond bearing," Anne murmured soothingly.

At that moment Cribbs returned, carrying a steaming flask and a tin cup in his mittened hand. "Made me pay fer the the cup," he explained. "Cut two lumps o' sugar—woman wouldn't let me have more. But if it ain't sweet enough . . ."

" 'Tis fine." Dominick took the flask and poured coffee into the cup. Holding it out to Anne, he offered, "Miss Morland?"

She shuddered visibly. "I think I should prefer to put nothing in my stomach this morning."

"Bertie?"

"Me neither."

Dominick shrugged, then took a sip of that hot liquid. "A pity, for it would warm your bones." With his free hand he wiped the steam from the window and pointed. "Miss Porter's is over there. As she drapes the door and windows with her latest cloths, 'tis dim inside. Not to mention that she's more than a trifle shortsighted from bending over her needle."

"Shortsighted or not, I cannot but think she will surely notice Mr. Bascombe's breeches on me," Anne pointed out reasonably. "Besides, what could I possibly tell her?"

He favored her with a decidedly pained expression. "You and Bertie are returning from a mill, and being in bad graces with your female parent, you are wishful of taking a peace offering home," he invented. "Show her the money, and let her greed do the rest."

"A dress for a gift? I don't think—"

"A dress, Annie."

"Never heard such a faradiddle in my life!" Bertie declared. "Buy m'mother a gown? I can tell you right now she wouldn't wear it!"

"Hopefully Miss Porter will not know that."

"Tell you what—you go in with her."

"I should be recognized on the instant."

Anne glanced down at the money in her hand with misgiving. "I am not used to lying, Mr. Deveraux. If this Miss Porter is any judge of character, she will see through this pretense on the instant. Besides, 'tis doubtful that she will have anything made up."

Bertie squinted out the window to read the sign on the shop. "Says 'gowns of the latest stuffs.' "

"Which means only dress lengths of cloth," she reminded him.

"She usually displays at least one gown on form to demonstrate her skill with her needle," Dominick answered. "How suitable it is could be quite another matter. In any event, she will come off price if you are willing to haggle."

"You seem rather well-acquainted with Miss Porter," she commented, eyeing the building doubtfully.

"My mother is cheese-paring enough to recognize a bargain, Miss Morland. Bertie, your comb."

"I ain't sharing it. Dash it, but—"

"Bascombe—"

"Oh, all right! Damme if I got anything left to call my own," he complained. Reluctantly he reached into his pocket, then dropped his comb into the other man's hand. "There's a bit of pomade on it," he muttered. "Make her hair flatter'n it already is, if you was to ask me."

"It cannot look worse." Dominick set his cup on the seat beside him and leaned forward to drag the teeth through her tangled hair. When she winced, he apologized. "Sorry. I cannot say I am any hand at this." Giving up on the comb, he ran his fingers beneath the disorder, lifting her flattened curls. Pulling some of them forward, he sighed. "You do look like a grubby schoolboy, you know."

"Thank you," she retorted acidly.

Bascombe shook his head. "Look like you was in the mill rather than watching it."

Dominick drew out his watch and laid it on the seat beside his cup. "You can have fifteen minutes."

"*Fifteen minutes?* Plain you ain't got any sisters, else you'd know it takes longer than that to rig 'em up," Bertie snorted. "Takes m'sister Gussie hours to get ready to go to the demned lending library!"

"Fifteen minutes."

Favoring Anne with a look of long suffering, Bascombe demanded, "Are you m'nevvy or m'brother? And who the devil am I, anyway?"

"I don't care—I shall feel the veriest fool, sir." Clutching the money in her hand, she reached to open the door. "If I am not clapped up in Newgate, 'twill be Bedlam," she predicted direly.

"Guess you are m'brother," Bertie decided, heaving himself after her. "Make it easier to explain. But I ain't this Wrexham fellow—don't like the name." Casting a surreptitious look down the quiet street, he started for the draper's. "Think I'll be Bales."

"Bales?"

"M'valet. Deuced starchy fellow—serve him right if I was to get in a scrape with it. Now, I don't want you a-saying anything. We ain't got time to chaw with the woman, you know."

Dominick watched them disappear into the tiny shop, then leaned back wearily. He ought to be glad to be rid of both of them, but somehow he wasn't. Now that he was nearly there, he did not relish the thought of going home. He sipped his coffee slowly, wondering if Annie Morland could be persuaded to stay with his mother. No, he decided, for she had said she wished for an employer of better disposition than the Philbrook woman, and he could not offer her that.

Once inside the small shop, Anne had to blink several times to adjust her eyes to the dimness. Taking a deep breath, she approached a woman she supposed to be the proprietress and blurted out, "We are come to buy a dress."

"Name's Bales," Bertie announced hastily.

"Mr. Bales."

"He's Bales also—'m'brother.'' As the woman's eyes took in Anne's disheveled appearance, he added, "Been to a mill, you know."

"I see." Her mouth drew into a thin line of disapproval. " 'Twould appear, young man, that you are more in need of a tailor than a dressmaker."

"Oh, it isn't for us," Anne said quickly.

"Right," Bertie agreed. "Got to take m'mother something to keep her from cutting up a devil of a dust, don't you know?" He peered past her curiously. "Ain't you got anything as is ready—I mean, ain't you got something as we could just take?"

"Mr. Bales, I assure you that I am noted for the fit of my gowns. I could not possibly—"

"Could we perhaps see what you have?" Anne asked.

"Well, there are the fashion plates, of course, and I can show you how the latest taffeta is made up, but I am sure your mother—"

"Taffeta? I don't—"

"We'll take it," Bertie told the woman. "And a petticoat and whatever else goes underneath."

"Slippers," Anne remembered. "We must have slippers. But I am not at all sure that Mama would like taffeta, John. Perhaps a muslin? A dress length even—and a package of needles and thread."

"Huh?" Perceiving that somehow Anne Morland was going to throw a spoke into the wheel, Bertie insisted, "Now, dash it, but you know she'd like a fancy gown! Bound to! Besides, you ain't got the time to have anything made up." Before either woman could demur, he declared, "We'll take the demned taffeta! I ain't got all day, you know. Give her the blunt."

The promise of immediate money held great appeal for the seamstress, but she was not about to part with what she considered nothing less than an artistic creation for less than satisfactory remuneration. "Well," she began slowly, "I do not in general sell my sample, sir. Perhaps you would prefer

something else—a fur muff perhaps,'' she added shrewdly.
''Unless your mama is a female of excellent taste . . .'' Her
voice trailed off. ''Well, I could not part with the dress, Mr.
Bales—nothing less than forty guineas would persuade me.
'Tis in the latest French style, after all.''

''Got twenty pounds says you sell the gown—and that
ought to buy whatever goes under it. Ain't got time to haggle.
And we got to have slippers,'' he recalled.

It was obvious that he'd struck a vulnerable spot. Though
it was less than half what she'd asked, it would be immediate.
''Twenty pounds?'' she asked. ''Scrip or bank draft?''

''Got the blunt right here,'' he assured her.

''Even so, I'm afraid I should have to fit your mother—
my reputation quite depends on the appearance of my
dresses,'' she said, wavering.

''If it don't suit her, she'll come in and have it adjusted,''
Bertie promised. He turned to Anne. ''Give the woman the
money.''

''Don't you think we ought to see the dress first?'' Anne
asked meaningfully.

''It don't matter. If she ain't got but one made up, then
that's what we got to buy. Here . . .'' He reached to take
the banknotes from her hand. ''Tell you what—you wait in
the carriage.''

''I'd rather not.''

''Box your ears if you don't,'' Bertie threatened. ''Go on.''
He counted twenty pounds into the bemused dressmaker's
hand, then told her, ''If it ain't ready in fifteen minutes—
no, best make that ten—I want my blunt back.''

The woman looked at the money before capitulating. ''All
I have are black cloth slippers, and I'd have to have extra
for them. Five shillings, I think. As for the petticoat—''

''Twenty pounds is it,'' Bertie insisted.

''Could we *see* the dress first?'' Anne repeated.

''Told you—it don't matter!'' For once in his life, Bertie
felt assertive. Taking hold of Anne's coat sleeve, he propelled
her forcefully to the door, leaning close enough to whisper
for her ears alone, ''Dash it, but I ain't having Dominick

angered 'cause you wanted to gape! Go on. Tell him I'm coming as soon as Miss Porter bundles the dress.'' Pushing the remaining money into her hand, he said, ''Here—for the coach fare and food.''

''Is aught amiss?'' the seamstress inquired suspiciously.

''Lud no! M'brother ain't been around females enough to know as what they'd like,'' Bertie explained, turning back to her. ''Ain't a man of the world like me.''

As Anne climbed back into the carriage and leaned once more into the now-familiar squabs, Dominick Deveraux lifted one eyebrow quizzically. ''Am I mistaken, or are you out of reason cross, my dear?'' Then, his eyebrow moving even higher, he observed, ''I don't see any boxes, Miss Morland.''

''I have been sent out like the veriest schoolboy,'' she retorted. Looking through the window once more at Miss Porter's, she added acidly, ''You behold a female about to be outfitted according to Mr. Bascombe's taste.''

''Egad.''

''Yes.'' Passing a weary hand over her aching brow, she forced a rueful smile. ''I shall appear a shocking fright on the mails—I know it.'' A resigned sigh escaped her. ''But 'twill be all of a piece anyway, won't it? 'Fugitive murderess taken in taffeta,' or some such, I suppose.''

''Taffeta?''

'' 'Tis all the woman has. With my continuing good fortune, I shall be riding the common stage in a country ball gown.'' Her gaze dropped to the wrinkled bundle on the floor, and she could not quite keep the regret from her voice. ''At least my own dress, however poor it must seem to you, could be worn almost anywhere.''

They did not have long to wait. Albert Bascombe emerged triumphantly from the shop carrying a box crammed so hastily that a pink satin ribbon trailed from it. As he tossed it into the carriage, it fell open to reveal Miss Porter's best imitation of a French evening gown. As Anne stared at it in dismay, Dominick lifted it, holding it up. The pink taffeta swished as the slender skirt unfolded from beneath a decidedly low bodice. There was more material in the tiny ruffled sleeves than in the top, which seemed to rely on strategically placed satin rosettes to cover the wearer's bosom.

"Definitely not the thing for the mail coach, my dear," Dominick murmured.

"Egad. I didn't look at the demned thing—place was deuced dark. Well, I ain't taking it back," Bertie declared. "The woman's too nosy by half—had a devil of a time describing m'mother to her whilst she was wrapping the thing."

Anne looked to the money she still held. "Perhaps if I purchased a shawl," she said doubtfully.

"No." Dominick refolded the gown and stuffed it into the box. "There is no help for it, I'm afraid—you'll have to come to the Haven with me."

"Oh, but I could not."

"Dash it, but she cannot go barging in on a sick woman, Deveraux!" Bertie protested. "It ain't done!"

"Do you have a better notion?"

Nonplussed, the younger man looked from Anne to Dominick. "No," he admitted. "Made a devil of a mull again, I guess."

"Not at all," Dominick murmured, his mouth twitching. "If Miss Morland ever wishes to attend a party, she has but to add a bit of modesty to the top, and she is ready for it."

Bertie brightened visibly. "Well, daresay she could do that." Then, as the full import of Dominick Deveraux's words sank in, he sighed. "But I guess you do not go to many parties, do you, Annie?"

"Not often." Nonetheless, she felt for him. Impulsively she reached to touch his arm. "The dress is quite lovely— truly it is," she lied. "I shall cherish it."

"Almost forgot." He fished in his pocket and produced a thin paper wrapped packet and a spool of thread. "Here—I bought the needles you asked for. Made Miss Porter throw 'em into the bargain."

"Mr. Bascombe—Bertie—I could kiss you," she declared thankfully.

Reddening, Bertie shrank back. "I pray you won't—ruin everything if you was to do that."

"A figure of speech merely, I suspect," Dominick said soothingly. His eyes met Anne's briefly. "I doubt she is any more like to kiss you than me, which is not at all—am I right, Annie?"

It was her turn to color. "Actually, I am not in the habit of kissing anyone. You are quite safe in my presence, both of you. Having no expectations, I do not engage in dangerous games."

"More's the pity, my dear."

She carefully unwrapped the square of paper and drew out one of the needles. "At least I shall be able to wear my own gown until something else can be contrived."

Bertie eyed the rumpled taffeta on the floor doubtfully. "I dunno. Have to say you was in an accident if you was to wear that." He looked across at Dominick. "And what about a maid? Dash it, but we cannot take her into your mama's without an abigail. It ain't done."

"I assure you that I look hagged enough to be taken for an ape-leader," Anne declared flatly. "If Mr. Deveraux thought me five-and-twenty yesterday, I must surely appear thirty today."

"Miss Porter thought you was a schoolboy," Bertie reminded her.

"Miss Porter is half-blind," she shot back.

"When we get to the Haven, I will procure a spinster's cap for you, if you wish," Dominick promised.

"Ought to do the trick." Bertie shifted his weight and leaned against the side panel. "Though why we are racketing about the country with *any* female ain't going to be easy to explain to m'father."

Anne stared soberly out her window. Somehow the thought of wearing a spinster's cap in the presence of Dominick Deveraux was more lowering than Bascombe's breeches or her own torn, soiled gown.

7

The atmosphere was decidedly subdued within as the carriage rolled up the drive through the Haven's park. The giant oaks on either side twined their bared limbs above, creating a lattice of shadows on the road below. In the distance, high on a hill, stood a monolithic mansion of gray stone. Staring dispiritedly out of the coach window, Anne thought it not unlike the setting of a gothic novel. All it needed was a rocky, precipitous coast above crashing waves, which, being in the Midlands, it did not have.

She had no business going home with Dominick Deveraux, and she knew it. But she was more than one hundred twenty miles from London, and whether she wished to admit it or not, she quite literally had nowhere else to go. Except jail. Still, she felt a very real sense of unease, not because she feared the self-styled rogue across from her, but rather because she found herself quite drawn to him. And sensible females of no means knew better than to cast lures at any man, for the result was destined to be disastrous.

Glancing surreptitiously at him, she wondered what he was thinking. He was a strange and moody man, she mused to herself, one whose acts of kindness seemed determinedly offset by a certain derisiveness, as though much of what happened around him was but life's bitter jest. Asleep he looked even younger than his twenty-seven years. Awake he looked older, more weary, more worldly-wise. Just now, the small wry smile was missing, and he appeared almost haunted.

His eyes were fixed on the house ahead, and his face was set. He'd been a fool to come, a fool to trade his safety for a woman who begrudged him his very life. Why had he done it? Guilt? Duty? He could not answer. If she yet lived, he

did not even know what he would say to her. He was, by
her own account, the greatest disappointment in her bitter,
unfulfilled life. And it did not help that the Almighty had
seen fit to create him in his father's image rather than hers.
For that alone she'd damned him.

"Dashed big place—thought Trent had the family seat,"
Albert Bascombe observed finally.

Dominick continued to stare out the window. "He does.
My mother brought the Haven with her on her marriage."

Bertie hesitated, then blurted out, "I been thinking—maybe
men Annie ought to go on as soon as she's got rigged up
right. I can put her on the coach bound for London, you
know. Draw a bank draft in Nottingham."

"I was under the impression you were without identifica-
tion."

"Egad—hadn't thought of that. But you can vouch . . ."
Bertie stopped guiltily. "Oh, guess you cannot, can you?"

"No."

"Guess we are still in the basket, ain't we?"

"Yes."

"Somehow it does not seem quite right to present ourselves
as guests," Anne said. "And I tend to agree with Mr.
Bascombe. In your mother's condition, perhaps we ought
to go on. I still have passage money left from Miss Porter's."
She looked down at her sadly mended and much-creased
dress. Her fingers scratched at a bit of dried mud. "I can
think of something to tell my fellow passengers. Really, there
is no need to impose further on your kindness."

"As my father's heir, the house is mine, Miss Morland,
and I am free to bring home whomever I choose." He was
silent for a moment, watching the road as the carriage made
the last turn. " 'Tis misnamed, you know," he said finally,
his voice so low she had to strain to hear it. "Of all the things
it is, 'tis scarce a haven." Tensing suddenly, he muttered,
"Damn," under his breath.

Curious, Anne tried to follow his gaze, and saw a tall
black-haired man emerge from the house. As the coach rolled
to a halt before the large portico, the gentleman looked up,

and she was struck by his resemblance to Dominick Deveraux.

"Your brother?"

"Trent. My only brother died some years back."

"I'm sorry—I did not know." So that was the notorious marquess. She didn't know what she'd expected, but he did not appear nearly as old as she'd imagined him. "There is a family resemblance between you."

He laughed harshly. "Not anymore, I'm afraid. Since he wed, Trent fancies himself the pattern-card of respectability." Sucking in his breath, then exhaling fully, much in the manner of one girding himself against something unpleasant, he reached for the door handle, ordering tersely, "Wait here, both of you."

Bertie exchanged a nervous glance with Anne. "If I'd known he was here, I'd have stayed in Nottingham. Trent," he pronounced solemnly, "is said to be demned disagreeable. Worse than Rotherfield, if half the stories can be believed."

"I suppose it comes from being a Deveraux."

"Eh? Not like that, it don't. Don't know him well, but even I can tell you Dominick's a hothead. But Trent—Trent's downright *cold*. *Everybody* says so, you know."

Her eyes still on the two men outside, she ventured slowly, "I shouldn't think that. I mean, he did marry Ellen Marling, and everyone said 'twas a love match, despite the fact that she had been wed to Lord Brockhaven."

"Humph!" Bertie snorted. "*On-dit* behind the hands was that he scared the baron witless to get her an annulment. When Trent wants something, he gets it."

"You seem to know the marquess rather well."

"Me? Don't know him at all—and don't want to neither. Know *of* him, that's all. Uh-oh."

She could not help hearing bits of the angry exchange on the portico steps. The marquess flung words like "young fool" and "damned hothead" at Dominick, while the younger man answered defiantly, "If you did not want me to come, you should not have written!" Then their voices lowered, and she watched nervously as they obviously discussed her and Albert Bascombe. No doubt Dominick was trying to explain how he'd come to bring them home with him at such a time.

Finally he returned, his face grim. Opening the door, he reached for Anne. "Brace yourself," he muttered. "It appears as though I've brought you to a damnable reunion."

She glanced at his scowling cousin and started to demur. "Really, I cannot feel right intruding."

But he caught her at the waist and lifted her out. Leaning close, he said low, "No, you don't, my girl. If I am to be surrounded by my relations, I'd as lief have a friendly face in the place. Come on, Bascombe."

As the marquess's cold blue eyes took in her dirty, hastily repaired gown, Anne wanted to sink from sight. But Dominick's hand on her arm propelled he forward.

"Miss Morland, may I present my cousin Trent? Alex, Miss Morland."

The black head bent over her hand politely. "Dom tells me you were in an accident."

"Fell from the carriage," Bertie said, speaking up quickly.

For the briefest moment the marquess's fingers tightened over hers. "Really? I was under the impression that the mishap occurred on some stairs."

For a moment Bertie was nonplussed; then he blinked. "Er . . . 'twas the carriage steps—fell right into a puddle, didn't you, Miss Morland? See, mud's all over her dress."

"So I see. Well, Miss Morland, once you are rested, bathed, and in a fresh gown, no doubt you will feel more the thing," Trent murmured. Releasing her hand, he stepped back.

"Uh . . ." Remembering the pink taffeta, she glanced up at Dominick in dismay. "Really, but I cannot stay, my lord. I . . . uh . . ."

"Nonsense," Dominick declared flatly. "You are most welcome." The way he said it, it was as though he dared his cousin to dispute it.

"She ain't got no clothes," Bertie reminded him. Then,

perceiving that the marquess's gaze had shifted to him, he colored uncomfortably. "Lost 'em."

"Lost them?"

"Trunk fell open into the mud also. Couldn't save anything but an evening gown." He looked to Dominick for aid and found none. "Had to leave the rest—fit for nothing but the trash heap," he decided. "Ain't that so, Deveraux?"

"Precisely."

"I see. Well, perhaps Miss Mitford will be able to supply the lack. No doubt she will welcome the company, in fact," Trent said dryly.

Dominick's eyebrow rose. "Miss Mitford's here? Whatever for?"

The marquess favored him with a pained expression. "I would think the reason obvious, Dom, but Aunt Charlotte insists 'tis that she needs a companion. Given Miss Mitford's singular lack of spine, I cannot think the association is a happy one. If the girl has any conversation, I've not heard it."

"Lud, no. Mama plays the cat over the mouse with her." The younger man shifted his weight uneasily, as though he feared to put a question to the touch. Speaking almost casually, he managed to ask, "I collect Mama must be recovering if she can still bullock Margaret?"

Trent's mouth curved downward, again reminding Anne of his cousin. "The physicians said it was a brain seizure, and when I wrote you of it, she was affected by a loss of speech and movement. Now she is merely angered with the world."

"Poor Miss Mitford—and Ellie also, of course," Dominick added politely.

"I did not bring Ellen. And if any good can be said for your arrival, 'tis that I may go home ere she is brought to bed with the child." Once again Trent's eyes rested on Anne. "Perhaps you ought to take Miss Morland inside, Dom, for she looks worn to the nub. Her maid can discover something from Miss Mitford, I should think."

Bertie looked to Dominick, and when the other man said

nothing, he uttered, "Oh, she ain't got an abigail! That is
. . . well . . . had to leave the maid behind. No room, you
know." When Trent's eyebrow rose incredulously, Bertie
explained defensively, "Well, there was the dashed dress
box, after all."

"I see," the marquess murmured, his face suddenly quite
bland. "After you have delivered Miss Morland to Miss
Mitford, Dom, no doubt you will wish to see your mother."

Dominick hesitated. He didn't know what he'd expected.
Perhaps it had been but the hope for a final understanding
between them, but if his mother's temperament was worse
. . . A wave of defeat washed over him. If he were more
the coward, he'd head straightaway back to Lyons. Schooling
his face into indifference, he reached again for Anne
Morland, taking her elbow.

"Buck up, Annie," he muttered grimly. "At least Miss
Mitford will have something you can wear, for you are nearly
of a size. Though if you can get her to say much of anything
to you, 'tis more than I have ever had of her. Trent's right
on that head, at least."

It was not until they were at the door that she dared to
ask, "I collect Miss Mitford is your mama's companion?"

"My mother's goddaughter." He turned back briefly.
"Coming, Bascombe?"

"Bascombe and I will share a glass of port," Trent
answered. "Later Wilkins will show him upstairs to a
chamber."

"You cannot leave Bertie with him," Anne whispered.
"There's no telling what he will say."

"At this point, my dear, I am beyond caring. I do not mean
to stay above one night anyway."

Having bathed and redressed in her ruined gown, Anne
sat on the edge of a tapestry-covered chair in the elegant
bedchamber, watching as Margaret Mitford held up the first
of several dresses. Had she not been quite so pale or quite
so slender, the fair-haired girl would have been passably
pretty. As for her lack of speech, Anne certainly did not

notice it. To her, it seemed Miss Mitford rattled on far too eagerly.

The girl shook the folds from a blue-checked gingham gown almost apologetically. " 'Tis not very fashionable, I am afraid, but I like it."

"If it is your favorite, I'd not wear it," Anne demurred.

"Oh, no! That is to say, I do not mind in the least. 'Tis enough that you are come to the Haven, Miss Morland. I vow I shall like it excessively that there is another young female here." Laying aside the gingham, she lifted a pink figured muslin. "This one does not become me at all, I assure you. But if you do not like it, there is the green twilled cotton that Aunt Charlotte ordered from London."

"Miss Mitford, I would not borrow something that is a gift. 'Tis enough if you have anything I may wear on the mails."

"Oh, I daresay she will not even note it, for I am quite certain that she has forgotten it already. Since the . . . since she has been ill, Aunt Charlotte's memory is not the best."

"Still . . ." Anne eyed the green dress longingly. "No, I cannot. 'Tis too lovely."

"Well, if 'tis your preference, take it. And when we have contrived to get you something of your own, you can give it back, if you wish."

"But I will not be staying that long, Miss Mitford. Perhaps the gingham would be best, after all."

The girl's face fell, betraying her dismay. Oh, but you must! That is, I should like having someone besides Aunt Charlotte to talk with," she said wistfully. "She does naught but complain, you know."

"Mrs. Deveraux is your aunt also?"

"Oh, no—did I say that? No, she is merely my godmother, but she insists I call her Aunt." Margaret sighed. "Why, I am sure I do not know, for we do not deal well together. Were it not for her hopes of me, she would not like me in the least. Indeed, but I should like to go home," she confided artlessly. "Alas, Papa will not hear of it."

Anne rose to inspect the gingham more closely. "Why not?"

"Because he is possessed of five daughters to fire off, and I am the eldest," she answered simply. "We are not well-fixed, I am afraid."

Anne nodded sympathetically. "And so he expects you to earn your own way, and you find yourself employed by Mrs. Deveraux. Believe me, Miss Mitford, but I quite understand."

"I would it very only that," the girl declared fervently. "But Papa and Aunt Charlotte have quite settled between them that Mr. Deveraux will wed me when his salad days are over." She put the figured muslin on a chair and picked up the green cotton. "Here . . ." Holding it up to Anne's shoulders, she decided, " 'Twill most likely fit, for we are of a height, I think. Actually, as you are not as thin as I am, 'twill probably look better on you than me, for it positively hangs on me."

" 'Tis lovely."

"Yes, it definitely becomes you better than me."

Looking from the mirror to the pale girl beside her, Anne could not help asking, "Then you and Mr. Deveraux have an understanding?"

"Oh, no! Indeed, I should be mortified if he knew why I am here!"

"He's an exceedingly handsome man," Anne pointed out judiciously. "And one cannot always judge another by his reputation, after all."

"I wish he had stayed in France!" Margaret declared fervently. "Your pardon, Miss Morland—I should not have said that. 'Tis just that . . . well . . ." She colored uncomfortably. "I know I should not say it, but—"

"Miss Mitford, I assure you there is no need to explain to me."

"Papa and Aunt Charlotte say I am but missish, but I should rather die than wed with Mr. Deveraux! There, I *have* said it!" the girl declared dramatically. "But they cannot understand that I would hate being married to him, Miss Morland." Then, peceiving that she had disclosed too much, Margaret turned her attention to the green gown. "Do try it on, I beg of you."

"Oh, I could not . . . my hair." Anne touched her still-damp hair. "I have but bathed and washed it. Really, I should not wish to spot the dress."

"Pooh. If it suits you, you may have it."

"Well . . ." Unable to deny that she longed for it, Anne worked at the hooks on the back of her ruined dress. "Do you mind, Miss Mitford?" she asked finally.

"Of course not! Here . . ." The girl moved behind her and deftly unfastened them. "This must have been a lovely dress once. I have always liked the silk nankeens myself, for they hang so nicely, if one has the figure for them. Though I cannot think I would wish to travel in such a gown. I should freeze, you know."

"Yes. Yes, it was a trifle cold," Anne admitted. "But it was quite the best thing I owned, and I did not expect to journey nearly so far. And when I began, I had a heavy shawl."

Margaret surveyed the dress again, then sighed, " 'Tis a shame, for 'tis quite beyond repair."

Unable to bear the other girl's sympathy, Anne pulled her gown over her head and turned away to discard it. Straightening, she adjusted the new petticoat from Miss Porter's. Margaret Mitford lifted the twilled cotton and hung it around her neck. Stepping back shyly, she waited for Anne to put it on.

" 'Tis the color for you, Miss Morland—indeed, 'tis not too far off-shade from your own."

Anne stared at her reflection in the cheval mirror for a long moment before she dared to speak. The dress was rather plain, with a demure rounded neckline, plain sleeves that ended above her elbows, and a skirt that fell straight to her ankles. Its only adornment consisted of a velvet band of a darker hue that crossed beneath her breasts. Yet, despite the circles under her eyes, despite the ragged mop of hair that clung to her forehead, she had to admit the dress looked quite good on her. "I couldn't, Miss Mitford," she managed finally.

"Nonsense. While you are here, 'twill be like having a sister again. Indeed, should not not mind it, I'd be called

Meg. Miss Mitford is so very formal, and I cannot say I like Margaret very much either.'' She surveyed Anne critically, then blurted out, ''Besides, the gown is the very thing for you. You are so much fuller in the bosom than I, you know.''

Anne turned around before the mirror, enticed by her appearance in the gown. ''Well, if you are to be Meg, then I must be Annie.'' But even as she spoke to the girl, it was Dominick Deveraux's words that echoed in her ears. *You are not as flat as I thought.* She colored, remembering how he'd laced her into the zona. It had all been so improper, but he'd not even seemed to note it. Briefly she wondered what the girl before her would say if she knew Anne's story; then she forced such thoughts from her mind. ''Why is it that you have taken Mr. Deveraux in dislike?'' she found herself asking. ''I'm sorry—'tis none of my affair, really, and I should not stick my nose where it cannot be wanted.''

Margaret moved behind her and twitched the skirt into place. ''I should not say 'dislike' precisely. 'Tis just that . . . well, 'tis that he *terrifies* me—yes, that's the word, I think.''

''*Terrifies* you?''

''They all do—Trent, Mr. Deveraux, all of them. The men of this family, Miss Morland—Annie—are so . . . so very *volatile,* you see. I cannot think they make comfortable husbands. And neither Papa nor Aunt Charlotte cares in the least that I have no wish to reform a . . . a confirmed rakehell! I'd rather lief not have a man who has no heart!''

''Well, I would not characterize him as heartless, precisely,'' Anne murmured. ''And I cannot think comfort the greatest requirement in a husband.'' Yet as she said it, she could hear Dominick Deveraux's words again. *I have no intention of making any unfortunate female a difficult husband.*

''Well, they are rich enough, of course,'' Margaret conceded. '' 'Tis all that Papa can see.''

''I was rather thinking of tender passions, but perhaps you worry for naught anyway.''

The girl shuddered. ''I doubt Mr. Deveraux capable of any tender anything. There is a . . . a temper that quite precludes tenderness. Indeed, but he is positively disagree-able.'' She caught herself and flushed guiltily. "There I go rattling again, I'm afraid. 'Tis just that I never get to say anything before Aunt Charlotte. She thinks she is so very different from him, but she's not."

"Alas, but I have not met her."

"Well, I cannot think you would wish to." Margaret started for the door, then turned back. "After you have rested, perhaps we can enjoy a comfortable coze ere dinner." She smiled hopefully and added, "Do wear the dresses, for Aunt Charlotte has bought me far too many."

"But I shall not be staying," Anne reminded her again. "I simply cannot."

But the girl was gone, leaving Anne to puzzle over her confidences. Taking off the dress and laying it carefully on a chair, Anne moved once more to the mirror to survey herself critically. What she saw there did nothing to raise her spirits. With her cropped hair, she looked more like an elf than a beauty. She rearranged the unruly brown hair with her fingers and sighed.

Margaret Mitford was a strange one if she could not find Dominick Deveraux attractive, Anne mused. Disagreeable? Sometimes. Volatile? Perhaps. A rakehell? No, she did not think so. She rather preferred his own characterization of a rogue. But it didn't matter what she thought of him, she reminded herself forcefully. On the morrow she would be bound for London—and jail.

With that less-than-comforting thought she went to lie upon the carved poster bed. Staring at the gilt-decorated plaster rosettes on the ceiling, she thought of Quentin Fordyce, and felt an overwhelming sense of defeat. Unlike her, at least Dominick Deveraux was not alone. Forcing her thoughts from that also, she tried to recall her mother's face, to see again the triumph of the small, lovely woman born with a voice from heaven.

And yet as Anne closed her eyes, 'twas Dominick Deveraux she saw, and he was running back into the inn for her dress. Despite the barbs he'd cast her way, his action had been kind. He could have abandoned her, after all, but he hadn't. And for that at least she felt an intense gratitude.

Bertie clutched his wineglass tightly and watched the marquess warily. He felt like a mouse beneath the eye of a cat. When Trent continued to say nothing, Bertie downed his port in a gulp, then rose.

"Got to run, I'm afraid."

"Sit down, Bascombe." Trent stretched booted feet toward the warmth of the fire. His fingertips met over his chest. "I find myself intrigued. I'd hear your side of the tale."

"You would?" Bertie dropped to sit nervously on the edge of the chair. "I couldn't tell you anything if I was to want to," he declared. "Damme if I know anything."

"I did not know that you and Dominick ran together."

"Eh? Don't."

"Do you know the penalty for abetting a fugitive?" Trent asked suddenly.

"Don't say as I do—and I don't want to neither." Bertie leaned forward to ask anxiously, "I say, but you ain't giving me over, are you?"

"No. In fact, I am relying on you to get him back out of the country."

"Me? I ain't got nothing to do with anything!"

Without rising, Trent poured two more glasses. Lifting his, he held it out toward Bertie. "To your continued health, Bascombe."

"Dashed well hope so." The younger man again downed his wine quickly. "Good stuff."

"You might as well sit back, you know." The marquess regarded Bertie, and his mouth quirked quizzically. "I have never been known to kill anyone inside—'twould ruin the carpet."

"Eh?" For a moment Bertie's face betrayed alarm; then he sank back. "Daresay you was funning with me, wasn't you?"

"Perceptive of you. I knew you could not be the slowtop I'd heard."

"You did? Dashed decent of you to say it! Get tired of everyone thinkin' I'm half-empty in the cockloft, don't you know? Even m'father . . . Well, I ain't the fool everybody thinks!''

''You could not be,'' Trent murmured, refilling Bertie's glass. ''Suppose you start from where you met my cousin.''

''Ain't nothing to tell.'' Squirming beneath the marquess's steady gaze, he drank deeply. ''I was going to France. M'father's got this maggot in his brain that I ought to step into parson's mousetrap without a whimper, don't you see? And Miss Brideport ain't got nothing but breeding to recommend her, I can tell you,'' he added with feeling. ''Screeches when she talks, in fact.''

''So you were eloping with Miss Morland?'' Trent prompted impatiently.

Bertie blinked and stared for a moment. ''No! She ain't with me—that is, she ain't exactly . . .''

''Are you saying she's with Dominick?'' the older man asked, lifting his brow. ''Somehow I cannot think she is quite in his style.''

''It ain't like that! And if you was a-thinking Miss Morland is his fancy-piece or something like that . . . well, she ain't!'' Bertie declared forcefully. ''She's a lady! Ask Deveraux—he'll tell you she ain't fast in the least. General Morland's grandddaughter, in fact.''

The eyebrow rose higher. ''Morland's granddaughter? I was unaware the old martinet had one. In fact, I was under the distinct impression that there are but a couple of grandnephews.''

''You know the old gent?''

''Slightly. Actually, Aunt Charlotte knows him better than I. In fact, I believe he attended the memorial service when Cass was killed.''

''Cass?''

''My cousin Casimir—Dom's brother.''

''Oh . . . didn't know.''

''I shouldn't expect so. He was rather older. Unfortunately, he lost his life quite early in the war—at Vimeiro.''

''Long time ago,'' Bertie murmured.

Trent drained his glass and nodded. ''Dom was still at Oxford when it happened.'' For a moment he stared soberly into the fire. "After we buried Cass, Dom wanted to fight the French, but I stood against him. I considered that Aunt Charlotte had lost enough." He sighed, then straightened. " 'Twas a mistake—I should have supported him."

"Ought to be grateful he didn't go—deuced nasty business, from all I ever heard." Bertie shuddered and reached to pour himself another drink. "Glad Boney's gone, though. Dashed loose screw, if you was to ask me."

"Back to Miss Morland," Trent said. "You still haven't explained how you met my cousin—nor how Miss Morland comes to be here under what can only be considered peculiar circumstances."

"Told you—aint nothing to tell. I was a-going to France. Met 'em at this inn called the Blue Bull in Southampton, and when they was about to be taken by the constable, Dominick commandeered my carriage. Made m'driver bring 'em here."

"Miss Morland was with Dominick? And why Southampton for any of you? I should have thought Dover."

"Don't know why they was there. Me, I thought m'father wouldn't think I'd leave from the place. But it don't matter—I didn't get to France anyway."

"You were telling me about discovering Miss Morland and my cousin, I believe," Trent prompted.

Bertie squirmed uncomfortably. Not wanting to give Anne's circumstances away, he answered evasively, "Uh . . . yes . . . in a manner of speaking, I guess you could say that."

"Bascombe—"

"Dash it, if you was a-wanting to know about Dominick and Miss Morland, you ought to ask them! Damme if I know anything! I just had the horses, that's all." He rose unsteadily, nearly spilling his wine. "Ain't right asking me, 'cause I don't know what to say." The port seemed to have gone to his head, making the room spin around him, forcing him to close his eyes to steady himself. When he opened them, Trent still regarded him. "Look, Miss Morland's a lady, and Deveraux's a gentleman," Bertie declared. "Ain't anything havey-cavey there. He holds her in the greatest regard, in fact. More'n that you'll have to get from him."

Trent let him go, then sat alone before the fire, trying to make sense of the sapskull's most unedifying disclosures. If Bascombe could be believed, his hotheaded cousin had either behaved most improperly with Miss Morland or finally thrown his hat over the windmill for the girl. And somehow Trent could not bring himself to think it was the latter. He sighed heavily. The burden of being the lately respectable head of a disreputable family was becoming rather onerous. Then the irony of it all came home to him, and one side of his mouth curved downward wryly. Given his own very blemished past, he reflected that taking Dominick to task for Miss Morland would be a case of the proverbial pot calling the kettle black.

8

He'd delayed as long as he could. Having bathed, shaved, and changed into a loose-fitting cambric shirt, fresh breeches, and a smart pair of Hessians, he was as presentable as he wanted to be. For a long moment he stood silently outside his mother's bedchamber; then, settling his shoulders manfully, he rapped on the door.

There was no answer.

When he rapped again, this time more loudly, the door opened and a maid slipped hastily past him. Peering into the dimness, he could see that the draperies were drawn against the gray day.

"Mother?"

The figure seated before a small fire did not move. "They told me you had come," she said.

There was no warmth, no welcome in her voice, but then, he'd not really expected anything more than she gave him now. Closing the door carefully, he walked inside to face her. She looked up, her eyes darting like a small bird's; then she turned her attention back to the fire.

"If you are taken, I'll not forgive the scandal," she said tonelessly.

"Trent wrote that you had suffered a seizure, that you might be dying," he replied, ignoring her words.

"He was mistaken. I cannot think why he came either."

"Possibly duty."

"For all that I bear the name, I am not a Deveraux, so he need not have bothered." There was a strained silence between them. Once more her eyes darted upward, only to drop again to the fire. "You'd best go back to France."

"Mother—"

"Go on— you have done your duty also. You have seen that I live. I do not expect more of you."

"Cass would have expected it."

"Casimir is dead."

"And I am alive."

Her lips pursed, then were pulled back into a thin straight line. "I hear also that you have brought your doxy with you. And Haverstoke's heir. I don't want them here."

He smiled wryly. "I can tell the maids have been busy. But alas, as is usual, they are but half-right. Miss Morland is not my doxy."

"Bascombe's then."

"No. Neither of us is so lost to propriety as to try to foist a barque of frailty on you." He moved around to stand before her, blocking the fire.

" 'Twould be all of a piece," she snapped irritably. "Your father—"

"I'm not Papa," he retorted angrily. "Look at me—for love of the Almighty, look at me, Mother! Do you truly see Papa? 'Tis Dominick, not Nicholas."

Ignoring his outburst, she fixed her eyes on his feet. "I will not have her here, Dominick—not in my house. I have borne far too much already."

His jaw working as he sought to control his temper, he managed more evenly, "The house is mine, I believe. And once you have seen Miss Morland, I defy you to call her a doxy."

There was a brief flicker of interest. "She is a plain female?"

"Not plain, perhaps, but rather unremarkable in looks. I should not be surprised if she wears a mobcap when she meets you."

She looked up at that. "She's an older female? Betty did not tell me."

"Two-and-twenty, I believe."

"Too young to be traveling unattended by an abigail in your company, in any event," she observerd tartly. "If she manages to leave without a scandal, I shall be thankful."

"There is always the possibility you might like her."

"I shouldn't think so." She moved uncomfortably in her chair. "Betty!" she called out. "Betty! Wherever is the little goose *now*, do you suppose? Betty! Ring for her, will you?"

"Could I help you?"

She favored him with a withering look. "If you could, would I ask for the maid? I've got to stand. Since the str . . . since the feeling has returned to my leg, my hip pains me when I sit overlong." Not waiting for him to ring the bell, she struggled to her feet. "Never mind," she muttered. She teetered briefly, then leaned on the chair. "My cane, Dominick," she ordered imperiously.

"Where do you want to go?"

"Don't want to go anywhere—getting into bed."

He slipped his hand beneath her elbow to steady her, and he felt her tense. For a moment he thought she'd pull away, but she didn't. "Ready?" he asked.

"Yes."

She didn't like leaning on him, and he knew it. Still, as she took a few unsteady steps, her thin fingers grasped his arm. Her frailty surprised him. All of his life, she'd been the tartar, the woman he could not please, and somehow he'd expected her to live forever. Now it came home to him with cold clarity that she wouldn't.

It was not until she sank to sit upon the edge of her bed that she spoke. "I've got the Mitford chit dancing attendance on me."

"Trent told me."

"A trifle too biddable, I own, but respectable. Not a gamester or a duelist on either side of the blanket." She looked up almost slyly. "Quiet girl. Not likely to cut up a dust over a man's inamoratas."

"Which translates into a total lack of conversation, I presume?"

"You could do worse."

"As I am a fugitive in my own country, I scarce think Miss Mitford would entertain the notion. And," he declared flatly, "I require a little life in my females. We should be a greater mismatch than you and Papa."

"You always were a grubby, disagreeable boy," she grumbled.

"Unlike Cass," he murmured.

"Unlike Casimir." She stared vacantly for a moment, her eyes welling with tears; then she recovered. "You never had any sense of the proper, Dominick—look at you," she said almost angrily. "Did you never learn to wear a coat? 'Tis indecent to run about in your shirtsleeves, particularly before Miss Mitford."

One corner of his mouth quirked downward. "And Miss Morland—you are forgetting Miss Morland," he reminded her.

"I forget nothing, Dominick—nothing. Ere you are come down to dine, you will wear a coat in my house."

"My house, Mother."

"Aye, you'd like it if I left it, wouldn't you?"

He appeared to examine a thread at the gathered wrist of his shirt. "I might be home more often," he admitted. "But, no, I don't want you gone. There have been times I have wished you at Jericho, Mother, but unlike you, I have never wished you dead."

"Casimir was the better son."

"I don't deny it." The gulf was too wide to breach, and he knew it. No matter what he said, no matter what he did, he'd never been able to please her. Age had not diminished her ability to wound. An impotent anger rose within, making him reckless, but his face did not betray his ire. Turning to leave he tossed back almost casually, "I am tired of running, Mother. Now that I see you are better, I am considering contacting the magistrate to give myself up." Swinging back to face her, he saw the stunning effect his announcement had had on her, and he took an almost perverse pleasure in it.

What little color she had drained from her face, then rose again, spotting her cheeks. "You will do no such thing, Dominick! Have you no decency at all? Is there naught that is proper in you?" Her voice rose shrilly. "I forbid it!"

"Oh, I shall be exonerated, Mother. There are those who can swear Beresford fired ere the signal was given." Bowing slightly, he favored her with a small smile that did not warm his eyes. "Besides, 'tis not your name that will be dragged in the mud, is it? As you are wont to remind me, you weren't born a Deveraux," he said softly.

"Dominick—"

"Until we sup, Mother."

As he let himself into the hall, he could hear her calling after him. For once, he'd gotten the better of her, he told himself as he walked away.

"Dominick! Dominick! *Dominick!*"

He'd not intended to turn himself in, he'd only said it to vex her, but as he trod the steps, the idea began to have a certain appeal to him. Once the Beresford matter was laid to rest, he would no longer need to run. He could be as other men. He stopped for a moment. No, he couldn't, he conceded. Whether he wanted to be or not, he was what she thought him, a rogue beyond redemption.

Anne woke, startled by a woman's cries, and lay there trying to gain a sense of where she was. As her eyes took in the elegance of the room, the rich sheen of the dark wood furniture, the heavy *matelassé* draperies, she was at a momentary loss. Then she remembered. The Haven. She'd come with Dominick Deveraux and Albert Bascombe.

She had no idea of the hour, only that she'd slept. She rose and moved to the dressing table, where she found a silver-spined comb. Deveraux was right, she had to admit it—the haircut was a disaster. She had neither the right sort of hair nor the right face for it. But it would grow, and where she was going, she doubted any would particularly care what she looked like. Still, as she stared at her reflection, she could not help wishing that somehow just once Deveraux could see her as she secretly yearned to be, fashionable and pretty.

A scream shattered her reverie, pulling her back to reality. Someone was in the hall, crying loudly, calling for aid.

"Oh, Lor, 'tis the mistress! Someone . . . Mr. Wilcox! Miss Mitford! God aid her, but the mistress is dead!"

There was no time to dress. Anne grabbed a wrapper the maid had brought while she slept, and tying it around her,

ran barefoot into the hall. When the hysterical maid saw her,
she clutched at Anne's arm, pulling her.

"She fell—Lor, but I think 'er's dead!"

Disengaging herself from the girl, Anne hurried into the
bedchamber. An older woman lay in a crumpled heap upon
the floor, staring. Kneeling, Anne bent her head low to listen
for breath. It was ragged and labored. When she leaned back,
her eyes met the woman's, and she saw the terror there. She
clasped a frail hand and murmured soothingly, "Help is
coming, help is coming—you are going to be all right," over
and over again. The woman did not move, but continued to
stare into her face with an expression Anne would never
forget.

"We got to move 'er—'tis drafty on the floor," the maid
mumbled behind her. "Oh, Lord, is she . . .?"

"Can you hear me?" Anne asked the old woman. There
was no answer. "Can you hear me?" she repeated more
loudly. Still nothing. "Can you close your eyes?" she asked
finally, groping for some means to communicate. The eyes
blinked. Anne looked up at the maid. "Fetch someone, will
you? I believe she has had a stroke." Leaning over the
woman again, she squeezed the bony fingers. "We'll have
you in your bed in a trice, and then the doctor will come.
Until then, you must be calm."

"Ahhh . . . ahhhh . . . ."

"No, do not try to speak."

"Aunt Charlotte!" Margaret Mitford knelt beside Anne.
"Oh, dear."

"Hold her other hand, will you? She needs comfort more
than anything now."

"But . . . Aunt Charlotte, what happened?"

"She cannot talk just yet. Keep your voice low and soft."
Demonstrating, Anne bent lower. "Mrs. Deveraux, Meg is
here with you also, and your son is coming." Of Margaret
she asked, "Can someone get a pillow for her head?"

Margaret sat holding Charlotte Deveraux's other hand.
"Betty, fetch a pillow," she said as calmly as she could.

"Oh, Lor, what's to do, miss?"

"The pillow," Anne said firmly.

It seemed like an eternity before the others came, when in truth it could not have been above a couple of minutes. It was not until Anne looked into polished boots that she dared to sigh her relief. The marquess dropped down beside her. "Aunt Charlotte . . ."

"Er's stroked plumb out of it!" Betty wailed.

"If she cannot cease that, send her out," Anne muttered. "It alarms Mrs. Deveraux."

"Betty, go fetch Dominick, will you?"

"I'm here, Alex."

Dominick stood there gazing down at his mother, and guilt flooded through him. Once more he ought to have held his tongue, and he hadn't. "What happened?" he asked.

It was Anne who answered. "I believe your mother has suffered another seizure. She cannot speak, but she can hear," she added meaningfully. "Here—no doubt she would rather hold your hand than mine."

"Shouldn't we get her to bed first?" he inquired, hesitating.

"I don't know," she answered truthfully. "I have cared for only one stroke victim in my life." She leaned over Dominick's mother once more. "Mrs. Deveraux, would you prefer to be in bed?"

"Thought you said she couldn't answer." Albert Bascombe spoke up from across the room. "Heard you say it."

"She can open and close her eyes. Mrs. Deveraux, if you wish to be moved to your bed, blink."

The eyes fluttered.

"Very well, then. Your nephew and your son and Mr. Bascombe will lift you gently and carry you there. You will be all right until the doctor comes."

As Anne started to disengage her hand, the frail fingers tried to close. "Ahh . . . ahh . . ."

"What's she trying to say?" Bertie wondered.

"She is merely frightened, I think. Gentlemen, be careful, for I don't believe she can help you."

With Anne still clasping Charlotte Deveraux's hand, Trent took the old woman's shoulders, Dominick her torso, and

Bertie her feet. Carrying her gingerly, they managed to lay her upon the bed. With her free hand Anne tried to pull the covers from beneath her and couldn't.

"Someone get a blanket over here—she may be chilled. And throw another log on the fire."

"I thought you were a companion rather than a nurse," Dominick murmured at her shoulder.

"Is everything a jest to you?" she demanded angrily. Then, realizing that perhaps he did not know what to say, she apologized. "Your pardon, Mr. Deveraux—I should not have said that. Here, hold her hand whilst I get some laudanum."

His eyebrow shot up. "Laudanum?"

"When Mrs. Cokeham had a seizure, the physician prescribed it, saying that the greatest danger was in the agitation of the brain. 'Twill soothe your mother."

He made no move to take his mother's hand. Finally Anne quite literally thrust it at him. "Tell her something meaningful," she suggested. "Something that will reassure her."

The thin fingers were cold against his, and not at all responsive. He held them awkwardly, wondering if she recoiled and he could not feel it. What could he say—that he was sorry for causing her to have a seizure? That he was sorry for everything? That, like her, he wished he'd died instead of Cass? 'Twas the only thing she would wish to hear, and he knew it. And even that could not bring Cass back for her. The gallant, good son was gone, leaving only the rogue, and there was no help for it. Maybe death was what she wanted; maybe she yearned still to be reunited with her beloved Casimir.

When he looked up, Anne Morland was watching him expectantly, and he felt a surge of anger. She knew not what she asked of him. Swallowing it back, he managed to tell his mother, "You are going to be all right. You cannot die, else I shall have everything."

He stood there holding his mother's hand, wishing he were almost anywhere else, until Anne found the laudanum and brought it back. Measuring out four drops into a small amount of water, she restoppered the bottle and handed it to the maid. Looking directly at him, she spoke rather bitingly. "I do not suppose it too much to ask, surely, but would you lift her head? And if she begins to choke, she must be raised immediately." Then, "Meg, will you stand ready with a napkin should she not be able to swallow?"

She poured carefully, giving but a tiny bit at a time, testing for throat paralysis. At first she thought it hopeless, for the liquid seemed merely to lie in the old woman's mouth, but finally there was an involuntary swallow. It was a painstakingly slow process, one that left Anne wet with perspiration before she was done. A great sigh of relief escaped her as Deveraux eased his mother back against the pillow.

"Came as soon as the horse could carry me," she heard someone say behind her. "Daresay she's had another one."

"Found 'er on the floor," the maid explained.

"Thank heaven you are here, Dr. Rand," Margaret said fervently. "She cannot even speak."

"Don't do her any good to have everyone standing over her, I'll be bound," Bertie declared. "Scare me if I was to wake up in this."

"Quite right, young man," Rand said. "Miss Mitford will stay whilst I examine Mrs. Deveraux. The rest of you ought to have a bit of brandy."

Meg hesitated nervously, then demurred. "I think it ought to be Miss Morland—she's ever so much better at this than I."

"Nonsense. Don't know her." Turning his attention to Trent, he urged, "Go on, my lord, and take 'em all with you. If there is anything that needs to be said, I'll send to you."

"Her son is here," Anne pointed out.

"I saw him."

It was not until they were out in the hall that Dominick hung back to speak with her. "My thanks, Annie."

"If you were my son, I should cheerfully strangle you," she muttered. "Telling someone she cannot die else you will have everything is scarce my notion of comfort, Mr. Deveraux."

For a long moment he stared down at her, his face sober. "Had it not been a capital offense, Miss Morland, I am certain my mother would have tried," he said evenly. Turning on his heel, he started the other way down the hall.

"Wait." He barely hesitated, then went on. And once again, she felt regret. "Please."

"Miss Morland. I am mortal man—not a saint."

"I'd apologize, sir." When he swung back to face her warily, she nodded. " 'Tis not my place to criticize what I do not know."

"No, 'tis not," he agreed.

"I know not why I say such things to you, for I seldom speak my mind to anyone anymore."

"As you can see from Dr. Rand, you are not alone in your opinion of me. One word of advice, however: never apologize for what you believe to be the truth. It ill becomes you."

"Still, when I leave with Mr. Bascombe, I'd remember the adventure rather than the rancor, sir."

The almost familiar smile twisted his mouth for a moment, then disappeared. "I forgot—you are the romantic Miss Morland, are you not? My dear, you have a lot left to learn in this life. Not everything is as it seems here."

9

A pall hung over the great house, making it seem even darker than it was. And it did not help that as the supper hour approached, a late-afternoon rain poured steadily outside. As Anne came down the stairs, a flash of lightning lit the panes that lined the sides of the outside door.

Looking upward toward the chandelier that illuminated the foyer, she saw the row of paintings, all men but one. And she could not help noting the tall portrait of the handsome, elegant woman on the wall. There was a vague familiarity about it, something that possibly reminded her of Dominick Deveraux. It was not the coloring, for the woman's hair was fair, her face was more oval than his, and though her eyes were blue, there was a softness to them.

" 'Tis Aunt Charlotte," Trent murmured beside her. "Done many years ago by Gainsborough—one of the last, I believe."

She turned around, meeting his eyes. "She was lovely, wasn't she?"

"If the artist can be trusted. Actually, I am told she was, but by the time I came to know her, I could scarce see it." He stared upward at the woman on the wall. "Life changes one, I suppose." He shrugged and returned his attention to her. "You are down early, Miss Morland."

"Actually, there was not much to do upstairs, my lord."

"Perhaps you would care to join me in a glass of punch before we sup?"

"Well, I . . ." She'd heard so many tales of him, of his opera singers and other bits of fluff, that she hesitated. "I don't think . . ."

He favored her with Dominick's twisted smile. "Miss

Morland, I assure you that my salad days are behind me. You behold a man utterly besotted with his wife.''

''Oh, I did not think . . . that is, I assure you—''

''Yes, you did,'' he told her bluntly. ''And I cannot say I blame you for it. A man's rep, once earned, is deuced long-lived.'' He opened a saloon door and held it for her. He waited for her to enter, then walked past her to a steaming punch bowl on a table. Filling a cup, he handed it to her. ''Actually, I am quite eager to make your acquaintance, my dear.''

''I cannot think why, my lord. You behold an utterly ordinary female.''

''Let us just say that you pique my curiosity, Miss Morland.' Lifting his own cup, he looked over the rim at her. ''You were quite efficient upstairs this afternoon.''

''I am not without experience in the care of elderly females, sir,'' she said simply.

''Nonetheless, you have my compliments. Between the ninnyhammer and the hysterical maid, I doubt either would have done much for my aunt had you not been there.'' Continuing to regard her, he sipped the hot, spicy liquid. ''Which brings me to a curious point, Miss Morland—how do you come to be here?''

She colored uncomfortably beneath the marquess's gaze and wondered what plausible story she could tell. She'd been truthful with Dominick Deveraux—prevarication was rather alien to her nature. And she did not want to spin a pack of lies now.

When she did not immediately answer, Trent observed wryly, ''Somehow you do not seem the sort of female to be in Dom's company, you know.''

''I am not quite certain whether I ought to be gratified by that opinion, sir,'' she answered a trifle tartly.

''You mistake my meaning, my dear. 'Tis that my cousin is not particularly noted for his association with respectable women.'' Gesturing to a chair before the fire, he said. ''Do you mind sitting down, Miss Morland? 'Tis a deuced nuisance having to stand with you. Go on, please—I have left the door open should you wish to bolt.''

She took the chair and placed her cup on the small reading stand between them. "There is much about you that reminds one of Mr. Deveraux, you know," she told him. "I suppose it is the bluntness usually missing in polite discourse. Or perhaps the spoiled nature of very rich men."

"I should never consider Dominick spoiled, my dear— quite the opposite, in fact." A corner of his mouth twitched. "As for me, when one has dealt with Miss Mitford for nigh to a week, one loses the will to be overly polite."

Anne looked down at the green gown and felt the need to defend its donor. "Miss Mitford is possessed of a kind and generous nature, but is perhaps overwhelmed by your presence here. From what she has said to me, she is merely shy before men."

"Coming it too strong, Miss Morland. Had she come down before you, I should be alone and grateful for it. The girl is as empty in the cockloft as Bascombe, if the truth were known." This time, when his eyes met hers, there was a glimmer of amusement in them. "But I shall not be fobbed off so easily by you, my dear. Drink up, then tell me of your journey here."

She eyed the punch suspiciously. "I do not deal well with spirits, my lord. Nor with wine," she added.

"There's scarce more than drop of rum in it," he assured her. "Just enough to warn the bones against winter's chill. 'Tis mostly apples and spices, Wilkins tells me."

He was waiting expectantly, and she knew it. Capitulating, she took the cup and sipped gingerly. The sweet and spicy liquid warmed her throat as it slid down. It was exceedingly good. She set the cup back.

"Somehow I did not take you for a coward, Miss Morland."

"I've no wish to be foxed with you, my lord."

"And I've no wish to see you foxed either—I'd hear a lucid tale, believe me."

"There's naught to tell," she began evasively. "I am but on my way to London."

"By way of a wharfside inn?" His eyebrow lifted incredulously. "My dear, that much of the story I had of

Bascombe. He said you and Dominick were attempting to escape from the authorities.''

"Not precisely. That is, it was not my intent to run, my lord.'' Not knowing what Albert Bascombe might have said, or how he might have missaid it, she twisted Miss Mitford's handkerchief nervously in her lap. "Really, my lord, but I shall be leaving in the morning, and I cannot think it any of your affair.''

"If you are in truth General Morland's granddaughter, I might be willing to help you.''

Her eyes widened; then she recovered. "He had no right to tell you that, sir.''

"*Are* you General Morland's granddaughter?'' he asked, persisting.

"Yes, but . . . Oh, 'tis too long a tale! And . . . and I've no wish to share it.''

There was silence for a long moment, and when she looked up again, she saw unexpected sympathy in his eyes. "In the basket, Miss Morland?'' he said softly. "While I cannot claim a close association with your grandfather, I should not hesitate to offer my assistance.''

"I am beyond assistance, my lord. Suffice it to say that.''

"If my cousin has wronged you, I am prepared to see that he acts responsibly in the matter.''

She blinked blankly; then, as his meaning sank in, the blood rushed to her face. "You think that I . . . that Mr. Deveraux and I . . . ? Oh, no! 'Tis nothing like that, I assure you! Mr. Deveaux has ever been the gentleman to me.'' But even as she said it, she knew that was not quite true. "Well, if not the gentleman,'' she conceded, "certainly he has never threatened my virtue.''

"You relieve my mind.''

He sat back and propped his legs up, much in the manner Dominick had done in the carriage. "The mysterious Miss Morland,'' he murmured. "I wonder.'' Abruptly he sat up again. "I'd still know how you came to be with my cousin.'' When she stared into the fire rather than speak, he said gently, "Whatever you tell me will not go beyond this room unless you wish it. Word of a Deveraux.''

She twisted the handkerchief more tightly and sighed. "When you have heard the tale, you will no doubt call the constable."

"I think not, my dear, for then I should have to give over Dominick."

There was no sound beyond the rain against the windows and the popping of the fire as she considered all manner of things to tell him. Finally she decided to believe him and tell him the truth.

"Very well, my lord, but I would prefer to close the door, I think."

A long time after she left him, ostensibly to return upstairs to find herself a cap, Trent contemplated the fire. Anne Morland's story was a preposterous one, and yet he believed it. He sipped his fourth cup of tepid punch and considered what he could do for her. Ordinarily he would have said nothing, and he would have done nothing, but there was a quiet calmness about the girl that reminded him of his wife.

"Oh, your pardon, I . . ."

He looked up to see Margaret Mitford backing out the door, her face paling at the sight of him. Every time he saw her, she took on the appearance of a cornered rabbit, and he'd not done a damned thing to frighten her.

"Would you care for some punch, Miss Mitford?" he inquired politely.

"Oh, no! I thought that perhaps Miss Morland . . . But I quite see I was mistaken . . . uh . . ."

With that, she turned and fled, leaving him to shake his head in disgust. How Charlotte Deveraux ever thought she could foist the hinny on Dominick was beyond his comprehending. Dom was too much like the rest of the Deveraux—and Margaret Mitford could not hold his attention above two minutes, if that long, making any marriage between them utterly disastrous. Trent would have thought from her own experience that Charlotte would not wish such a fate on the girl. But there was little danger of its coming to pass anyway. It would take more than mere breeding to leg-shackle Dom. Dom was too much like him—he would require someone like Ellen, someone possessed of common sense, wit, and passion.

Trent's thoughts returned to Anne Morland, and he mulled over in his mind everything she'd told him—how Dominick had dropped her off the roof, had dressed her in Bascombe's clothes, had paid for the unsuitable taffeta dress, and finally had brought her and Haverstoke's heir home with him. She'd not even spared herself the details of Quentin Fordyce's attack, nor had she glossed over his possible death. And she'd not failed to tell of getting disguised with the two men over the port. His mouth curved into a smile as he recalled the way she'd described their flight. Most females of his acquaintance would have played the tale for his sympathy, but she had not. She could in truth be compared to Ellen.

He sighed. He was homesick for Ellen, and it was beginning to make him maudlin. He wanted to be with her before the child came, but he could not rely on the little mouse to keep peace between Dom and Charlotte. Charlotte's stroke had thrown a spoke into his and Dom's wheels, tying them inexorably to her until the last. What she'd not wanted in life, she was like to have in death.

"Oh, I didn't know you were down, Alex," Dominick murmured, coming into the room. "I'd thought perhaps to find Bascombe or Miss Morland." He poured himself a glass of punch and sprawled wearily in the chair opposite. "Devil of a coil, isn't it?" He closed his eyes briefly. "Never thought I'd be glad to have you, you know, but I don't think I could stand being here with Miss Mitford."

"Your Miss Morland was quite prompt with her assistance this afternoon," Trent observed casually.

"She isn't my Miss Morland, Trent."

"So she says. And Bascombe insists she isn't his either."

Dominick brushed a stray black lock back from his forehead wearily and opened his eyes defensively. "If you are meaning to pry, Alex, I can tell you I am too tired to answer anything right now." Taking a swig of the punch, he made a face. "Must've been better hot," he muttered. "Too sweet by half."

"Miss Mitford is no hand at all with your mother."

"Who is?"

"Betty didn't know what to do, you know."

"I daresay 'twas the first time she saw her speechless."

" 'Twas the second. But this is worse, I believe."

"Mother will recover," Dominick predicted flatly. "She could not bear to go and leave it all to me."

"A harsh judgment, Dom."

"Is there another?" the younger man wondered bitterly.

"Given the circumstances, why did you come back?"

Dominick stared into the amber liquid for a long moment, then sighed heavily. "I don't know. Perhaps I had hopes that the stroke had mellowed her. Maybe I was enough the fool to think there could be peace between us yet."

"It isn't too late."

"The devil it isn't! No, nothing's changed, Trent. Only a fool could fail to see that."

"At least you brought Miss Morland—and Bascombe, of course."

Mistaking his cousin's meaning, Dominick snapped, "I had no choice in the matter. I couldn't in conscience put her on the mail coach like that. And I had to bring Bascombe— 'twas his carriage."

"A stroke of fortune, don't you think?"

Dominick glanced at Trent suspiciously, but the older man's expression was bland, betraying nothing. "What difference does it make to you?"

His cousin sat up abruptly and leaned to place his cup on the table. "I need to go home, Dom. I need to be with Ellie."

"Mother would not expect you to remain. I cannot say that she likes you much better than me, you know." Rising, Dominick walked to the window and stared absently for a time. "Miss Morland will say she cannot stay," he said finally. "Though I cannot deny she'd be welcome."

"Because of the Fordyce thing?"

Dominick gave a start, then muttered, "Someone ought to put a plaster on Bertie's mouth. I don't care what he told you, you cannot believe it. Ten to one, he got the tale wrong."

"I had it of Miss Morland. General Morland's grand-daughter, I believe," Trent added softly.

"He doesn't claim her."

"More's the pity."

"She wants to turn herself over," Dominick said slowly. He swung around to face his cousin. "Much as it may surprise you, I've thought a great deal on the matter, and I cannot think such a course wise." His eyes met Trent's soberly. "For one thing, if he is not dead, Fordyce is apt to seek revenge on her. And he will no doubt seek her at Mrs. Philbrook's."

"Mrs. Philbrook?"

"Her employer."

"Ah, the old tartar."

"Yes."

"Perhaps you could persuade Miss Morland to wait until Fordyce's fate is known."

" 'Twill not be long." A wry, almost rueful smile curved the younger man's mouth. "I'd thought of that also, you know, and have dispatched one of the grooms back to the Blue Bull to make an inquiry."

" 'Tis to be hoped he is discreet."

"He will be. His instructions are merely to remain there overnight, to tipple a bit, not flash much money, and listen. Even in the Blue Bull, a dead toff must surely be much discussed, I'd think."

"One would think so. And another day or so cannot make much difference to Miss Morland. Surely you could offer . . . perhaps even employ her here whilst she waits," Trent ventured. "Your mother—"

"I would not wish Mother on the lowest creature, Alex," Dominick declared with feeling. "And certainly Annie is not that."

"Annie?" Trent's eyebrow lifted. "Annie?"

"Miss Morland."

Trent rose to refill his cup. "More punch, Dom?"

"No."

"Oh, I'm sorry—'twas not my intent to intrude," Anne

apologized. "I was merely looking for Miss Mitford, and her maid said she had come down."

"Alas, but Miss Mitford fled," Trent murmured, rising. "But do come in, my dear—we were just speaking of you. You ought to wear green often, don't you think, Dom?"

Dominick stared at her in surprise. Miss Mitford's gown actually became her, and in it she appeared almost elegant. His gaze traveled over her trim, slender figure, up to her face. "Most definitely," he answered. Her clear dark eyes met his for a moment; then she dropped them politely. It was then that he noted the ruffled and starched mobcap on her head. "Where the devil did you get that thing?"

His tone spoiled the effect she'd hoped to have, and for a moment she was at a loss. "Well, the dress is Meg's, of course," she began defensively.

"Not the gown—the silly cap."

Her hand crept to the offending garment. "You dislike it? I thought—"

"Makes you look like a damned housekeeper. In the carriage, my dear, I merely jested."

"Well, I had it of the upstairs maid. And if you must know, I am wearing it to signify that I am quite on the shelf, Mr. Deveraux," she told him severely. But there was no mistaking a certain twinkle in her eyes as she explained, "Indeed, since my arrival in your and Mr. Bascombe's company, I have received the most censorious looks from the staff. No doubt your rogue's reputation makes my conduct suspect."

"Coming it too strong, Miss Morland."

"Yes, well, rather than have them believe me fast, I should prefer to be old, I think," she added sweetly. "It helps explain my lack of an abigail, don't you think?"

"I think—"

His answer was cut short by the appearance of his mother's doctor. "There you are—both of you." His manner grave, Rand walked into the saloon. "Do sit down, sirs."

"I shall see you at supper," Anne murmured, turning to leave. To her surprise, Dominick's hand rested on her arm, holding her back. "Really, I'm quite sure you will wish to be private, and—"

"No, not at all, Miss Morland."

"Has there been any change, Doctor?" Trent inquired, cutting to the heart of the matter.

"Er . . ." Rand cleared his throat and looked at Anne.

"Miss Morland is a friend of the family. Do go on."

"Yes . . . well, 'tis quite serious, my lord. That is to say, I think perhaps we ought to prepare ourselves for the worst."

"She isn't going to die," Dominick declared.

"Alas, I wish you were right, sir, but cannot hold much hope at the moment." As the younger man's eyebrow rose skeptically, he cleared his throat again. "You see, usually if the seizure is not severe, the patient will begin to recover certain functions within a matter of hours. In Mrs. Deveraux's case, there has been no improvement—in fact, 'tis quite the opposite. I wish I could wrap it up in clean linen, but I cannot. Alas, sirs, but I should expect her to slip away rather quickly."

"But not all cases are alike," Anne protested. "Surely 'tis too early to tell. That is . . ."

He favored her with the patient look he reserved for imbeciles. "Young woman, I have treated many such seizures in my career, and I can assure you that I know of what I speak." Turning back to Trent, he continued, "It is my opinion that she will continue to have these seizures until the brain can sustain no more."

"There is no hope, then?" Dominick asked hollowly. "None?"

"One cannot say death is an absolute certainty, of course, but in my opinion, we should expect it."

"How long . . . how long does she have?"

"That, Mr. Deveraux, is in the hands of the Almighty."

Anne looked up, seeing that the color had drained from Dominick's stricken face, and there was no mistaking the pain there. Without thinking, she dropped her arm, sliding her hand into his. His fingers gripped hers convulsively, holding them tightly for a moment; then he pulled away. Turning on his heel, he left the room.

"I'm sorry, Mr. Deveraux," the doctor called out to him. Turning back, he addressed the marquess. "Your pardon, my lord. Perhaps I ought to have broached the matter a trifle more delicately, but, well . . . I'd not thought the attachment a deep one. Perhaps a bit of laudanum—and some rest, of course." He hesitated. "Should I go after him, do you think?"

"No," Trent answered curtly.

"Well, I'd not expected . . ."

Anne stared at the open door, torn between following Dominick and leaving him alone in his grief. It was not her place to intrude on him, she decided rather reluctantly. Then, remembering the terror in the old woman's eyes earlier, she asked suddenly, "As you are down here, sir, who is with Mrs. Deveraux now?"

"Her maid. But 'twill make no difference, I think. The poor soul is utterly senseless, may God give her rest."

"What sort of doctor are you?" she demanded almost angrily. "Whilst a body breathes, there should be hope rather than defeat, don't you think? Were you my physician, I should wish you to fight for me! I should wish you to at least attempt to save me!"

The physician reddened uncomfortably. "Miss Morland, you are overset merely. I assure you—"

She'd overstepped herself again, and she knew it. Taking a deep breath, she let it out slowly. "Your pardon, my lord—'tis not my intent to interfere."

Though she'd spoken to Trent, Dr. Rand said stiffly, "I shall choose to count that as an apology, young woman. Now, if you will excuse me, my lord, I shall go home."

"Go *home*?" Anne asked incredulously.

"Miss Morland," he answered icily, "I assure you that only God can do more than I have done this night."

After the physician left, Anne stared silently into the fireplace for a time, and the room was quiet save for the crackling flames and an occasional gust of rain-laden wind against the windows. " 'Tis my accurst tongue," she said finally. "After years of saying nothing, I seem to be unable to contain myself now."

"You appear to think there is hope," Trent observed soberly.

"I don't know, my lord. 'Tis just that I cannot bear to see him give up so easily." She turned around to face him. "I was once employed to companion an elderly female, a Mrs. Cokeham, and while I was there, she suffered much the same sort of seizure." She waited but briefly for him to digest the import of what she said, then plunged ahead. "Though she was far older than Mr. Deveraux's mother, she regained part of her strength and lived another year after. Her doctor, however, never despaired. 'Twas always that she might recover."

"You think Dom ought to request a consult?"

"Yes." She hesitated, her eyes troubled; then she blurted out, "Where do you think he went, sir?"

He regarded her soberly for a moment, then shook his head. "I think I should leave him to himself for a while, Miss Morland. He can, upon occasion, have a devilish bad temper."

"Well, you know him best, of course," she conceded slowly. " 'Tis just that were I he, I should not wish to be alone. Well . . ." She sighed. "In any event, I probably should discover Miss Mitford and apprise her of the situation. And I will, of course, offer to help Betty tonight."

He watched her go, thinking he ought to have appealed to her to stay at the Haven. But, he reminded himself, it was not his place to ask. That would have to come from Dom. And unless he mistook the matter, ere long his cousin would be in no condition to do so.

10

Supper was a strange, stilted affair, with the marquess presiding at one end of the long, highly polished table, Bertie Bascombe at the other, and the two women in between. A footman moved silently to serve them, and much of the time there was little sound beyond Bertie's determined slurping of his soup, Miss Mitford's occasional furtive sighs, and the clink of silver against china.

Dominick Deveraux was nowhere to be seen, and it seemed as though everyone was taking care not to remark it. Even Bertie appeared unusually subdued, and between him and Miss Mitford there was not a word. In fact, aside from asking Anne to pass the peas, the girl said nothing to anyone. Trent, on the other hand, punctuated the silence with comments to Anne, and she tried heroically to carry the conversation to the others. It was a futile attempt and was soon abandoned in favor of merely eating.

Finally, as the dessert plates were being removed, Trent cleared his throat. "Would any of you care to join me in the saloon? Wilkins assures me there is ratafia for the ladies."

Miss Mitford bowed her head before shaking it. "I am rather tired, my lord," she mumbled. "I should like to be excused."

"I dashed well am too, Miss Mitford," Bertie agreed, eager to escape. "Think I'll retire early. Got to, you know—me and Miss Morland got to get back to Nottingham in the morning, don't you know?" Waiting politely for the pale girl to rise, he turned back to Anne. "Wilkins says the Royal Mail departs for London at ten sharp."

"Miss Morland?" Trent inquired politely.

"I rather think I ought to look in on Mrs. Deveraux again."

"Has there been any change?"

"Well, I did not stay, of course, for Betty insisted I should sup with everyone else. However, Mrs. Deveraux is now unresponsive."

"What do you think?"

"My opinion has not changed, my lord. I still believe 'tis too early to know much of anything."

Trent cleared his throat again. "Miss Morland, I should like nothing more than to go home to my wife," he declared, "but in good conscience I cannot leave Dom at a deathwatch with naught but Miss Mitford for support."

"No, I suppose not," she agreed noncommittally.

"I do not suppose that you could be persuaded somehow to stay?"

"Not above a day or so, sir, for there is still the matter we spoke of this afternoon. The longer I delay, the worse 'twill surely look for me."

"Dominick—"

"Mr. Deveraux has far more important matters to concern himself with than me, my lord," she said definitely. "I cannot embroil him in my affairs further."

He sensed that he ought not to press her, that he ought to leave it to Dominick to tell her of his inquiry at the Blue Bull. He inclined his head slightly. "Perhaps you will wish to take your ratafia later?"

"I should not wait for me," she advised. "Much depends on Mrs. Deveraux's condition . . . and on Betty."

"The ninnyhammer could sit with my aunt, you know. She at least owes Aunt Charlotte something."

"Miss Mitford, I suspect, is one of those females who cannot cope with illness."

"Miss Mitford, my dear, cannot cope with anything." He moved closer, and for a moment she thought he was going to touch her. Instead he raised his hand in a sort of salute. "You, on the other hand, appear to have a great deal of sense. You remind me very much of my wife."

"I shall take that as a very great compliment, my lord."

Yet, as she climbed the stairs, she could not help shaking her head. Sense? If she'd had any sense, she would never have gone with Quentin Fordyce, she would never have found herself in such a pickle. Sense? He gave her far too much credit.

As for staying, she could not deny the appeal of that. When she viewed her own disquieting future, she had to admit it was tempting to remain in hiding at the Haven, to pretend she'd not struck Quentin Fordyce in the head, but it would not be right. And moreover, she'd meant what she'd told Trent: if she were to be caught later, the very fact that she had hidden would no doubt be construed as proof of guilt. No, she had to go.

Betty came to the bedchamber door when Anne knocked. Behind her, a brace of candles flickered at Mrs. Deveraux's bedside, casting eerie moving shadows on the papered walls. An ormolu clock ticked on the mantel, keeping time to the steady beat of rain against the tiled roof. Water coming down the chimney hissed and sizzled when it hit the fire.

Anne's gaze moved to the woman in the bed. She was propped up amid a bank of pillows, her gray hair spilling over them and tangling at her shoulders. The only color in a seemingly bloodless face was the reflected yellow of the candlelight. As Betty stepped back, Anne entered the room and walked to stand over Dominick's mother.

Looking downward, she saw nothing of the beautiful girl in the portrait below, and she felt a rush of pity for the frail, still woman lying there. Reaching to smooth the gray hair back from a translucent, almost alabaster forehead, she felt the cool skin. To her relief, the woman's breathing was not labored.

"She ain't moved in hours," Betty told her.

"Did Dr. Rand give any instructions?"

The girl shook her head. "Un-uh. Just to give her the laudanum. Said 'twas the end—said she'd not likely waken."

"Hush." Lifting a candle from the stand, Anne leaned forward to study Charlotte Deveraux. " 'Tis possible she can hear you."

"Shouldn't think it," Betty muttered, peering over Anne's shoulder. "Never thought it'd be like this, ye know. Thought her'd go in a fit—not quiet-like."

Very carefully, holding the candle so that it would not drip onto the bed, Anne used her other hand to raise one of the woman's eyelids. The pale eye was glassy, but as the light struck it, the pupil contracted.

"Take this," she ordered tersely, handing the maid the candle. Possessing one of Charlotte Deveraux's cold hands, she tried to feel the pulse in the wrist. When she could not count it, she leaned over to run her fingertips along the woman's jawline, discovering the stronger one there. It was relatively steady.

"Have you tried to give her anything to drink? Can she still swallow?"

"Ain't had nothing but the laudanum."

"That I gave her?"

"No, miss—Dr. Rand gave 'er another dose."

"How much?"

"Six drops. Twice." Still holding the candle nervously, the maid eyed her mistress with great misgiving. "Told you, she ain't going to wake up."

After sixteen drops of laudanum in but a few hours, neither you nor I would wake either—not for a while, anyway," Anne muttered dryly. She turned to face the girl. "I would you did not give her any more tonight."

"But Dr. Rand said to dose her every four hours."

" 'Tis only useful for pain and agitation, and at this point Mrs. Deveraux appears to suffer neither. I should think she ought not to have any unless she is restless."

"Ye ain't the doctor," Betty grumbled under her breath.

"No, but I have seen this sort of thing before. Mrs. Cokeham had an excellent physician, the best to be had in London, and he insisted that the best thing to do was to encourage her. A very great deal depends on Mrs. Deveraux's will to survive."

"Encourage her?" The girl eyed her mistress with disbelief. "But she ain't . . . She can't . . ."

"It was Dr. Morse's opinion that the last sense is that of hearing, Betty. We must speak to Mrs. Deveraux as though she can hear everything we say." To demonstrate, she leaned over Dominick's mother again, this time to pull the covers up over her cold hands. "Mrs. Deveraux," she said clearly, " 'tis Anne Morland. I have asked Betty to keep you warm, and I shall be back directly to bring you a drink and sit with you. Hopefully, you will feel more the thing in the morning."

"You going to stay with her tonight?" the girl whispered.

"For a while, I think."

"Thought you was leaving on the stage."

Not wanting to answer that, Anne merely murmured, "I can sleep on the mail coach, if necessary. Until I am come back tonight, I'd have you get someone to build up the fire. And perhaps you ought to put another blanket on the bed."

Outside the chamber door, Anne stood for a moment, feeling quite helpless. Mrs. Deveraux would either get better or she would expire in a matter of days, and despite what Anne had said to Betty, she really had no idea which would happen. And while none of the people in the house seemed inclined to like the woman very much, the terror she'd seen earlier in Charlotte Deveraux's eyes still haunted her.

Her heart went out to all of them—to the prodigal son come home too late, to the mother he apparently could not love, to the marquess yearning for his wife. And to Miss Mitford even, for the girl seemed to be fearful of everything.

As she made her way down the stairs again, she supposed she ought to report her observation of Mrs. Deveraux to Lord Trent. Afterward she would get herself some tea and possibly a book before returning once more to the sickroom. Hopefully, ere she left the Haven, she would see some improvement in Dominick's mother, some indication that she'd been right.

The saloon was dark, and there was no sign of the marquess. He had, she guessed, chosen to retire also when there was none to keep him company. It didn't matter—she could tell him in the morning, and perhaps then the news would be better.

A door opened, throwing a slice of light into the dimly lit hall, and Wilkins, the ever-present footman, emerged. When he saw her, he shook his head.

"Four bottles, and he'd have another," he grumbled.

"Ain't like him to be a sot." With that rather oblique observation, he started past her.

"Wilkins?"

He stopped. "Aye?"

"I mean to sit awhile with Mrs. Deveraux, and if 'tis not excessively troublesome, I'd have a pot of tea up there."

"Aye."

"And I don't suppose Mrs. Deveraux has anything I could read, do you think?"

"Got anything as you'd want, miss, but . . ." He hesitated momentarily, then blurted out, "But I wouldn't be a-going in there—not tonight."

"I'm afraid I don't understand."

He jerked his thumb toward the door he'd come out. "The library," he said succinctly. "Master Dominick's in there—and he's in a real taking." Then, thinking he'd perhaps said too much, he started back toward the kitchen. "Bring you the tea upstairs," he promised.

"Yes. Yes, that will be fine."

Alone in the hall, she stood contemplating the light beneath the library door. She ought to leave well enough alone, she supposed, but somehow she could not. Telling herself she was but a meddler, she pushed the door open and eased gingerly inside.

Despite the light from the fire and from several braces of candles placed about the room, the tall rows of filled bookshelves gave it a dark, musty appearance. As her gaze swept across it, she thought that Wilkins had misled her, that the room was empty. And then she saw the booted feet.

Dominick Deveraux sat, or rather lay back, in a wing chair, his legs sprawled before him. His black hair was disordered, his face was flushed, and his closed eyes were like bluish smudges above the strong cheekbones. Rather than being in a taking, he appeared to have passed out.

"Mr. Deveraux . . . Dominick," she said softly.

There was no answer. She was disappointed, but it was just as well, she decided finally. He was in no condition to discuss anything relevant anyway. But as she stared down into his handsome face, she felt a pang of regret—somehow it did not seem right that a man as young as he should be so very torn. Spying a plaid woolen shawl draped over another chair, she picked it up and laid it gently over him. In the morning he was going to pay dearly for his night of folly.

Disengaging a candle from one of the braces, she carried it with her to the bookcases, exploring the seemingly endless rows for something likely to keep her interest. Mrs. Deveraux, or whoever maintained the library, did not seem much inclined to the newer novels. Finally, after a great deal of indecision, she selected Blake's *Songs of Innocence,* his much-acclaimed but somewhat dark volume of poetry. At least it would suit her mood.

"Bookroom thief," he uttered behind her.

Startled, she dropped the candle onto the rug. Before she could bend over to retrieve it, he'd lurched to his feet. Swaying, he stamped at the flame, grinding the burnt wick and the wax into the expensive rug.

"Trying to burn the damned place to the ground," he mumbled thickly.

"You startled me." Then, looking down, she apologized. "I'm terribly sorry about the rug. Perhaps if 'tis rubbed with soda . . ."

"Hang the rug. Buy another." For a moment his bleary eyes focused on her, and he shook his head. "Ought not to be here. Not a pretty sight, am I?" Stumbling, he managed to find his chair and sink into it again. "Where the devil's Wilkins?"

Ignoring the question, she sat down opposite him and leaned forward. "Mr. Deveraux, I have been to see your mother," she began, "and I think—"

"Wilkins!" he shouted. "Wilkins!"

"Mr. Deveraux," she tried again, "she's too heavily drugged to respond to anything. I should like your permission to discontinue the laudanum until 'tis absolutely necessary."

He blinked. "Don't matter. You heard him—she—she's dying."

"Perhaps . . . and perhaps not. I think only the next day or so can tell that, sir."

"Here's your . . ." The footman stopped. "Oh." There was no mistaking the disapproval on his face when he saw her.

"Give it over, man." Dominick looked upward, scowling. "And I am in no state to compro . . . to compromishe anyone, I asshure you."

"Bring the pot of tea in here, will you? And two cups," Anne added significantly. "He does not need any more wine."

"Don't want tea! Wilkins, d'ye hear me? Don't want tea!"

"Coffee, then."

"Wilkins!"

"I shall bring both, miss."

"Wilkins! Dammit!" Dominick called after the retreating footman. Slumping back, he eyed Anne balefully. Lifting his empty glass, he sneered. "To Mish Annie Morland, a due-deuced managing female. Interfering female, thash what you are." He waved the glass for a moment, then flung it past her. It broke against the marble facing on the fireplace. "A pox on females," he muttered.

"Wilkins says you are not usually a sot."

With an effort, he lifted his brow at that. "Don't know me—not anymore."

"I'm trying to tell you that your mother may not die, Mr. Deveraux. She may, of course, but then, she may not—'tis too soon to know."

"Rand—"

"Dr. Rand appears a trifle pessimistic to me."

He appeared to consider that, then shook his head. "Doeshn't matter. She doeshn't want me here. Wants to die without me."

"I cannot think anyone would wish to die alone."

"Mush you know about it, Mish Morland. Hates me." He blinked again and moved his head, trying to focus on her. "You know why? Wanna know why?" he demanded truculently. " 'Cause I'm alive! Good, hanshome Cassh is dead, and I'm alive!"

She sat quietly, not knowing what to say, hoping Wilkins would return quickly with the coffee. Across from her,

Dominick rambled almost incoherently, and she did not try to stop him. It was hard to follow him, and often she didn't know to whom he referred. For a time it was as though she were not there.

"I look like him, you know—not like her and Cassh. Devil take him. Devil take her too. Don't care anymore." With that pronouncement, he slumped down and closed his eyes.

Out of the corner of her eye she could see Wilkins carrying in the tray. She rose quickly to intercept him and took it.

"He all right, miss?" the footman asked.

"He's just in his cups."

"I dunno, maybe you ought not—"

"I am all right," she assured him. "He is overset because the doctor has given him to believe Mrs. Deveraux will not survive."

"Humph! He ain't going to miss her, if you was to ask me."

"Wilkins, I hardly think—"

"I know it ain't right to speak wrong of the dying, miss, but she ain't exactly been right to him neither." He turned to leave. "Call me when he'd go up to bed."

"Mr. Wilkins, who is Nicholas?" she could not help asking.

"His father."

"Cass was his older brother?"

He nodded. "Died in Boney's war. Right at the beginning.

She let him go, and she carried the tray to set it upon the reading table. Moving matter-of-factly, she poured steaming coffee into one of the cups, broke off a lump of sugar from the block, and stirred it in. "Cream, Mr. Deveraux?" she asked loudly.

One eye opened briefly, and there was no mistaking the hostility there. "No."

She held out the cup, and for a moment she thought he'd knock it from her hand. "I put just a bit of sugar into it," she coaxed. "Here—'twill clear your head."

"Don't know many sots, do you?" he muttered. "Still drunk—jusht awake."

"Please."

"Who made you my guar . . . my keeper? Go to Nottingham . . . go to London . . . go on."

"In the morning," she promised. "But for now, I'd talk with you."

"Nothing to say," he mumbled. Nonetheless, he took the cup unsteadily, spilling some of the hot liquid on his expensive breeches. He did not seem to notice. Taking a sip, he burned his mouth and winced. "Satishfied? Go on . . . leave."

"Not yet." She moved to pour her tea, adding sugar and cream to it; then she sat again opposite him.

"Too foxed to talk," he grumbled.

Sipping the hot sweet liquid, Anne tried to discover the means to reason with him. But he was staring sullenly into the fire, and the prospects for civilized discourse did not look at all good. Somewhat daunted, she nonetheless said quietly, "I could stay, I suppose." Even as the words came out, she felt quite foolish and forward. "That is, I am not without experience in the care of a sick person. There was Mrs. Cokeham, and before that my own mother, Mr. Deveraux. And I cannot think Mrs. Philbrook means to welcome me anyway." She felt like a rattle, for there was no indication he even attended her. "Mr. Deveraux, I should like to help you," she added lamely. "I think you need me."

His head turned slowly, and the expression on his face told her she'd been wrong. Instead of gratitude, there was anger. He lurched to his feet, reeling drunkenly over her. "Don't need your pity!" he flung at her. His lip curving into a bitter sneer, he demanded, "You think I need anything, Mish Morland? Dom Deveraux doeshn't need anybody! Go on to London and leave me to my cups! I don't need another managing female!"

Turning back, he swept the coffee cup onto the floor, where the brown liquid pooled across a rose woven into the woolen rug. He stared down briefly, then staggered from the room, leaving her. She sat motionless, the blood rising in her cheeks, feeling quite humiliated.

She could hear his bootsteps on the stairs, his voice bellowing in the hall above, and her chagrin turned to anger also. He'd made it abundantly clear that her offer meant nothing to him, and hell could freeze ere she repeated it. Let Lord Trent, Miss Mitford, and Dominick Deveraux take care of his mother. She was going to London and forget she'd ever met the boor.

A door banged somewhere above her, followed by the sound of muffled voices. But she no longer cared. Whatever Dominick Deveraux did was none of her affair. She laid the book on the tea tray and carried the whole up with her.

In the dimly lit upstairs hallway, several people stood uneasily watching Mrs. Deveraux's door. Bertie Bascombe, his slight body encompassed in a nightshirt, his head covered in a sleeping cap, complained, "Fellow can't sleep here—place is a deuced Bedlam! Damme if I know what's going on!"

Miss Mitford, her pale hair streaming about her shoulders, emerged, her hands gripping her wrapper tightly over her gown. "Whatever . . . ?"

"Damnable commotion!" Bertie told her with feeling. "That's what it is! Bedlam," he repeated. "Bedlam."

"Came in like the devil was with him," Betty insisted, "and I wasn't stayin'."

"What happened?" Anne managed to ask.

"Mr. Deveraux's in there," the maid answered. "Told me to get out, he did." She looked up to where Trent had come to stand behind Anne. "My lord, I couldn't—"

"You going in, my lord?" Wilkins wondered.

There was no sound coming from the bedchamber now, and as Trent stared speculatively at the door, the rest strained to hear his answer. "Go on to bed, all of you," he said finally. "Apparently Mr. Deveraux wishes to be private with his mother."

"But—"

But the marquess had already turned on his heel and headed back down the hall, making dispute difficult. One by one, the others shrugged and started returning to bed. As Margaret Mitford passed Anne, she shuddered. "I told you he was possessed of a volatile temper, Miss Morland. I shall be quite glad when 'tis all over. How Papa could ever think—"

"Get the door for you, Miss Morland," Bertie offered when he noticed the tray. Waiting until she was nearly into her bedchamber, he leaned to tell her, "I ain't going to miss this place. Be glad to get out of here in the morning. Daresay the Frenchies ain't any more havey-cavey than the Deveraux."

"Good night, Mr. Bascombe."

"You going to be ready early?"

"Yes."

Although a fire had been laid in the ornately faced fireplace, Anne undressed hastily, drew on her borrowed nightrail, buttoned it to her chin, propped up her pillows, and climbed into bed. Still seething, she poured another cup of the tea and tried to calm herself. Sipping the tepid beverage, she opened Blake's volume and forced herself to read.

Rain sprayed the paned window like sand hitting the glass. On the morrow she would be gone from this miserable place. And the day after, she would be in London. Her anger faded, replaced by a sinking feeling. In London she would turn herself in, and after that . . . well, she did not want to think about it.

She turned the pages, looking for the familiar poem, and found it.

> Tiger, tiger, burning bright
> In the forests of the night,
> What immortal hand or eye
> Could frame thy fearful symmetry?
>
> In what distant deeps or skies
> Burnt the fire of thine eyes?
> On what wings dare he aspire?
> What the hand dare seize the fire?
>
> And what shoulder and what art
> Could twist the sinews of thy heart?

She paused and stared toward the fire, seeing the images of beauty and of destruction. A metaphysical interpretation of man's condition. Whether it was what the poet intended,

Anne saw in it not a tiger, but rather human suffering. *And what shoulder and what art could twist the sinews of thy heart?* 'Twas the pain one gave another. Like Dominick Deveraux and his mother.

She sipped absently, thinking of him. He called himself a rogue, but in truth he was more of an enigma. While possessed of wit, looks, wealth, and occasional charm, he was also arrogant, cold, intemperate and bitter—and it was difficult to tell whether he loved or hated his mother.

But from what Trent, Betty, Wilkins, and Miss Mitford had intimated, 'twas possible that Charlotte Deveraux did not deserve his love. Still, whenever she thought of the old woman, she saw only the fear, the terror in her eyes. Charlotte Deveraux was afraid to die.

It was odd that she was so old, old enough to have been painted by Gainsborough, while her younger son was but twenty-seven. He must have been born after she was well into her thirties, perhaps even forty. Or else she had been one of those females who did not age well. Because she had been ill, 'twas difficult to tell.

It didn't make any difference, Anne reminded herself. She had no place there, no business even being there, and Dominick Deveraux was ready to wash his hands of her. For her attempt at kindness, she'd received a total rebuff, and she was not the sort of woman to stay where she was not wanted.

Sighing, she returned to the poem, scanning it the rest of the way through, seeing it end as it had begun.

> Tiger, tiger burning bright
> In the forests of the night,
> What immortal hand or eye
> Dare frame thy fearful symmetry?

Downstairs, someone pounded on the outer door. And once again there was movement in the hall, the shuffling of feet on the stairs, the creak of the door opening below. As it was now quite late, Anne thrust back the covers and padded to peer out the window. The light from a hastily lit lamp on the porch reflected off ice like a candle on crystal. It had not been rain she'd heard—it had been sleet.

There was a murmur of voices below, more feet coming back up the stairs, a great deal of shuffling and whispering in the hallway. A door opened, shut, and opened again. And finally there was a soft rapping at her door. Thinking perhaps that Mrs. Deveraux had taken a turn for the worse, that the doctor had been summoned, she threw on her borrowed wrapper and went to answer.

The marquess was scarce half-dressed, with his shirt not yet tucked into his breeches. The print of his bedclothes was still clearly visible on his cheek. Behind him, his valet cried his boots and his coat.

"What . . . ? Oh, dear, is aught the matter, my lord?"

"Have you seen Dom? No . . . no, of course you have not. Did not mean that as it sounded." He looked haggard, harried, and worried. "I have to return home. Word has come that Ellie—my wife—is brought to bed early."

"I'm sorry. I wish her a safe delivery."

"As do I," he said fervently. "I've not the time to find Dom, but tell him if he has need of me, he has but to send to the Meadows. Once I know Ellie is all right, I can return." Grasping her hand, he pressed several banknotes into it. "I don't know what Dom was able to bring with him, and you may need this." He did not wait for her to respond. "Ready, Crawfurd?" he addressed his valet.

"Really, my lord, but I cannot—"

He was already halfway down the hallway. Knowing that he was terribly hurried, she closed her hand over the money and said nothing more. Later, before she left, she would give it to Wilkins to return. She started to shut her door again, but Bertie had come out.

"What the deuce *now*?" he demanded querulously. "Place is like a demned inn! Worse, in fact. Don't know how—"

"Trent is leaving."

"Eh? Trent is leaving?" he repeated. "*Now?*"

"His wife is in childbed, and I expect he cannot wait for the storm to pass."

"Can't say as I am not glad he's going," he admitted,

turning back to his own room. He froze suddenly. "What storm?" he asked hollowly.

" 'Tis sleeting, Bertie."

His slender shoulders settled, conveying the impression that the unwelcome storm was all of a piece. "Don't care if it comes a foot of ice, I ain't staying," he declared. "It ain't right to intrude on a dying woman—and I'll be hanged if I'm going to try to talk to Miss Mitford anymore." He looked back. "You're going with me, ain't you?"

"Yes."

"Good girl. If it wasn't for m'father, I'd take you back to London myself. You ain't like the rest of 'em, Annie."

"Bertie, have you seen Mr. Deveraux?" she could not help asking.

"Been trying to sleep," he reminded her. "Hopeless," he added glumly, "but I go to try. Demned long way to France."

Once back in the warmth of her bed, Anne still could not sleep. She lay there wondering about Dominick Deveraux, wondering why he'd not come out. Surely with all the noise, he ought to have known something was afoot. Well, it was not her affair, she reminded herself. He didn't seem to want any sympathy or aid from anyone. Yet as she thought of him, she realized that her earlier anger had faded, and she could not help feeling sorry for him. For all his faults, there was something about Dominick Deveraux that drew her to him, and she did not seem able to help that either.

The room was dark save for the fire that blazed warmly in the hearth. He half-stumbled, half-reeled to stand over the bed. His mother lay as still as death, her face as pale as the bank of pillows behind her. For a long time he stood there staring down, trying to feel, but whether 'twas an excess of wine or a dearth of soul, he could summon nothing.

He told himself there ought to be something. The frail woman lying there had borne him more than twenty-seven years before. But she hadn't wanted to—she'd made that so plain in the intervening years. Maybe that was the difference between them.

Finally, unable to stand it, he reached to touch her hand where it lay against the folded coverlet. It was bony and cold, and for a moment he thought he'd been cheated again, that she'd already died.

"Mother . . ."

There was no sign that she heard—no flinch, no recoil—nothing. He moved his hand to her face, tracing her profile with his fingertips from her forehead to her nose. And he felt the faint rush of her breath.

"Mother." Dropping to the chair Betty had kept by the bed, he leaned over her. "Mother, 'tish Dominick—'tish Dom. Your other son." Again there was only the spitting, crackling logs and the faint ticking of the clock.

He ran his fingers through his hair as though he could somehow clear the fog in his head. For once she was going to hear him out, for once she was going to know. And he would not have to listen yet again to her bitter tirades against his father. He began to talk to her, pouring out his own bitterness, his own pain, in a lengthy, rambling discourse.

"Wasn't me that left you, Mother," he reminded her. He leaned forward again, so close that his face was but inches from hers. "Not Nicky Deveraux, Mother—never was—jusht looked like him. Dom never left you, for all that you wished he would."

He paused, drawing in his breath, then exhaled heavily. He could scarce hold his head up now, but he didn't want to stop—not yet. "Hell, Mother—you gave me hell—d'you know that? You wouldn't let me mourn my brother, Mother—you wouldn't even give me that. What did you think I did—jusht live to spite you? Man ought to think someone lovesh him, you know."

His head had fallen into his hands, and it seemed too heavy to lift, and yet he had to see that she'd heard him. Forcing himself to lean back, he looked once more into her still face. She couldn't hear him. Once again she'd cheated him, and he knew it.

"Damn you!" he shouted at her. "Damn you! Even now, you will not let me be a son to you!"

Struggling to his feet, he lurched toward the door. The

room spun around him, and for a moment he thought he was going to be sick. She wouldn't want that. He fell back into the chair, then leaned to cradle his head in his arms on the side of her bed.

The morrow, he promised himself, would be better. Annie Morland would be gone, and that he regretted, but a fugitive had no business even looking at a respectable female. As long as he had to run, he could not afford to get attached to her. As long as he had to run, there was no room in his life for her. But he would apologize for what he'd said ere she left. She'd deserved better of him. Finally, unable to sort it all out, unable to reason rationally, he turned his head against his sleeve and slept.

The room was cold, the sleet pelting the windows when he woke. And at first he could not place where he was. It was dark. He moved his hand from beneath his head and felt along the covers until he reached his mother's arm. Wincing, he sat up gingerly, trying not to shift the ache in his pounding head. It was as though the pulse in his temple was a hammer.

The fire had died to embers. Shifting his gaze back to his mother, he could barely make out her face. Touching it, he felt a sense of shame flood through him. Whatever she'd done to him, she'd still borne him, and he ought to honor her for that at least. He did not have to love her.

He rose unsteadily, this time taking care to hold his head, and an imperfect memory of what he'd done returned. Vaguely he remembered that Annie Morland was leaving, and he knew he didn't want her to go. She had to wait. She had to wait until he knew if Fordyce was dead. Forgetting that he'd decided she could not stay, he flung himself into the hallway, then stood until the pain in his head subsided.

Groping his way down the dark passage, he beat on her door. "Annie!"

She woke with a start. Her heart pounding, she tumbled from bed to find the wrapper. Pulling it on, she managed to light a candle from the fire and hurried into the hall. "Whatever . . . ? Mr. Deveraux! What is it—is your mother taken worse?"

"Got to stay until Burton comes back. Got to find if Fordyce is dead."

"What? Who is Burton?"

"Cannot go," he insisted.

"Mr. Deveraux, you are foxed," she told him severely.

"Dishguised," he agreed.

"Cannot this wait until morning, sir? You are in no condition to ask anything just now." Despite the soft slur of his speech or his disordered, almost wild appearance, there was a certain boyish appeal to him. And she felt almost angry with herself for responding to it. "You won't even remember this when you wake," she muttered. "Go on to bed."

The flickering light of her candle reflected in his blue eyes. "Like me, you know—got nowhere to go, Annie."

"What a lowering thought, sir."

"Could've left you at the Blue Bull, but didn't."

"Well, if this don't beat the Frenchies!" Bertie declared, disgusted. "Don't anybody but me want to sleep?" He regarded Dominic Deveraux peevishly. "Ain't at all the thing to be standing yallering in the hall in the middle of the night. Ain't at all the thing to be standing out here with Miss Morland neither." He turned to her. "If you was a-wanting to, I'd demned near as lief leave now. Get more sleep in the carriage anyway."

"Morning will be soon enough, I think."

"What the deuce is he thinking of?" he demanded plaintively. "Making a racket at . . ." Abruptly he disappeared back into his room, then returned with his pocket watch. "It ain't but three o'clock!"

"Mr. Deveraux is merely foxed. No doubt he will feel more the thing after he has slept. Though I am not quite sure how to get him to his bed." She looked at Bertie hopefully. "I suppose between us—"

"Eh? No, you don't. It ain't done—be the talk of the house if you was to be in his chamber." Bertie peered up and down the hallway as more discreet observers retreated behind their doors. "Never a footman or a valet when a man needs one," he complained under his breath. Reaching for Dominick's arm, he sighed. "Come on, sleep it off. Wait . . . don't lean on me." Favoring Annie with a look of long suffering, he pulled manfully. "Don't know what you was thinking of," he told Deveraux. "Gel's half-asleep, and shouldn't wonder at it. You want to talk, talk in the morning." As they reeled unsteadily down the hall, the smaller man trying to steer the larger one, she could hear Bertie say, "You're a demned lost soul, you know."

It was some time before he came back alone. Anne heard him stop outside her door, then heard him say, "Annie?"

"Yes?" she answered.

"If anybody else's to knock, don't come out."

"I quite agree, Mr. Bascombe."

His door had scarce closed before she heard the tap. Sighing, she answered it, and Margaret Mitford slipped in. "Are you quite all right, Miss Morland—Annie?" the girl asked, whispering.

"Yes."

"You must stay—you must! With Trent gone, I cannot bear to be left with Mr. Deveraux!"

"Meg, 'tis three o'clock," Anne reminded her. "Can we not speak of this a bit later in the morning?"

"Oh. Oh, yes, of course."

It wasn't until she was back in bed that Anne came fully awake. Lying there beneath the warmth of the thick covers, she pondered Dominick Deveraux's strange behavior. After what he'd said to her in the library, why had he asked her to stay? Was it pity?

Like me, you know—got nowhere to go. Could've left you at the Blue Bull, but didn't. She had somewhere to go, all right. She was surely bound for Newgate. And who was Burton? *Got to stay until Burton comes back. Got to find if Fordyce is dead.*

Finally, unable to sleep after all that had happened, she rose reluctantly and went to the window. The sleet had ceased, but the sky was nearly white with heavy snow. She stared out into the cold, pristine beauty of it, thinking Bertie would surely be cast down when he saw it. Then she thought of Lord Trent and his precipitate race home, and she offered a small, silent prayer that he made it safely.

Throwing on the wrapper yet again, she picked up her book and let herself out into the hall. If she could not sleep, she could at least be of use to someone. Besides, if she were to read aloud to Charlotte Deveraux, it might do both of them some good. At the very least, it would relieve her own mind for a while.

11

Bertie came down early, only to be greeted by the news that snow had been falling for hours. Staring glumly out the saloon window, he had to admit he could not see much beyond twenty feet. It was all of a piece, he decided irrationally. His flight to France had been doomed from the start. He wouldn't even put it past his omniscient parent to have ordered the ridiculous sequence of events that brought him to the Haven.

"I feel like a demned Greek," he muttered. "And the Fates has caught me." Turning around, he sighted Wilkins. "Anybody down yet?" he asked.

"I don't believe so, sir. But if you are wishful of breakfast, naught's to say you cannot be served now."

"I *am* deuced hungry," Bertie admitted. "And there ain't nothing else to do."

It wasn't until he was already into the dining room that he realized Wilkins had been mistaken. Margaret Mitford was already there. He considered bolting, then decided if either of them was to give up breakfast, it could be she. When she looked up, her eyes widened, then she dropped her gaze to her still-empty plate, saying nothing. He took the chair at the other end of the table.

" 'Morning, Miss Mitford," he said casually.

"Yes."

"Seen Miss Morland yet?"

"No."

"Deveraux?"

"No."

"Well, daresay 'tis just us, ain't it?"

"Yes."

"Havey-cavey business last night," he observed.

Apparently in the absence of a direct question, she did not
feel it incumbent to comment. He began to hope breakfast
was served soon. As the silence grew heavier between them,
he fidgeted uncomfortably. Finally he could stand it no
longer. "Hanged if I'm going to spend m'breakfast like
m'dinner, Miss Mitford."

She blinked. "I beg your pardon?"

"Look," he told her, "you ain't got nothing to worry
about from me. For one thing, I ain't much in the petticoat
line, and for another, I ain't got much conversation neither."

"Yes."

He eyed her suspiciously. "What's that supposed to mean?
I didn't ask anything."

Keeping her face averted, she said quite low, "I can tell
you are not an accomplished, flirt, Mr. Bascombe."

He brightened. "You can? See, told you—you ain't got
nothing to worry about." Twisting in his chair, he looked
toward the door. "Where the deuce is everyone, do you
think?"

"Possibly they are asleep."

"Oh. Yes. Shouldn't wonder at it, what with all the doings
last night."

Apparently that did not require a response from her either.
To his relief, Wilkins appeared with the coffeepot.

"Chocolate, Miss Mitford?" the footman inquired. "Quite
sorry, but I did not realize you were down."

"Yes."

After the man withdrew, Bertie studied her curiously.
"Was it yes, you was wanting chocolate, or was it yes, you
was down?"

"He knew what I meant."

Determined to pursue some sort of conversation, he stuck
his oars into the social waters manfully. "Place looks like
one of them gothic houses, don't it? Wonder Caro Lamb
didn't set that story here, don't you think? I mean, we got
a place filled with folks as don't talk to one another, and
Deveraux's running round as tragic as Byron. Got the old
woman a-dying upstairs. Give a man the dreads, if he was
to think about it."

"Yes." Then she asked suddenly, "Do you think Miss Morland will stay?"

"Eh? Well, she ain't going anywhere today, I can tell you. Ain't nobody going," he added glumly.

"No, I mean do you think she will stay after the storm is past?"

Recalling Quentin Fordyce's body on the tattered rug, he shook his head. "Can't."

"Why?"

"Just can't, that's all. Got business in London." He looked toward the door, wishing Wilkins back. "Place is like a tomb, ain't it? Don't know how you can stand it."

She stared down at the grain on the table, reddening. "My papa will not let me come home," she mumbled finally.

Before Bertie could digest that, the footman reappeared with her chocolate and the bread rack. The one he placed before Margaret Mitford, the other in front of Bertie. "Would you have your eggs coddled, sir?"

"It don't matter. I'd just have 'em quick."

When Wilkins left again, Bertie glanced down the table to where she sat. "You eating, Miss Mitford?"

"Just bread and jam. 'Tis all I take."

"Only brought one rack," he observed.

"Yes."

He eyed the vast expanse of table between them and sighed. Rising, he reached for the bread, the butter dish, and the jam pot and carried them all to her. Then he returned to retrieve his coffee and the pot. Moving them to the place across from hers, he dropped to a chair. She looked up curiously.

"Look, I ain't a-going to trot the food for you, so we might as well be civilized in the matter."

"Yes."

When she made no move toward the rack, he selected a piece of bread and began to butter it. "I ain't here 'cause I'm a-wanting to be either," he told her conversationally. When she said nothing, he gestured with his bread. "I got sisters, you know—you got any brothers?"

"No."

"Sisters?"

"Yes."

"Talk to 'em?"

She looked up at that. "Of course."

"Then you can talk to me. And I'll talk to you like you was one of m'sisters."

"How many do you have?" she asked timidly, her curiosity stirred.

"Three. Louisa, Fanny, and Augusta. Gussie's coming out this year. You come out, Miss Mitford?" he managed to ask between mouthfuls.

"No." She hesitated, then blurted out, "There are too many of us."

"Deuced nuisance anyway, if you was to ask me. Don't know why m'father's bothering, 'cause Gussie ain't going to take—carrot top, you know . . . spots too."

"Spots?" she repeated faintly.

"Freckles. Everywhere."

"How awful."

"Oh, m'mother tried bleaching 'em, but it lightened her skin also, so's they were even more in evidence. But you don't need to repine for Gussie, 'cause she don't care whether she gets an offer or not."

"I daresay your parents must care."

"Eh?" He stuffed another piece of bread into his mouth and began to chew. His mouth full, he had to drink from his coffee and swallow before he could answer. "Devil of it is, they don't," he admitted. "Fired off the older girls, but Gussie's not the same. Bit of a bluestocking," he added, as though that would explain it. "Ain't like me at all."

"You are an indifferent scholar?" she managed to ask.

"Ain't a scholar at all," he retorted.

"Well, I daresay that as you are a wealthy man, it does not matter."

"Humph! Everything I do matters to m'father, Miss Mitford—everything. M'father . . ." He paused to take another drink. "M'father ain't going to rest until I am leg-shackled." When he looked up, she was watching him, and then her eyes dropped. "Devil of a thing to be the heir, you know. I tell him I ain't got no address, and he tells me it don't matter—he'll take care of the business for me. Now, how the devil's he to do that, I ask you?" Not waiting for an answer, he rambled on, "Says he's an earl, I'm going to be one when he pops off, and there ain't many females as wouldn't wish to be a countess."

"Your papa is an earl?" she asked incredulously.

"Uh-huh. Haverstoke."

"He must be very rich."

He nodded. "Like a nabob."

"Well . . ." She could not help smiling shyly. "Your pardon, but you do not look much like an earl to me."

"I don't look like one to *me*," he said. "Thing is, I got no choice. Born to be one."

"I suppose you could count that a burden," she murmured.

"Deuced nuisance. Don't know if anyone's a-wanting to know me or m'father, you know. But it don't signify, I suppose—I ain't got too many friends anyway. Daresay you don't either."

"No."

He reached for another slice of bread. "Turnabout. Know I'm here 'cause I'm running from m'father, but what about you?"

She appeared to study the jam pot, then sighed tragically. "Between Papa and Aunt Charlotte, 'tis determined I am to fix Mr. Deveraux's interest, and I . . . well, I cannot."

He nearly choked. "Egad! 'Course you cannot! Ain't in his style, for one thing—have to be empty in the cockloft not to see that! Be like me throwing my hat over the windmill for . . . for . . ." He groped for some equally unsuitable example and was at a loss. "Princess Charlotte," he decided finally.

Stung, she reminded him, "She's dead—and one should not speak with levity of the dead, sir."

"Well, if she wasn't," he shot back, unrepentant. "What was they thinking of? Deveraux indeed."

Although she'd often reflected in much the same vein, she

could not help feeling he lacked sensibility in the matter.
" 'Twas hoped I would restrain his . . . his rather reprehen-
sible tendencies," she said stiffly.

"Be like setting the chicken under the fox's nose," he
snorted. "Ain't no match for him."

"So I have told Papa, but he will not listen. He says 'tis
up to me to make a good match, and . . . well, I cannot!
I should not know how to fix anyone's interest, Mr.
Bascombe!"

For a moment he thought she meant to cry, and he regretted
trying to talk with her. He groped for the means to pacify
her before she enacted him a tragedy. "Here, now, it ain't
all that bad," he murmured soothingly. "Daresay if you was
to talk up a bit . . . well, maybe some other chap—"

"I cannot! And I cannot abide the thought . . . the thought
of Mr. Deveraux! And if I am cooped up here, there is no
other chap!"

"Tell 'em you don't like him," he advised. "Tell 'em you
want to look about a bit for another fellow."

"Did that help you with your father?" she countered.

"No. Had to bolt."

"Well, I cannot, for we are rather poor. Papa has every
expectation of my snaring a rich husband. And, given my
circumstances, Mr. Deveraux is all I am ever like to see."

He considered her for a moment, then went back to his
coffee. "Then you got to learn to talk up. A man finds it
a deuced bore listening to himself. And Deveraux . . . well,
he's been with some high fliers, don't you know? That is
. . . Dash it, but he ain't going to . . . Well, it don't matter,"
he decided.

"Mr. Bascombe, I have told you: I cannot."

"Talked to me just now," he reminded her. "But your
papa's deuced simpleminded to think you can fix Deveraux's
interest. Got to get out of here and find another chap," he
repeated.

"Where? Papa cannot afford a Season, and even if he
could, I should die rather than be paraded about on the
Marriage Mart."

"Go to Bath."

"Bath?" she repeated faintly.

He nodded. "Pump Rooms. Ain't as starchy as London. Cheaper, too. Get your papa to take you for the Little Season. Know two fellows as went there last year and came back betrothed—said it wasn't as bad as London. Didn't like the water, though, but daresay it ain't much worse than the lemonade at Almack's."

"I don't think I could," she ventured doubtfully.

" 'Course you could! Miss Mitford, you ain't exactly an antidote! Just . . ." His pale eyes studied her for a moment. "Just too shy, that's all."

"You don't think me plain?"

" 'Course not. Look better'n Gussie, after all." He looked over at her, then nodded. "Yaller hair's all the crack, I'm told. Besides, you ain't got spots. Tell you what—you need to practice a-talking, you can practice on me. Don't have to impress me, you know, 'cause I ain't about to offer for you."

"Mr. Bascombe, I don't think I could. I mean, I—"

"Talking to me right now, ain't you?"

"Yes, but—"

"Thing is, you got to quit thinking about parson's mouse-trap and start thinking about what you got to say, Miss Mitford. Speak up—man don't want a female as don't have nothing to say, you know." Then, afraid he'd misled her, he added, " 'Course, he don't want one too forward neither."

"Mr. Bascombe, they are wrong about you—I don't think you are a slowtop at all." Realizing what she'd said, she turned a dull red. "That is, I did not mean—"

"It don't signify, Miss Mitford. I ain't exactly a downy one neither."

12

Anne's throat was almost sore, her voice husky from reading the poems aloud over and over, but she felt strangely elated. The snow had relieved her of the burden of making any decision about her future. It was out of her hands.

A footman came in to lay a fire in the hearth, and Betty drew the heavy draperies, flooding the room with the white light. Mrs. Deveraux was still relatively out of touch, but she was not precisely comatose. As the night had receded and the day begun, she seemed to be able to respond to light and possibly noise. Morever, she'd curled her fingers. It wasn't much, Anne admitted, but it was something positive to report to Dominick Deveraux. After all else that had befallen him, 'twas time he heard something good.

She rose and stretched cramped muscles, then crossed the room to the window. And what she saw below made her heart rise into her throat. Emerging from the billowing, swirling snow, half a dozen red-coated men rode down the carriage lane. She did not have to wonder why they'd come.

"Betty," she said, trying not to betray her alarm, "you must find Mr. Deveraux and warn him."

"Begging your pardon, miss?"

"There are soldiers coming."

The girl stared. "Oh, lud! Oh, me!"

"I would you went now. Try not to alarm the household."

It was futile warning, for as soon as the maid got into the hall, she began to shout, "The soldiers is coming! Mr. Deveraux . . . Mr. Deveraux! The soldiers is coming!"

Anne all but ran back to her bedchamber and, throwing the borrowed wrapper onto the floor, fairly dived into the green dress. Dragging the comb through her hair, she tried to make herself presentable. Frowning, she pulled the ruffled cap over the disarray. Dominick Deveraux had saved her once, and she would try to stall the soldiers for him. Hopefully, he could either hide or else he could escape. Not that she had much hope of the latter, for the snow would give evidence of any flight.

Her heart pounding in her ears, she made her way downstairs just as the elderly butler was opening the door. A gust of bitter wind blew in, carrying snow across the polished marble floor. An officer, his face ruddy from the cold, stepped inside and stamped his booted feet. Behind him the other soldiers did the same.

"A most dreadful day for traveling, sirs," she said. She patted the cap, hoping he would take her for a sensible, mature female.

"Mrs. Deveraux?"

"No. She is unable to receive anyone just now, I am afraid." Anne forced herself to move forward and held out her hand calmly. "I am Miss Anne Morland."

He assessed the green dress before bowing over her hand. "Miss Morland, I am Gareth Collins—Captain Collins."

"Wilkins!" she called out clearly. "Do come serve these gentlemen some hot punch in the front saloon."

"Aye, miss," he responded promptly.

"I say, but—" Emerging from the dining room, Bertie paled when he saw the officer. "Lud."

"Mr. Bascombe, may I present . . ." Anne looked at the fellow expectantly, all the while praying that Bertie would not give Dominick away. "I'm dreadfully sorry, sir, but I did not note the name clearly."

"Collins—Captain Collins," he supplied shortly. "And I cannot—"

"Nonsense," she declared briskly. "We are quite civilized here. Mr. Bascombe is, after all, heir to the Earl of Haverstoke."

"You don't say."

The color returned to Bertie's face. "Just so," he managed weakly.

"Do come in, Captain Collins—and your men also. Naught's to say that they would not enjoy a bit of hot punch also, is that not so, sirs?" Not waiting for an answer, she ordered crisply, "Wilkins, tell Cook to heat the cider, if you please."

"Really, but there is scarce the time—"

"Cold out," Bertie maintained. "Deuced cold. Can't think why a man'd be out in this, if you want my opinion. Bound to be frozen to the marrow."

"Yes, but I'm afraid—"

"I am certain the captain will apprise us as to why he is here directly—after the punch," Anne said smoothly.

"Actually, we—"

"In due time, sir." Noting that Meg had appeared also, she continued to delay. "Mr. Bascombe, perhaps you would wish to present the captain to Miss Mitford?"

"Shouldn't think she . . . Oh . . . uh-huh. Miss Mitford, this is Captain Collins. Look, we ain't done with breakfast but—"

"Servant, Miss Mitford," the captain said gallantly.

The girl colored and stammered something utterly incoherent. "Shy girl," Bertie explained. "Come on, Miss Mitford. Daresay they ain't going to mind if we was to eat."

"Breakfast can wait, Mr. Bascombe," Anne told him meaningfully. "Your pardon, Captain, but you find us at sixes and sevens. Mrs. Deveraux suffered a dreadful seizure last evening, and I'm afraid none of us has had much sleep. Not to mention that Lord Trent was called away in the night most precipitately. His first child, you know, and his marchioness is brought to bed early."

"Lord Trent was here?"

"But of course he was here!" she retorted a trifle acidly. "His aunt had another stroke earlier and *someone* had to come. I mean, under the *unfortunate* circumstances . . ." She let her voice trail off, hoping she'd given the impression that there was no one else. Gesturing toward the open door, she directed him, "But go on in, sir, and I shall see to the punch." Then, realizing that would leave them with Bertie and Meg, she changed her mind. "Actually, Meg, why don't you go with Wilkins?"

"I don't—"

"Nonsense, my dear. Do join us, Mr. Bascombe."

"I . . . uh . . . dash it, but I ain't finished eating!"

"Bertie, dear boy . . ." Her voice rose slightly in warning.

"Well, daresay I ain't all that hungry," he conceded, "though what I am to . . . well, I am sure I don't know." Resigned, he sank into a chair. "So, gentlemen, what brings you here?" he asked in a manner that clearly indicated he didn't really want to know.

"Not *now.* You'll have the captain thinking us positively uncivil. Really, but give them time to warm themselves at the fire. In the absence of a proper host, one must do one's best to accommodate the unforeseen, don't you think, Mr. Bascombe?"

He was trying to follow her, but it was an effort. His pale brow furrowed for a moment, then lightened. "Oh, collect you mean me, eh?"

"Just so."

"Are you a relative of Mrs. Deveraux?" Captain Collins asked him.

"Lud no!" Then, realizing how that must sound under the circumstances, Bertie tried to recover. "Actually, m'god-mother," he invented. "Came when I heard she was sick. With Dominick out of the country, I . . ." He looked to Anne for help.

"You did just as you ought," she murmured soothingly.

"And you, ma'am?"

Clearly she was not dressed as an ordinary companion, and he was likely to note it. She smiled brightly and hoped God did not punish her for spinning lies. "Mrs. Deveraux is my godmother also." She looked to where one of the soldiers was edging closer to the fire. "Do warm yourself, sir. Dreadful out, isn't it?"

"Snow's deep," he muttered, stretching his hands toward the blaze. "And 'tis cold."

"Think the roads will be passable tomorrow?" Bertie asked hopefully. "I mean, I was thinking of going home, you know. Can't do anything here, after all. She don't know us," he explained.

Seeing the captain's questioning frown, Anne explained,

"I'm afraid Mrs. Deveraux is in a coma, sir. If you have come to see her, 'tis a wasted errand."

Wilkins returned bearing the steaming punch bowl, and behind him another footman carried cups and a ladle. Anne could see that the captain was torn between duty and the punch. She had to push him toward the latter.

" 'Tis quite good—an old family recipe of Mrs. Deveraux's, I believe," she murmured. "I am told that when he is home, Mr. Deveraux quite favors it over anything else—except his port, of course. That will be all, Wilkins. Meg, pour for the gentlemen, will you?"

"Uh . . ." The girl cast about for the means to escape. "Miss Morland—Annie—I cannot!"

" 'Course you can! Just put the punch in the cups," Bertie insisted. "Ain't nothing to it."

"Is she a relative?" Captain Collins asked.

"Aunt Charlotte is my godmother," Meg answered. Then, as he turned to look at her, she colored deeply, the red of her face in sharp contrast to the paleness of her hair. "Miss Morland . . ." she said desperately.

"Mr. Bascombe will assist you. Pardon me one moment, gentlemen." Before the girl could demur further, Anne slipped into the foyer. As she pushed the door nearly closed, she could hear the captain observe, "Mrs. Deveraux appears to be a most generous woman, Miss Mitford. I'd think few could claim the devotion of so many godchildren."

"Well, I . . ."

"Woman's a prince—er, a princess, that is—great affection for her," Bertie insisted.

"Wilkins," Anne hissed as she caught the footman, "have you see Dom—Mr. Deveraux?"

"Sent Beckman up, and he found him at his bath," he whispered back. "Said he was weasel-bit, but he knew what Beckman was telling him."

"Good. Tell him I am doing the best I can, but I fear Captain Collins grows suspicious. Whatever he means to do, he'd best do now."

"Yes, miss."

As she reentered the saloon, the captain asked, "Are you

quite certain Dominick Deveraux is out of the country, Mr. Bascombe?''

Bertie strangled on his punch and fell to coughing hard. Both Anne and Margaret hastened to pound him soundly on his narrow back. And after he caught his breath, he looked up reproachfully. " 'Twas too hot.''

"I didn't think it hot at all," one of the soldiers spoke up.

"Mr. Bascombe has a delicate palate—the nobility, you know," Anne said with a straight face.

"Are you the only gentleman here?" the captain persisted.

"He is definitely the only gentleman in the house—isn't that so, Miss Mitford?" Anne declared.

"Er . . . yes. The only gentleman."

"I believe Mr. Bascombe has a tongue, Miss Morland."

"Burned it," Bertie reminded him. "On the punch."

The captain drained his cup and set it on a small table. Reaching into his coat, he drew out an official-looking document. "As much as I regret the unpleasant task, I'm afraid I have a warrant for Dominick Deveraux's arrest." He paused briefly, letting his words sink in. "We believe he is in England, and most probably is either in this house or on his way here."

Trying very hard to appear shocked, Anne could only manage, "Oh, dear. Are you quite certain, Captain?"

"He came in at Southampton and was nearly taken there."

"But that does not mean . . . that is, 'tis a long way from Southampton, sir." Anne stopped, her mind racing for some means to question the legitimacy of the captain's authority. "Should not it be the constable who comes, sir? I should not think we are in your jurisdiction."

"Dominick Deveraux is a dangerous man, Miss Morland. According to the deposition against him, he shot a man who had eloped."

"Still, 'twas a duel, was it not? You have come after him as though he has committed treason. I am not at all sure—"

"Since you seem to be doing much of the speaking, Miss Morland, I shall address the matter to you." He handed her the warrant smugly. "Read it."

"I did not question your word, sir, but merely the irregularity of this."

"Nonetheless, I am afraid I must insist on a search of the house."

"Yes, of course. Though I cannot think you will discover Mr. Deveraux here. If you will but excuse me for a moment, I shall get Wilkins to show you about."

But this time Captain Collins followed her into the foyer, and as she was desperately casting about for the means to give Dominick more time, he looked up. "Miss Morland, I believe you are a liar," he announced coldly.

"Really, sir, but I find your accusation most offensive. I assure you . . ." She followed his gaze and her heart nearly stopped. "Oh."

Coming down the wide staircase was Dominick Deveraux. He was dressed in an open-necked cambric shirt, a patterned silk scarf knotted at the neck, exquisitely tailored buff breeches, and gleaming knee boots. Over his arm he carried a heavy cloak, and in his hand an old-fashioned tricorn hat. Despite the obvious fatigue in his face, he looked like a highwayman ready to ride. Weasel-bit or not, he did not show it.

"Dominick Deveraux?"

"Yes."

Captain Collins stepped forward. "Mr. Deveraux, I arrest you in the name of the crown. You are hereby charged with—"

"I am well aware of the charge, Captain," Dominick cut in curtly. Turning around, he gestured to a servant who carried a portmanteau behind him. "I shall, of course, require the services of a valet, and Beckman has kindly offered." His gaze shifted to Anne, and his expression softened perceptibly. "And you must acquit Miss Morland of any intent to deceive."

"She lied, sir," Collins retorted.

The Deveraux eyebrow shot up in exaggerated disbelief. "Is that true, my dear? What did he ask that you felt it incumbent to answer falsely?"

"He wished to know if Mr. Bascombe were the only gentleman left in the house."

"And you of course said he was?"

"Yes." Despite the terrible circumstances, she could not resist smiling at him. "I had it on good authority, sir, that you are a rogue rather than a gentleman."

"Exactly." He turned his attention to Collins. "Well, Captain, you behold that I have come down freely to give myself up. However, I should like a brief word with Miss Morland ere I go."

"I hardly think it necessary," Collins responded stiffly. "I have tarried overlong already, and the snow grows deeper even as we speak."

"I'd give instructions for my mother's care. Surely you would not deny a man's concern for a dying parent, Captain?"

The officer hesitated. "How do I know you will not bolt?"

Once again a single black brow rose. "My dear fellow, in this weather? I should leave a blasted trail, don't you think?"

"Still . . ."

"You may stand guard outside the door."

"Very well. Under the circumstances, I do not suppose five minutes will make much difference. But I must ask your word as a gentleman . . ." He stopped, seeing that Deveraux's brow had climbed even higher. " . . . as a rogue, then," he snapped.

"My thanks, Captain. Annie, the library."

"I shall be waiting directly outside," Collins reminded him.

"Of course."

Dominick held the door for her, and as Anne stepped past him, he said appreciatively, " 'Twas an extraordinary performance, my dear."

She half-expected him to somehow make a run for it, to perhaps escape through the window, and she was prepared to speak loudly until he was gone. But after he closed the door, he moved to face her soberly.

"I've not much time, Annie."

She nodded.

"First, I'd apologize for my abominable behavior last night."

"You were foxed, sir."

" 'Tis no excuse for rebuffing an offer freely given."

"Sometimes I should learn to hold my tongue. I *am* a managing female," she admitted. "And I should not have tried to talk to you then."

His mouth curved into the faint smile. "Never give coffee to a man in his cups, my dear. It merely irritates him." Abruptly the smile faded, and his expression sobered once more. "I was wrong—there are more than two kinds of females," he said softly. "You are an exception, you know, for you are possessed of a kind and generous heart."

"Stuff, sir." Then, realizing how ungrateful that must sound, she added, "I am quite ordinary, really."

"That, my dear, is the first lie you have told me." Despite his solemn mien, his blue eyes were warm, disconcerting her. "Annie, I am asking you to stay until I can return."

She looked away. "What about Mr. Fordyce? Naught's to say they will not come looking for me also. Mrs. Philbrook will recall I left London with him. Surely someone at the Blue Bull must make the connection, and . . . well, I'd cause you no more difficulty, sir."

"I have sent Burton to make a discreet inquiry, and he should be back in a few days. If Fordyce is dead, 'twill not matter."

" 'Twill matter to me."

"Wilkins will give you the key to my box," he went on matter-of-factly. "You may use the money in it at your discretion."

"You do not even know me, sir," she protested.

"I trust you, Annie." He slid his knuckle under her chin and lifted it. Before she knew what he meant to do, he'd bent his head to hers. His face blurred; then she felt his lips brush hers. "Take care of things for me," he whispered as he drew back. "Until we are met again."

He was leaving. "Wait—"

He swung back around. "What?"

"Why did you do it—let them take you, I mean?"

"I am tired of running, Annie. There comes a time when a man ought to get on with his life, you know. And I didn't commit murder." Somehow, in that moment, it became important that she believe in him. "Beresford did not elope, Annie—he fired ere the signal was given, and I can assure you he did not fire into the air."

Afraid for him, she could scarce form the words, but she managed to ask, "What will they do to you, sir?"

"Dominick."

"What . . . ?"

" 'What will they do to you, *Dominick*?' " he repeated. "I don't know. There will be a formal inquest, and a great deal depends on how much the witnessess lie."

"Your second? Surely—"

"My second disappeared." Once again he started for the door. At the last moment he stopped. "I shall be forever in your debt, you know. Good-bye, Annie."

She stood there rooted to the floor, listening as the door closed after him. She heard him tell Captain Collins he was ready, and then they were gone. She watched through the window as the soldiers' red coats disappeared into the blowing snow. Her hand crept to her lips in memory of the brief, warm feel of his.

Bertie came in, and Meg followed on his heels. "Are you quite all right, Annie?" she asked. "I vow I could have died when I saw the soldiers. I know not how you were able to be so . . . so *composed* about it."

"He kissed me," Anne responded absently.

"Oh, how awful for you! And you did not call for help?"

"Sometimes, Miss Mitford, females want to be kissed," Bertie reminded her. "If they don't, they let a man know it."

"No." Anne sighed, then collected herself to face him. "Mr. Bascombe—Bertie—I have decided to stay." Aware that he was looking quite askance at her, she sighed again. "I know. But 'tis not fair to leave Meg to bear the burden of Mrs. Deveraux's care."

"What about For . . . about the other matter, that is?"

"I am to wait until someone named Burton returns from

Southampton. After that, I don't know. I suppose 'twill depend on what he has learned. In any event, perhaps Mrs. Deveraux will be better by then."

Bertie took a deep breath, then let it out heavily. "Well," he conceded, "I ain't actually got any place to be neither. Besides, it don't seem right to leave two females alone." He looked to Margaret Mitford almost defensively. "Well, stands to reason, don't it? You ain't got a man in the house. Go on—go on back to eat. I'm going to be there in a minute also."

He waited until she'd left; then he turned again to Anne. "Guess I should've asked whether you wanted me here first, huh?"

"Bertie, I was going to ask you."

"You were?" He brightened. "Well, of course you were—need a man to take care of things."

"I need a friend."

"You got at least two of 'em, Annie—me and Deveraux. Come on—you got to eat."

"No. I am not yet hungry."

She sat alone, staring unseeing into the small fire long after Bertie left, mulling over those last minutes with Dominick Deveraux, reliving his words and his kiss until she caught herself guiltily. She ought not to refine too much on those things, she told herself sternly, for was he not a rogue? He had probably kissed a hundred women—or done a great deal more than that even with some of them. And it was wool-gathering to think he meant anything more than gratitude, for men of his stamp did not look twice at the Anne Morlands of this world. Or if they did, their intentions were seldom honorable.

Annie, I am asking you to stay. . . . You may use the money in it at your discretion. . . . I trust you. . . . He'd spoken of himself, of her, of her situation. But once alone, he'd said nothing of his mother. He'd only said, "Take care of things for me."

Well, she would do it. For now, she would do her best for his mother, but as soon as the roads cleared, she would send to Lord Trent. Perhaps he could exert some influence on the local magistrate ere Dominick was moved to London. And she would ask his aid in discovering a good solicitor for his cousin. Surely, with the family honor at stake, he would help her provide one.

13

To take her mind from that which she could not help, Anne wholeheartedly devoted her time and effort to Dominick's mother. For the first two snowbound days she spent nearly all of her waking hours in the sickroom, setting up a schedule whereby she chatted with, read to, and verbally cajoled the seemingly unresponsive woman at intervals. In between, she washed her, combed her hair, and patiently fed her a thin, sustaining gruel, taking care that Mrs. Deveraux did not choke on it. Sometimes she despaired, but then something would happen to encourage her. On this day, for instance the old woman had seemed aware when Anne spoke to her, and more than once she'd been able to exert pressure with her fingers. Regimen was important, Anne insisted to the skeptical Meg and Betty. Sometimes, when she would give Dominick's mother a rest, she would either catnap herself or sew.

Still determined to save her ruined dress, she had taken it completely apart at all the seams, sponged it, and was now using the quiet time with the old woman to work on it. It was, Meg insisted, an utterly hopeless undertaking, but Anne simply could not be brought to part with it. To her, the dress represented far too many hopes. But try as she would, she could not seem to restore it to its former glory.

"You ought to use Mr. Deveraux's money to buy yourself a gown," Meg told her. "If he could see what you have done for Aunt Charlotte, not even he would begrudge it."

"I haven't even looked in the box," Anne murmured, biting off her thread.

"Someday, when you are downstairs, I am going to throw that on the trash heap," Meg promised. "And then you will have to buy yourself something."

For a moment Anne sat, seeing Dominick Deveraux running back into the Red Hart to retrieve the dress for her, and she shook her head almost absently. "No. Even if I should have others, I should still want this one."

"But *why*?"

"Well, I cannot expect you to understand it, I suppose, but after several years of practicing the most shocking economies, I persuaded myself that I ought to have something quite nice to wear to meet my grandfather."

"The general?"

"I see you have been speaking with Mr. Bascombe," Anne observed dryly.

"But I think it quite romantic, truly I do," Meg insisted. "To have had a toasted opera singer for a mother, and a general for your grandfather. None of my relations has done anything."

Anne lifted her eyebrows in surprise. "He told you about my mother also?"

The girl colored. "Well, there is naught else to do, is there? You are cooped up here much of the time, and there is no other diversion."

"I did not think you cared for the company of gentlemen, my dear."

"Well, I don't, but I find Mr. Bascombe quite droll, actually."

Although Anne had developed a certain attachment for Bertie, she would not have precisely described him in that vein. "Droll," she repeated.

"Well, he is a sad rattle," Meg admitted, "but beneath that he is possessed of a great deal of practical advice, you know."

"No."

"Only fancy, when I would not speak with him, he told me I should pretend he was one of my sisters. And of course, since I am not expected to fix his interest, I could see he was quite right." She looked across at Anne. "He holds you in the highest regard, you know."

"Fiddle."

"Well, you could do a great deal worse," the girl retorted.

"He is, after all, Haverstoke's heir. And his papa is as rich as a nabob."

"Yes," Anne agreed noncommittally.

Meg eyed her suspiciously. "Are you casting out lures to him?"

At that, Anne laid aside her sewing. "I do not believe we should suit."

"Why?" the girl persisted. "You cannot say your affections are engaged anywhere else, can you?"

"No." Anne caught herself guiltily. "That is to say, I do not think so." Even then, she was not sure she did not lie just a little.

She was saved by a rap on the door, followed by Wilkins peering inside. "Miss Morland, I am to tell you Burton is back."

For a moment Anne's hands turned to ice, and she felt her stomach knot. "Already?" she said hollowly.

"Housekeeper's in a taking 'cause I told him to wait in the front saloon, but Mr. Deveraux said I was to see he came to you," the footman explained. "Says for you to hurry—he's dripping mud on the floor."

"Yes. Of course. Meg, do you mind sitting with Mrs. Deveraux for a while?" Without waiting for an answer, Anne rose. " 'Tis her nap time, in any event, so there is naught for you to do. In fact, there is a book on the table, should you wish to read."

The girl glanced at the slim volume of Shakespeare's sonnets and shuddered. "I should just sit, I think." As Anne left, she leaned back in the chair, a satisfied smile lingering on her lips. She did not note the old woman's eyes following the other girl to the door.

Dread and hope warred in Anne's breast as she forced herself to walk calmly into the saloon. The groom's back was to her as he stretched gloved hands toward the fire.

"Mr. Burton?"

"Aye." He turned around. "Heard they took Master Dominick. Bad business."

"Yes."

"Couldn't get back any faster," he apologized.

"Mr. Burton, I am amazed you made it at all. There's not even been mail for these two days past."

"Roads is bad," he conceded, "but I used Mrs. Deveraux's vouchers to change m'horse often enough. Get tired in the mud, ye know."

"Yes." Unable to bear the wait any longer, she could not help asking, "What did you discover at the Blue Bull, sir?"

"Nothin'."

"Nothing? How can that be? Did you not ask?"

"Nothin' to learn. I drank mysel' half under the table, miss, a-waitin' fer somebody to spill. Finally allowed as how they must not get many of the gentry coves."

"And?"

"Said they did sommat—not often, mind ye."

"Did you mention Mr. Fordyce?"

"Uh-huh. Never heard o' him. Last cove was a Smith, and he was gone. They was a-laughin' as to how some mort'd fleeced him."

"A woman fleeced him?"

"Aye—and left 'im fer dead. The cove woke up and wouldn't tell 'em nothin'. Said he fell on 'is 'ead."

"Are they quite sure this Smith was the only . . . er . . . cove lately?"

" 'Cept Master Dominick and Mr. Bascombe. Described 'em both—said Bascombe left light."

"Left light?"

"Wit-out 'is money, miss."

"Yes. Of course. But nobody was found dead?"

"No'm."

She hadn't killed Quentin Fordyce. She hadn't killed Quentin Fordyce. *She hadn't killed Quentin Fordyce.* An indescribable relief washed over her, leaving her unable to think of anything else for the moment. *She hadn't killed Quentin Fordyce.*

"Are you all right, miss?"

"Huh? Yes. Oh, yes!" It was then that she realized he was waiting expectantly. "Thank you, Mr. Burton!"

He shifted from one foot to the other. "Master Dominick said I was to have two quid fer me trouble, ye know."

"Oh. Yes, of course." She'd not even looked in Deveraux's box yet. "One moment while I get Mr. Wilkins to fetch the money."

She did not know what to expect when the footman brought it. Carrying the leather-covered box to a small table, she took the key Wilkins gave her and unlocked it. The hinges were old and stiff, making it difficult to pry open. Finally, after considerable effort, the lid came up, and she could not help gasping. Inside lay a thick sheaf of banknotes, a number of gold coins, and a heavy old ring. There appeared to be a fortune.

"There must be some mistake . . ." She lifted the sheaf of notes and began to count. There was at least a thousand pounds there, more than she could expect to see in twenty years, if not in a lifetime. "Oh, *my*!"

"Druther have the gold," Burton insisted.

"What? Oh." Laying aside the banknotes, she picked up two coins. "Be careful with them."

He doffed his cap and hurried out, ostensibly to show his fellows his money. Anne forced the lid down and quickly locked the small box. "Are you quite certain this is the box Mr. Deveraux meant?"

" 'Give her the box,' he told me, miss."

"Does he . . . ?" She cleared her throat nervously. "Does he always keep so much money in it?"

"Sometimes more. He took some with him when they came for him—said he might need to bribe somebody, I believe." Perceiving that she still stared at the little leather-covered chest, he shook his head. "That ain't nothing, Miss Morland. The Deveraux are rich," he declared. "Nicholas Deveraux left Master Dominick some twenty thousand pounds. And that don't count what came from his grand-fathers on both sides, nor this house neither."

"Twenty thou . . . *twenty thousand? Pounds?*"

He nodded proudly. "Pleasure to serve him, miss. Ain't a pinchfarthing like some of 'em, nor a gamester like old Nick."

She sank into a chair. "What am I supposed to do with this? I cannot keep it in my chamber—I should be afraid to be done in for it.'' But even as she said it, she could hear Dominick Deveraux's voice. *You may use the money in it at your discretion.*

"Miss Morland, nobody's going to steal anything at the Haven,'' Wilkins protested stiffly.

"No, no, of course not. 'Tis just that I do not believe I have ever seen quite so much at once, you understand.'' She looked up at him. "Where *do* we put it?''

"Well, Mr. Deveraux keeps it in the library wall, but he said I was to give it to you,'' he reminded her.

"I should very much rather you put it back into the wall.''

"He said I was to give you the key.''

"Well, I do not mind the key—'tis the money I'd not keep.''

She sat there staring into the fire for several minutes after he'd carried the box out. Over one thousand pounds. Why on earth had Dominick Deveraux done it? *I trust you. You may use the money in it at your discretion.* How did he know she would not take it and run? *I trust you. I trust you.* He could not know. *Take care of things for me.*

"You seen Miss Mitford, Anne?''

"Huh?''

"You seen Miss Mitford? Dash it, but it ain't like you to sit there a-gathering wool, Annie,'' Bertie complained.

"There is more than a thousand pounds in this box.''

"Whose box?'' Baffled, Bertie moved closer. "You ain't been tippling, have you?''

"No.'' She looked up. "Deveraux left me the key to his box, Bertie, and there is more than one thousand pounds in it.''

"Surprised there ain't more'n that. The Deveraux are deuced plump in the pocket, from all I ever heard.''

"He said I was to use it at my discretion.''

"For what?''

"I don't know,'' she answered slowly. "Unless . . .''

"Guess you could buy yourself a dress.''

It came to her then. "Bertie, how soon until the roads are passable, do you think?''

"I don't know." He regarded her strangely. "Look you ain't wanting to tip him the double, are you?"

"What?"

"Take the money."

"Of course nòt."

"Didn't think so. Didn't think I could be that mistaken in you."

"What I want to know is how to discover the best solicitor in Nottingham. Bertie . . ."

"How'm I to know that? No, leave it to Trent, Annie. Dash it, but I don't even like the fellows!"

"It could take days to hear back from Lord Trent. In the meantime, I think we should go into Nottingham, speak with Deveraux, then discover someone to represent him."

"Ten to one, he's got one." When he perceived she was indeed serious, he protested, "Dash it, Annie! Them fellows wants money!"

"We have Deveraux's thousand pounds," she reminded him.

"Look, I was only wanting to find Miss Mitford—thought maybe she'd play cards or toss dice with me, you know. I ain't wanting to get out in the mud." He looked out the window. "Besides, it's raining now. Snow's melting—roads ain't nothing but mudholes!"

"Burton made it in from Southampton."

"When?" he snorted.

"Just now. Besides, you have no business tossing dice with Meg."

He sighed. "You know what, Annie? You are a deuced managing female!"

"I know."

"When was you wanting to go?"

"What time is it?"

"It ain't late . . ." He stopped himself. "I don't know."

"Look."

He drew out his watch and squinted. "Eleven," he mumbled. "And I ain't missing nuncheon for nothing!"

"I can be ready within the hour." She rose. "I wonder

. . . should I wear the green dress or the checked one, do you think?''

"Wear something as can be walked in," he muttered glumly, " 'cause the carriage's getting stuck.''

She made her way back upstairs, her mind racing. As soon as she gave instructions to Meg for Mrs. Deveraux's program, she would get ready. Maybe, just maybe, Meg might even let her borrow a hat to cover her awful hair.

"Annie! Annie!" Meg ran from the bedchamber. "Annie, she's gurgling! Whatever do I do now?''

"Gurgling?''

Anne pushed past the girl and hurried to Charlotte Deveraux's beside. Taking the old woman's hand, she murmured soothingly, " 'Tis Annie-Annie Morland.'' The hand seemed to tighten in hers.

"Her eyes are open,'' Meg said behind her.

"They often are.'' Reaching behind Dominick's mother, Anne lifted her higher onto the pillows. "You are all right, Mrs. Deveraux.''

"Aaaaaahhhhhh . . . aahhhh.''

"What is she doing?''

"She's trying to talk. 'Tis all right, Mrs. Deveraux,'' Anne murmured, trying to keep calm despite the surge of elation she felt. " 'Twill come. Each day you will be stronger,'' she promised. "If you will but keep trying, 'twill come.''

"I thought she was dying.''

"No. She's getting better. I would that I were going to be home this afternoon. Meg, you will have to continue talking and reading to her. And do not be surprised if she attempts making words, but rather if she seems to want something, you must work to understand her.''

"You are leaving?'' the girl demanded incredulously. "Oh, but you cannot! No! I should not know how to go on without you! Annie—Miss Morland—oh, I pray you will not!''

"I shall be back to sup with Mrs. Deveraux—unless the roads are truly impassable.''

"Tonight? But what about this afternoon?''

"Bertie and I are going into Nottingham.''

"No!" the girl wailed. "I cannot!"

"Stuff." Anne leaned over Charlotte Deveraux and said clearly, "Meg will stay with you today. Your son has been taken into custody, and I am going to see a solicitor on his behalf. I shall also attempt to see him, and I will tell him you are much better. When I come back, I will report all I have discovered to you."

"Do you think you ought to have told her that?" Meg asked anxiously. "About Mr. Deveraux, I mean?"

"If she loves him, 'twill give her a reason to get well." She straightened and looked at the younger girl. "When you feed her, make certain she does not choke. Count at least to fifty between each spoon." Reaching to clasp the old woman's hand once more, she squeezed, then released the bony fingers. "Do not worry, Mrs. Deveraux. Your son shall prevail."

She started to leave, then remembered the hat. "As I shall be visiting Mr. Deveraux and then seeking out a solicitor, I do not suppose you would consider lending me one of your hats, would you? I rather think I ought to look as respectable as possible."

"But of course you must! You are welcome to anything I have, Annie," Meg answered sincerely. "I should not know how to go on without you here."

"Stuff, Meg—one does what one must. Otherwise, one must surely perish."

It was not until after Anne had left that Meg settled into the chair again. Sighing in resignation, she reached to pull the covers up to her godmother's chin. It was then that she noted that the old woman's eyes watered. For a moment she wondered if she ought to tell Annie, then decided it did not signify. Instead, she picked up the book Anne had left, opened it, and began to read aloud.

14

Owing to the muddy roads, it took nearly two hours to travel the eight miles to Notthingham, and much of the way Bertie Bascombe fretted about the effect of the mud on his carriage and his cattle. But Anne stared out the window, scarce hearing him, her thoughts on helping Dominick Deveraux. Her hands clasped her borrowed reticule tightly, afraid to set it down for fear of losing the hundred pounds inside.

As she passed the cottages of starving hosiers and weavers, she worried greatly about breaking down. That she was in the area of the great Luddite Rebellion but a few years back did nothing to reassure her. With thousands now on the poor rolls, it would not do to be discovered carrying money.

Even in the miserable weather, there was a commotion at the side of the road, and as they passed it, she could see a stockinger loom being repossessed. She sighed heavily, feeling for the family that stood watching it being loaded onto a wagon. If she were rich, she'd have tried to help them.

Finally, through the misting rain, she saw the town itself, its old castle rising above it, and she could not help recalling the story of how the evil, ambitious Earl of Mortimer had been taken there in adultery with Queen Isabella, the she-wolf of France, nearly five hundred years earlier. Below it, the Trent River meandered past, a gray ribbon threading through the dirty snow.

The carriage turned down a narrow street, passing a row of Georgian terrace houses, winding into the old town. "Have you ever been to a jail, Bertie?" she asked suddenly.

"Lud, no! Don't want to go now, if you want the truth of it, but you got this maggot in your brain—well, I told you what I thought. Leave it to Trent."

"I was just wondering what sort of place it is."

"Ain't anywhere you'd want to be," he declared. "If it was, nobody'd mind going there, don't you know?"

When the carriage stopped, Anne nearly wished she hadn't come. The soot-covered edifice appeared grim and forbidding. When Cribbs opened the door, she clutched the reticule even more tightly, something she'd not thought possible. Bertie jumped down and turned to help her out. Holding the skirt of Meg's checkered gown, she tried to step across the puddle.

"Well, we are here," she said, trying to keep her voice bright. " 'Tis not a pretty place, is it?"

"And we ain't been inside it yet," Bertie reminded her sourly. "Tell you what—we ask around for the solicitor first. Come back later."

"No. We have to discover of Deveraux whether he wishes one."

"Ten to one, he's got one already. If he ain't, Trent'll get him one."

"Come on, Bertie." Taking his arm, she started up the steps. "If you wish, I will do the talking."

"I ain't saying nothing."

Her fingers pressing into his forearm, she steered her reluctant companion to the nearest guard. "Your pardon, sir, but could you tell us if Mr. Deveraux is still held here?" she inquired politely.

His eyes raked over her insolently; then he jerked his head toward a man who sat against the wall. "Ladybird to see Deveraux!"

"Now, see here," Bertie began, bristling. "Miss Morland is a respectable female!"

"Is he here?" she repeated.

"Aye." The other man rose and walked toward them. Addressing Bertie, he asked, "You his relation?"

"No. Name's Bascombe."

"Only his relations get in."

"Mr. Bascombe is the Earl of Haverstoke's heir," Anne told him, "and we are come to see how Mr. Deveraux fares."

His eyes took in her form, then her face, but his manner was impersonal. "And who might you be, miss?"

"Told you she is Miss Morland," Bertie protested.

Anne exhaled, then managed to smile at the jailer. "I am Mr. Deveraux's betrothed," she announced baldly. Beneath her fingertips, Bertie gave a start. Her fingers closed, nipping him in warning.

"I dunno. Will! This lady says she's Deveraux's betrothed!"

Anne felt the blood rise to her face, but she tried to brazen her way in anyway. "Surely you will make allowance . . . that is, after all . . ."

"Will, ask him if he'll see her!"

As the other fellow disappeared, Bertie and Anne exchanged glances. "Make it sound like he holds audiences," Bertie muttered under his breath. "Wish you'd quit giving out about m'father," he added.

"Well, being an earl's son must be useful for something, don't you think?" she pointed out reasonably.

"You got gold?" the jailor asked.

"Well, I . . ."

"Give him the grease," Bertie hissed.

"I beg your pardon?"

"Got to bribe 'em."

"I thought you'd never been in a jail before."

"Ain't. But you got to grease the hogs everywhere, you know."

Aware that the jailer was waiting expectantly, Anne turned away, using her body to shield the contents of the reticule from him, and drew out several coins. Drawing the string closed, she held them out.

"Here."

"Five shillings!" he fairly howled.

"Annie, that ain't enough," Bertie snorted.

" 'Tis all I have," she lied. " 'Tis a week's honest wages, in any event."

"He says he'll see her."

The one apparently in charge slipped the money into his

pocket, muttering he'd get the rest from Deveraux himself. Jerking his thumb toward the door, he ordered, "Take her back."

"I say, but—" Bertie protested.

The jailer spat onto the dirty floor. "Didn't ask for you."

"Miss Morland is a respectable female!" Bertie called after her. "If aught happens to her, you'll answer to me—m'father too!" he added forcefully.

The fellow led her past a row of dirty cells, down a narrow passage, down a stairwell, and her resolve nearly deserted her. "Down here?" she asked faintly.

"Ain't any rats in the daytime," he reassured her. His dirty hand steadied her elbow. "Way's steep," he offered in understatement.

At the bottom was a door, and she envisioned a hellish dungeon behind it. But as the door swung inward, she was surprised to discover a large room. Her eyes darted around it nervously, taking in the cot, the table and chairs, the wine bottles, the chamber pot, and finally the man who stood waiting for her. He was freshly barbered and elegantly attired, and gave no appearance of having suffered in the least for his ordeal.

"Leave us," he ordered curtly, nodding to his valet. "You also, Will," he told the guard. As he turned his attention to Anne, one black eyebrow quirked upward and his mouth twisted wryly. "My betrothed, Miss Morland?"

"Yes, well, I apologize for *that,* of course. When we arrived, we discovered that only your relations could see you. I'm afraid I gambled a bit," she admitted ruefully. "I thought perhaps they might admit your intended." She managed a smile. "Well, you are looking rather well. Much better than I expected," she added lamely.

He shrugged. "I get on. For enough money, they provide whatever I need, and then I win the blunt back over cards. 'Tis tolerable, I suppose."

"I had to bribe my way in here. It cost you five shillings. You, sir, have completely corrupted me," she told him with feeling. "Before I encountered you, I did not believe I had told half a dozen falsehoods in my life, and since, I seem to have done nothing but lie.''

"The resourceful Miss Morland,'' he murmured, moving forward. She backed up a step. He stopped. "What—no kiss? What sort of betrothed are you, my dear? I was rather looking forward to that at least.''

"*Will* you be serious?'' she demanded crossly. "Ever since you left so precipitately, I have read to, bathed, fed, and tended your mother night and day, I have listened to Meg until I have wished her at Jericho, I have been cooped up in your house worrying over what has become of you, and you . . . you apparently have scarce been in jail! And . . . and I have ridden the worst roads in the mistaken notion that you might have need of aid!''

"Annie . . . Annie . . .'' he said softly. He reached for her, and would have drawn her into his arms, but she ducked away. "Annie, I am sorry for this, you know.''

The way he said it made her want to cry, which in turn made her feel utterly ridiculous. "Oh, stuff!''

He let her back up. "I collect this is not a social call, then? That you have not come merely to commiserate with me?'' he murmured regretfully.

"Not precisely. That is, I have come to discuss certain matters with you.''

"Very well, my dear. You behold a rather captive audience.'' His mouth twisted again, this time downward. "Ah, my lamentable memory. I forgot for a moment that you are not anyone's dear.'' He gestured toward the table. "Would you care to sit down, Annie? Alas, but I have no ratafia. However, there is a bit of port.''

"Yes, well, I should prefer to sit and not drink anything, I think.'' As she spoke, she took a chair. Looking away, she apologized also. "I am sorry about claiming a betrothal, you know, but I saw no other way.''

"I assure you I am not repining.'' He took the chair on the other side and leaned his elbows onto the table. For a time he sat there looking at her, saying nothing, thinking she was perhaps the best discovery he'd ever made. Finally, aware that she was watching him also, he smiled. "So . . . what is it that has brought you flying to my side?"

"The money."

"The money?"

"In the box. I should like to engage a solicitor with it."

"Burton's news was not good."

"Oh, no! 'Twas the best mine ears have ever heard, I assure you!"

"Fordyce lives?"

She nodded. "Apparently, though I cannot think how he managed to do it, Mr. Fordyce recovered his senses and refused to discuss the matter at all. And, as he had the foresight to sign in as a Smith, there's none to place me at the Blue Bull." She looked over at him to see the effect of Burton's information. "So you see, I have been a fugitive without reason."

"I'm glad. You relieve my mind."

" 'Tis for you that I should engage the solicitor, sir," she told him, returning to the matter at hand. "I owe you much for all you have done for me."

"Dominick," he reminded her. "Or Dom. Formality will be remarked between us."

"There's no one here," she pointed out reasonably.

"Practice brings fewer lapses—not to mention I should like to hear you say it."

"Can I not call you Deveraux? Dominick sounds so personal."

"Would you like to be called Morland?"

"No. *Do* you have a solicitor, si . . . Dominick?" she asked, determined to pursue her purpose. "I'd know before that horrid man returns."

"I have a man of affairs in London. But he is scarce the sort to represent one in a criminal matter, I suppose."

"Then do you object if I engage one? 'Tis possible he could delay your return to London. And more to the point, 'tis possible that bail can be arranged until your mother is better."

"Annie, I am ready to get this over. I don't mind going to London, you know."

"But she's better! And if you were home to encourage her—"

"She's better?"

"I think so. Her eyes focus now, and she tried to speak. And there is some control to her hands. But it will take time and a great deal of patience ere she regains what she has lost. She needs you, Dominick—she *needs* you!"

He snorted derisively. "You never had that of her, I can tell you."

"What is it that is between you? Your pardon. I should not have asked," she countered hastily. "I do not mean to pry, I assure you."

"Ah, but you do, Annie. There is that female mind in you that either will take me for an undutiful son or will know the tale, isn't there?"

"I don't want to hear it," she insisted.

"There's not much to tell anyway. We do not deal well together, she and I—we never have. When I was a small boy, I thought 'twas because I was bad. I have since realized that she made me what I am, Annie. She did not want me—she had her precious son in Cass."

"Sir . . . Dominick, there is no need—"

"Do you know what my great sin was, Annie?" he demanded. "I look like Nicholas Deveraux—I look like my father! There have been times when I would have ripped this face off for her, Annie—I swear it. But no more."

"You could not help your looks," she murmured. "And it would have been a shame to wish for any others."

"She left him, you know. The year before I was born, she left him and returned with Cass to her family. He was rather indiscreet, you see, and she could not stand his endless parade of lightskirts. Finally, when he brought one home, 'twas the end of whatever she'd ever felt for him."

"How awful for her."

"He wanted her to make the girl her maid, so I am told, and she left him for it." He reached to pour himself a glass of the port. Leaning his chair back, he ran his fingers through his hair, combing it. "The upshot of it was, there was a devil of a dust over it. Her father met my grandfather Deveraux, and between them 'twas decided she had to go back. Nicholas was to give up his bit of fluff in exchange for their clearing his gaming debts.''

"And she went back to him."

"She had no choice. Much as I would she hadn't, I know she had no choice. The devil of it is that I am the result of it." He made no move to touch the port he'd poured. Instead, he leaned back to stare at the ceiling. "Nicholas Deveraux was everything she ever called him, you know—and worse. I am told that about the same time Mother learned of me, she also learned that he still kept a woman in the village. And one in Nottingham. And several in London."

"It made her bitter, I suppose."

"Bitter? *Bitter?* Annie, you know not what bitter is! She left him again, and this time my grandfathers decided that for the sake of appearances, she would return to the Haven to have me. Nicholas, on the other hand, was forbidden to come back except for my christening." Abruptly he leaned forward, and the front legs of his chair hit the floor. "That, my dear Annie, is the tale. Charlotte Deveraux was never a mother to me, and I am not much of a son to her."

"Perhaps it is not too late for either of you," she said quietly.

"You cannot love that which you have come to hate."

"You can pity her."

"She could accept that less than love or hate. You do not know her."

"I know you risked your life to come to see her."

"To what end? She did naught but complain of it."

"She is your mother, Dominick."

Her words seemed to hang between them for a moment; then he looked away. "You give a man naught to save himself with, Annie, do you?"

" 'Tis not his words, but rather his heart that saves," she said softly. She reached out to him, touching his hand where it lay on the table. "I'm sorry—I did not mean to overset you."

He pulled away. "You know what you are, Annie?" he

demanded almost furiously. "You are a damned conscience!"

"I said I was sorry."

"You get into me, and you will not let me go!" He rose, nearly oversetting his chair. "Why did you come?" he asked, his back to her.

"I told you—I'd hire a solicitor to plead for you."

"No."

"But—"

He swung around. "I don't need another mother, Annie. I got myself into this, and I mean to get myself out of it."

"I sent for Lord Trent."

"Damn!"

"I thought you would wish it."

"Well, I don't. I am seven-and-twenty, you know, and I'd not hide behind his coat."

"Well, I'm sorry for that also, Dominick Deveraux!" She felt her own anger rising, but she didn't care. "What was I to think? You asked me to take care of things for you, you know! And you were here, and . . . and I had no way of knowing 'twas like this! I thought you were in a hole some- where, that you would wish out of it!" She rose and started for the door, calling, "Guard!"

"No . . . Annie!" He caught her from behind and held her. "Where the deuce did you get the bonnet?" he muttered. "Cannot see around the damned thing."

" 'Tis Meg's."

His fingers loosened the ribbons beneath her chin, then slid upward to dislodge the hat. Before she could catch it, it fell to the floor.

"You'll ruin it, and I cannot . . ."

Her words died as he turned her around. There was no mistaking the warmth in his blue eyes. His hands moved to cradle her head, and his face blurred before hers. This time, there was no gentle brush of lips against lips. He crushed her to him, and his mouth possessed hers eagerly, shocking her. For a moment she stiffened, then gave herself up to the sheer pleasure of his kiss. Her arms slid around his waist, holding him. She was breathless when he released her.

"Been wanting to do that since I bade you good-bye, you know," he murmured huskily.

She'd behaved like the veriest trollop, and she knew it. Blood rushed to her face, heating it. "Meg's bonnet," she said lamely.

"I'll buy her another—'twas worth the price."

"Time's up!" the guard called through the door.

"Damn," Dominick muttered. He leaned over to pick up the hat, then placed it on her head. His fingers fumbled, making a lopsided bow beneath her chin. "You know, I was wrong earlier—you are deuced pretty."

" 'Tis the hat," she managed, trying not to look at him. "It hides my hair."

" 'Tis you, Annie."

The door opened and the guard said gruffly, "Got to go, miss."

This time Dominick ducked beneath the brim to kiss her lightly. "Until we are met again, Annie," he said much as he'd said at the Haven. "Good-bye, my dear."

She started to follow the guard out, then turned back briefly, "Meg was right, you know—you are volatile, Dominick."

He bowed slightly at that. "At least I am not a dull fellow."

Bertie was pacing the outer room impatiently, but stopped when he saw her. "He all right?"

"Far better than I expected," she muttered.

"You all right?"

"No. We are returning to the Haven, Bertie."

"Thought you was looking for a solicitor. Had it from the keeper as there's this fellow—"

She cut him off. "Dominick Deveraux has no wish to be managed by an interfering female."

"He tell you that?" he asked incredulously. "Of all the ungrateful . . . Dash it, but we swam mud to get here!"

"Well, we are swimming mud back again." She swished past him into the street. "He can hang before I offer anything again." But even as she said it, she knew it was a lie. As her companion handed her up into the coach, she sank back against the squabs. "Bertie, do you think anyone could count me pretty?"

He tripped over her feet and righted himself with the pull strap. "Eh? Why'd you ask a thing like that?"

"Well, do you?" she persisted.

"With or without the hat?"

"Never mind."

He leaned back and looked at her for a moment. " 'Course I do, Annie—almost as pretty as Miss Mitford, in fact."

"Thank you, Bertie," she retorted sourly.

Turning her face to her window, she stared out, seeing not the dirty, muddy street but rather Dominick Deveraux, and hearing not the shouts of drivers maneuvering in the road but rather his voice again. *You know, I was wrong earlier— you are deuced pretty. . . . Been wanting to do that since I bade you good-bye. . . .* And she could not help wondering if he'd meant any of it. Stop it, she told herself fiercely. He was but a rake and a rogue, and no doubt he paid lavish court to every female he met. With that lowering thought she decided that as soon as Charlotte Deveraux showed sufficient improvement, she had to leave the Haven before she lost her heart. She had no wish to be anybody's ladybird. She caught herself again. Well, not a ladybird, anyway, and anything else was about as likely as an offer from the Regent.

15

Charlotte Deveraux improved steadily over the next few days, much of her progress being owed to Anne's stubbornness. When the old woman would not try to help herself, Anne alternately cajoled, pushed, and downright bullied her until 'twas easier simply to do it. It was a clash of wills, Meg told Bertie with awe, that Annie simply refused to lose.

As Charlotte's speech returned, she became more and more reluctant to use it, for her words were slurred worse than a drunkard's, she complained to Annie. As for her coordination, it was poor also, partly because of lingering paralysis on the right side of her body.

Deciding that the time for wholehearted sympathy had passed, Anne gave orders to everyone that if it was at all possible, Mrs. Deveraux was to do for herself. And she meant it. When she fed the woman, she would give her one bite, then make her take the next herself, eliciting a great deal of grumbling.

"Uh . . . uh . . . unnn-fee . . . ling," the woman managed to pronounce.

"You have to learn to do things again," Anne murmured, putting the spoon in her hand again, much in the manner of one dealing with an uncooperative child. "If you miss, I will wipe it up. Now, come on, and when we are done, we shall get you bathed and into a fresh nightrail," she promised. "And then I shall read to you until you are ready to sleep."

The woman's eyes flashed defiantly for a moment; then a shadow of defeat crossed her face. "Ca-aaan . . . ot."

"Of course you can. This *will* pass."

"No."

"Did I ever tell you about Mrs. Cokeham?" Anne asked, knowing very well she had *ad nauseam*. "Well, she was in the same case as you, you know, and within a month she walked. Not well, at first, I admit, but she walked. And before the year was out, she got around quite proficiently with a cane.''

"Don . . . Don't wa-aant . . .''

"Believe me, after a month in this bed, you will positively relish the thought.'' Guiding the old woman's hand, she managed to tip the spoon between her lips. "There. Now 'tis my turn.''

"Staaarve.''

"Not if you do your part.'' Anne dipped the spoon into the custard and carried it to her mouth. "Open.'' Leaning over her charge, she did not hear the door open across the room. "That's better. Here—you will need a drink to wash that down, don't you think?'' She paused, waiting for an answer, trying to force the woman to speak. "Tell me what you want.''

"W-wine.''

"Very good.'' Slipping an arm behind her, Anne raised her and held the cup to her lips. "A small swallow.''

He stood there watching her care for his mother, thinking she had the patience of a saint. He'd been greeted below by nearly everyone in the house, and each vied with the other to tell how she'd saved Charlotte Deveraux's life. And by the looks of it, she meant to win the battle for the quality of that life now. Even as she coaxed his mother, she seemed a restful, caring person. And God knew he needed that. He was certainly tired of the other. He knew he could do a lot worse.

He cleared his throat. "I am come home.''

Anne nearly dropped the cup. Turning in her chair, she tried not to betray the surge of elation she felt. How . . .?''

He crossed the room and leaned over his mother. "Feeling more the thing, are you?''

"No.'' Her eyes sharpened when she saw him. Rolling them toward Anne, she uttered, "A-a-bominable. Tortures me.''

"Somebody ought to.'' He looked to Annie and favored

her with his oddly twisted smile. "You are not the only liar, my dear."

"I beg your pardon?"

"I am released on my word as a gentleman—and one hundred and fifty pounds to the magistrate. He wouldn't take the word of a rogue, you see."

"You bribed the magistrate?" she asked incredulously.

"I posted bond, my dear. I am to travel to London next month, where the matter will be resolved." He reached into his pocket and drew out an envelope. "By the by, this ought to be of as much interest to you as to me."

Mystified, she opened it. " 'Tis from Lord Trent."

"Yes. He rather thought I ought to let you know Ellie was safely delivered."

She scanned the bold handwriting. " 'Twas a daughter named Anne Amelia Caroline," she murmured. "And he says your second, upon hearing of your arrest, has come forward."

"A stroke of luck," he acknowledged, his mouth quivering at one corner. "But do go on, my dear."

She continued to read, then reddened. "Well, I shall not expect you to refine too much on the rest of it."

"The part about what an unexceptionable wife you would make me?"

She dropped her gaze to the floor, fixing her attention on one of the roses in the rug. "Yes."

"My dear Annie, for all that he would do it, I have not the least intention of letting Trent run my life." He turned to his mother again. "Trent has a daughter named for Annie."

"Not for me, surely," Anne protested.

"You certainly impressed him. Full half of that page extols your virtues, my dear."

"I assure you I said nothing to warrant his regard."

"You did not have to."

He was too close to her, too real. "Unless you have a wish to be private with your mama, I should like to finish her meal."

"I'll wait."

"I cannot think you would wish to. I mean, you would have quite enough time to get dressed for dinner ere I am done."

"Can you believe this, Mother? My betrothed cannot rid herself of me quickly enough, 'twould seem. Very well, Annie, but after dinner I shall not be fobbed off so lightly." In full view of his mother, he leaned to peck Anne's cheek. "Buck up, my love," he murmured, grinning.

She sat still as stone until she was quite certain he'd left. Then, aware that Charlotte Deveraux's bird-bright eyes were on her, she hastened to assure her, "Tis no such thing, you know, and I cannot think why he would wish to overset you . . ." Her color deepened with the realization of what she'd said. "That is, I hope you will not think me unspeakably fast, ma'am, but 'twas the only way I could see him in jail. Oh, dear, I am making a mull of this, am I not? Perhaps I ought to tell you the whole. And then you must try harder to help me, for I do not think I ought to stay here much longer."

In the upper hallway, Dominick encountered Meg stealing out of Annie's bedchamber. She glanced furtively one way, then back to him. "Oh! You startled me, sir." As she spoke, she whisked something behind her. A piece of green silk slid to the floor. "Oh, dear."

He bent to pick it up. "You are sneaking cloth from Annie?" he asked, lifting his brow.

"Not cloth precisely." She looked down guiltily. " 'Tis what is left of her dress. We thought . . . that is, Betty and I thought that perhaps in the excitement of your return, she might not note it was missing. And by the time she does, 'twill be quite burned on the trash heap."

"You are stealing Miss Morland's dress? Why?"

"She keeps sewing on it—and 'tis hopeless! 'Tis time she got another. Even Bertie says so," she finished almost defiantly. "But she will not do it. I do not believe she has spent anything of the money you gave her. There—I have said it!"

"You seem to have discovered your tongue, Miss Mitford," he observed dryly.

"I have had to. Now, if you will pardon me, I must get this out before I am seen."

Remembering how Annie had run back toward the Red Hart, he shook his head. "No."

" 'Tis naught but a rag, sir."

"I know. I'll take it."

"You, sir?"

"Yes. What were you going to do when she looked for it, by the by?"

"None of us were going to admit seeing it."

"See that you don't." He reached around her to take the piece of silk. Rolling it into a ball, he started toward his own chamber.

"But—"

"I will tend the matter, Miss Mitford. But do tell Bertie I should like a word with him ere we sup."

Everyone was already down by the time Anne made her way to the dining room. For some perverse reason, she'd taken longer than usual to dress, and she'd even allowed Betty to try her hand at the curling tongs. The result was a riot of short curls that made her feel ridiculous, but by then there was no time to soak them out.

"Oh, Annie—your hair!" Meg breathed when she saw her.

"Perhaps I ought to go back for the cap," Anne decided.

"Oh, no! It looks lovely, doesn't it, Bertie?"

"Looks like that Greek," he declared gallantly.

"What Greek?" Anne asked suspiciously. "I am not aware of any Greek noted for her hair—except Medusa, and I don't believe she was a Greek precisely."

"That's the one."

"My dear Bertie," Dominick murmured with a straight face, "Medusa had snakes growing out of her head."

"That settles it. I am going back for the cap."

"Wasn't Medusa," Bertie insisted. "Can't remember her name, I guess."

"Perhaps you are talking of Medea. Sit down, my dear. You actually look quite fetching," Dominick said, holding her chair for her. "Word of a Deveraux."

"Do," Bertie agreed. "Meant you was like one of them statues."

"I think perhaps you ought to cease complimenting me while I am still speaking to you."

"That's what I like about you, Annie," Bertie declared sincerely. "You ain't one of them females as expects a man to be on ceremony with you."

She sighed. "It would not help if I were. Somehow I cannot imagine you as my gallant, you know."

"Well, I think Mr. Bascombe is quite"—Meg groped for a word—"quite accomplished!"

"You do? Egad." Nearly overcome, he lapsed into momentary silence; then he could not resist asking, "In what?"

"Well . . . that is . . ."

"Knew it was a hum," he muttered.

"You make people feel comfortable around you," she blurted out finally.

"A rare talent," Anne agreed, smiling. "And you have a kind heart."

"Me? No, I don't. Surely not."

Dominick poured the dinner wine into the glasses. Picking one up, he offered a toast. "To kind hearts." As the others drank, he looked to Anne and grinned. "And to my betrothed."

"Oh, Annie!"

She choked and nearly strangled on her wine. " 'Tis no . . . 'tis no . . ." Unable to go on, she fell into a fit of coughing.

"I own, my dear, I should have rather chosen somewhere besides the Nottingham jail for the announcement, but I accept the rather peculiar circumstnaces." He lifted his glass again. "To Annie—a most unexceptionable female," he said softly.

"To Annie!" Bertie cheered. "Best gel I know!"

"To Anne," Meg murmured with a sudden lack of enthusiasm.

Still coughing, Anne grabbed her napkin and ran from the room. Bertie set down his glass and exchanged an uneasy glance with Dominick.

"What the devil ails her?"

"I fear I am about to be jilted. Er . . . if you will excuse me . . ."

"Looked downright queasy, didn't he?" Bertie observed to Meg. "Makes a man not want to cast his hat over the windmill. Ain't seen one yet as did not make a cake of himself."

"Is she engaged to him?" Meg demanded. "She never said a word to me. Whenever did he ask her?"

"Eh?" Bertie shifted in his seat uncomfortably, uncertain what to say. "Must've been in Nottingham."

"Aunt Charlotte is going to be mad as fire," Meg decided, warming to the idea. "You know, at one time I thought Annie was trying to fix your interest."

"Me? Lud, no! Where'd you get a bird-brained notion like that? Just friends, that's all."

Dominick found Anne sitting before the fire in the library, in the very chair where he'd drunk himself into a stupor that night. Closing the door quietly, he crossed the room to stand over her. Ignoring him, she pulled the plaid wool shawl from the back of the chair and wrapped herself in it.

"Annie—"

"How could you?" she demanded furiously. "Betrothed indeed!"

"It seemed like a good idea to me." He grinned crookedly. "So I accepted. Come on, Annie—am I that hard to take? 'Twill be all over Nottingham within the week anyway."

"I never asked you. 'Twas a ruse to get into the jail, and well you knew it." She looked up at him. "You scarce know me, and you cannot even pretend to love me. Besides, everything is a jest to you."

"I admire you more than any other woman I have ever met."

"I want more than that."

"What *do* you want, Annie? What would you have me say to you?"

She wanted to shout that she wanted passion, that she wanted romantic love, that she wanted to be wanted, but she could not do it without sounding like a wicked wanton. Instead she lowered her head and stared unhappily into the fire. "If I told you, 'twould serve no purpose. You would give me my words rather than yours."

Given his experience with all the women who'd cast out lures to him, her attitude was unexpected. "Annie, we should suit. You are good and kind and sensible—all the things I am not. You rein in my wilder impulses," he argued.

"And you think that is what I wish to do?" she asked incredulously.

"You have nowhere to go. You don't want to be a companion to my mother while you wither, and I'd not ask it of you. Let me repay you for what you have done here."

If she had wavered at all, that decided her. Of all the reasons to be wedded, the worst she could think of was gratitude. "You saved me at the Blue Bull, sir, and therefore we are even. And like you, I have no wish for pity."

"Annie—"

"As for having nowhere to go, I think I should finally like to meet my grandfather. No doubt he will not wish to further the acquaintance, but at least I will have seen him. After that, I will go back to London."

"And do what? Feed pap to elderly females? I'll say one thing for you, Anne Morland: you certainly know how to give a man a set-down."

" 'Twas not meant as one."

" 'Twas so taken. Very well, if my suit is repugnant to you—"

"Not repugnant precisely. Not that."

"You will hear no more on that head from me. I had but thought to make life easier for you, that's all. But I can see you think me merely a frivolous fellow."

She heard the door slam behind him, and it was as though every recess of her mind cried out, "Fool" to her. As much as she'd tried to deny it, she'd cherished silly, romantic notions of him almost from the first. If only he'd said he cared for her, she would have closed her eyes and followed him almost anywhere. But he hadn't. He was merely grateful.

Pulling the shawl closer, she drew up her knees into the chair and laid her head on the arm. Whether she wanted to or not, she was going to engage in a good bout of tears.

In the dining room, Bertie heard the door slam also, and he sighed. "Looks to me like we got a lot to eat between us," he told Meg. "Went about it all wrong, you know."

"I beg your pardon?"

"Man ought to determine what she's going to answer before he asks. Saves a lot of trouble for both of 'em, you know."

16

Easing Charlotte Deveraux's dependence on her, Anne set up a schedule for the rest of them to follow, with each taking turns doing things with the woman. She spared no one: Meg was to assist her in relearning to knit; Betty was to assist her at her food and her bath; Bertie, who'd begged off reading in horror, was impressed to play cards; and Dominick was to bring her downstairs twice each day. But Anne still sat with her, practiced her speech with her, and read to her each night before she retired. And the results were promising: Charlotte Deveraux was slowly regaining much of what she'd lost. Anne could see the time coming when she would be more of a hindrance than a necessity.

Yet when she mentioned to Bertie about leaving the Haven, he put her off. First they could not go because it rained, then 'twas the fog, and finally 'twas simply that it was winter. He would not even entertain the notion of taking her into Nottingham to catch the mail. There was no hurry, he told her, particularly since his father had failed to discover him there. In fact, he admitted, the bucolic life was beginning to suit him. He finally had two players in Meg and Mrs. Deveraux he could defeat at cards.

As for Dominick Deveraux, he was polite and pleasant, but never quite the devilish fellow she'd known before his disastrous proposal, or rather the lack of it. He came and went, seeing her when he visited his mother and at meals, but in general his manner was impersonal. Within the week of his second homecoming, Anne was longing for a return of the rogue she'd met at the Blue Bull. Finally, scarce able to stand the stranger he'd become, she took to avoiding him.

A new winter storm blew in, bringing another bout of sleet and snow, isolating the Haven from the outside world, making her suddenly restless. The days and weeks of pushing and coaxing Mrs. Deveraux were taking their toll—she was tired, she was beginning to think herself superfluous, and she was ready to leave. When she saw Dominick she was uncomfortable, and yet when she did not, she could not help wondering where he was, what he was doing. She was, she told herself severely, beginning to feel like a moonling calf.

On this evening, as the snow piled up in the corners of the windowpanes and the fire popped in the hearth, she was particularly low, a condition not improved when Mrs. Deveraux, who was sitting across from her, asked, "Tell me, Miss Morland, do you think there is any hope for Meg?"

Though the woman's voice was still a little slurred, it cut into Anne's own rather morose reverie, startling her. She'd thought his mother dozed before the fire. "I beg your pardon?"

"Do you think he has finally noted her?"

"Who?"

"Dominick." The old woman frowned. "Sometimes, Miss Morland, I think you are not here at all," she chided peevishly.

"I cannot think they would suit," Anne muttered.

Mrs. Deveraux's bird-bright eyes narrowed. "And why not, pray tell me? She is a most biddable, agreeable girl."

"Because he has too much levity. 'Volatility' is perhaps a better word for it." Exasperated, Anne tried to turn the subject away from him. "How long do you think it means to snow?"

"I am sure I do not know, dear. But do you not think perhaps Meg's quietness could civilize him?"

"I don't think a saint could civilize him," Anne managed through gritted teeth. She rose and moved to peer out the window. "By the looks of it, we are snowbound forever."

"I shouldn't think so. Storms seldom last here," Mrs. Deveraux observed. "Indeed, aside from the awful winter of 1814, there is but a week or so when 'tis safe to skate. Now, that year 'twas frozen for a month."

"I was in London then. We had a wonderful frost fair on the Thames, for it was quite turned to ice." Anne sighed regretfully. "I was with Mrs. Cokeham then, and her maid and I went to it. I can still remember the brandy balls and the gingerbread from the stalls."

"What . . . what happened to Mrs. Cokeham?"

"She died. But not from the stroke, of course. 'Twas said that her heart gave out."

"Oh."

"But she was much older than you are," Anne hastened to add.

"I am not young, my dear." It was the woman's turn to sigh. "I have not aged well, you know." Then, "How old do I appear to you?"

"I am not a hand at guessing such things, ma'am."

"About sixty?" Charlotte Deveraux persisted.

"Well, as your son is but seven-and-twenty, I should not think so. And as your older boy would be but in his thirties . . ." Her voice trailed off.

"I am sixty-one, Miss Morland. I was thirty-four when Dominick was born. 'Twas an ill stroke of fate, 'twas what it was."

" 'Tis never quite fair to blame the sins of the father on the son," Anne murmured, forgetting herself.

The woman's head came up, and she stared hard at Anne. "He told you of it, did he?"

"He has no love for his father."

"And none for me." Abruptly the sharpness left her voice. "I gave him no reason to care."

"Perhaps 'tis not too late," Anne said softly.

"No. When one has hated a lifetime, one cannot love."

Despite everything Anne knew of her, she could not help pitying the woman. "If one cannot love, one can understand."

"Do you think I do not understand him, Miss Morland? He is as Nicholas was—he has vexed me at every turn!"

The vision of a black-haired little boy, unloved by either parent, came to mind, routing her pity for the woman. "A child is what one chooses to make of him, Mrs. Deveraux, and if he has not pleased you, perhaps you did not let him," she said acidly. "He was but a child!"

"He was Nicky's son."

"And yours. Tell me, Mrs. Deveraux, did you ever cradle him, did you ever soothe his pain? Did you ever offer him any reason to love?" Anne's voice rose with her indignation. "What did he ever do? Did he bring his lightskirts home? Did he gamble away his substance?"

"He killed three men, Miss Morland," the old woman retorted.

"He did not murder them." Recalling Bertie's defense of him, Anne added, "Perhaps the quarrels were forced on him. Because you hate the father, you must not hate the son."

Charlotte Deveraux's gaze dropped to the fire. "You mistake the matter, Miss Morland," she said low. "I loved Nicky. 'Tis that Dominick has the look of him."

"He is flesh of your flesh!"

"Do you think it serves to shout, Miss Morland?"

Both women gave a start at the sound of his voice, and an awkward silence ensued. As the blood crept to Anne's cheeks, his mother asked calmly, "Did you enjoy the sleigh ride with dear Meg?"

"It did not last long, Mother. Miss Mitford complained of the wind ruining her hair, and Bascombe complained of his boots."

"Oh, you took Bertie, did you?"

"Bertie, despite what you think him, can be counted on to prattle, which rather fills in Miss Mitford's silence in my presence."

"Perhaps you ought to have taken Miss Morland also."

"Miss Morland does not seem to favor my company."

"Are you come to sit with me?"

"I am come to put you to bed."

" 'Tis just as well, I suppose. Miss Morland seems a bit cross today."

"So I have heard."

"Yes, well, now that you are here, sir, I think I shall go," Anne decided. "I have a bit of sewing I should like to do. Meg has given me a gown's length of calico, and I will have need of the dress when I leave."

She rose quickly and started for the door. He moved just as quickly to open it for her, forcing her to duck beneath his arm. "If you were a solicitor, my dear," he murmured as she passed him, "I should take you to London to plead my case."

As she looked up, she caught a trace of his once-familiar smile. "I expect I shall be gone ere that," she murmured, fleeing.

Instead of carrying his mother to bed, he dropped into Anne's chair, and for a time there were no words between them. The gulf was so wide he could feel it, an abyss of pain he no longer wished to cross. Despite everything, or perhaps because of it, he was too mind-weary to fight.

"The girl's got a tongue to her," his mother said finally.

"Huh?"

"You are not deaf."

"No."

"Do you know anything about her family?"

"Miss Morland's?"

"She's the only one with a tongue in this house," she retorted.

"I own I had not noted that," he muttered dryly.

"Well?"

He had no wish to discuss Anne with her, and yet he knew if he did not answer, she would pester the story of Bertie, and God only knew what poor Bascombe would tell her. Stroke or no, she still could think rings around that rattle. He stretched his long legs toward the fire, crossing his boots at the ankle.

"Well," he began slowly, "she's Old Morey's grand-daughter."

"Old Morey? General Morland?"

"It surprises you."

"Well, yes—of course it does." She regarded him suspiciously. "What sort of faradiddle are you telling me?"

"None at all."

"If she is General Morland's granddaughter, what is she doing passing herself off as a nurse?"

"Not a nurse—a companion."

"You have always made me pull every word out of you," she told him sourly.

" 'Tis a lifetime of habit, I suppose."

"Not a becoming one, I am afraid."

"Anne Morland is General Morland's granddaughter, Mother—the product of a legal but unblessed *mésalliance* between Morland's son and Eliana Antonini."

"The opera singer?"

"You've heard of her, I collect."

"Heard of her? I have heard *her*! Your father . . . Well, it doesn't signify."

"If you mean to tell me she was one of his paramours, Mother, I'll not believe it."

"No, of course not. As far as I know, there was never a scandalous word about her. But he took me to hear her once, when . . . in better times," she finished lamely. "I have never heard a better voice in my life, Dominick—never. But she must have made a fortune."

"Nicholas Deveraux was not the only bad husband, apparently. I understand Miss Morland's father gambled the money even more quickly than the Antonini earned it."

"Does the girl sing?"

"She says not."

"A pity. I should have liked to hear her also."

Once again silence lay like a blanket over the room as both stared into the licking flames. Finally he heaved himself from the chair to tower over her.

"I'd best get you to bed, Mother."

"I suppose."

He bent to lift her, sliding his arms beneath her frail body. "You could help, you know."

"My limbs are not what they used to be." Nonetheless, she reached an arm around his neck and held on. As he carried her across the room, she murmured, "I cannot think General Morland would wish her to earn her bread."

"I don't know that he knows it." He laid her down and pulled the covers up to her chin. "But I have written to him, apprising him of her situation."

She looked up at him. "I don't suppose 'twould do any good to say that I shall hate to see her go?"

"Why? You cannot bullock her."

"I am grateful to her."

"I cannot make her stay." He started to leave, then stopped. "You will be pleased to know she refused my suit."

He had the satisfaction of seeing her eyes widen. "Why would that please me? If you cannot like Meg—"

"There was never any question of Miss Mitford, Mother."

He crossed the room, and his hand was on the door when he heard her say, "You never did have any address, did you?"

"Being a Deveraux, I never needed any," he reminded her.

As he passed Anne's door, he could hear her voice rising from inside. "If you do not know what happened to it, and Meg does not know what happened to it, then who does?"

"Lor, miss, but I dunno!"

He knocked. "Is aught amiss, Miss Morland?" he called out.

She opened the door, and he could see she was nigh to crying. "My dress—'tis missing!"

"The cloth? Did you ask Meg?" he inquired innocently.

"Oh, Mr. Deveraux, her's accusing me o' stealing it, she is!" one of the maids wailed.

"I didn't accuse you," Anne insisted. "I merely asked if you'd seen my green gown."

"The one you had of Meg?"

"No—mine." She retreated into the room and sank onto her bed. " 'Tis the first time I have had to work on it in two weeks, and 'tis gone—gone! I cannot think . . . Who? Meg said she would take an oath that she didn't have it, but . . ."

"I told her mebbe the scrapman . . ." the maid said.

"Ten to one, you have but misplaced it," he murmured soothingly. "You still have the calico for your needle, don't you?"

"Misplaced it? Where? Look about you, sir—there are not many places to mislay anything! 'Tis gone!"

"For all you have done here, I'll buy you another," he offered.

"It was mine! There is no other like it!"

"Fetch Betty and get some brandy, will you? Miss Morland is having a bout of hysterics."

"Yessir."

"I am *not* having hysterics! 'Twas all I have that was mine, and 'tis stolen! Stolen!"

He sat down on the bed beside her and patted her shoulder. " 'Tis not a tragedy if it is, Annie. There are a dozen gowns where that one came from."

She sniffed. "I made it. I was repairing it, and at least I would have been able to wear it at home."

"You sent for me, sir?"

"Betty, have you seen Miss Morland's green gown—the one she wore here?"

"No, sir—and so I have told her."

"Here's the brandy, sir." The other girl held out the decanter and a glass.

"I don't need any brandy! I want my dress—is there none here to care that it has been stolen?"

" 'Twas a rag, if you was to ask me," Betty said under her breath.

"Not to me," Anne reminded her. Tears welled in her eyes, and one rolled down her cheek. Brushing angrily at it, she muttered, "Go on—I shall no doubt get over it."

"Take this," Dominick murmured, sliding an arm about her shoulder and holding the glass to her lips. " 'Twill make you feel more the thing."

"I don't want to feel more the thing," she retorted. "Can you not go away and leave me to a bout of tears?"

"No. Come on—just a sip," he coaxed.

Goaded, she took a swallow, and as the fiery liquid slid down her throat, she choked, and the rest of the tears spilled over. He handed the glass to the girl and drew Anne to him. At first she stiffened; then, as his arms closed around her, she leaned into him and sobbed.

"You are just tired, Annie—and 'tis no wonder. Go on, cry. That's the girl."

His body was remarkably warm and solid, his voice oddly reassuring. She allowed herself the luxury of being held, of feeling the strength of him as long as she dared. Then she sat up guiltily and wiped her streaming eyes.

"I've ruined your coat," she said foolishly.

"I've got others."

"I feel positively idiotish, you know. She's right—'twas a rag—and 'tis wrong to take excessive pride in things."

"It was yours, Annie."

Somehow she managed to smile. "I've not forgotten how you went back for it."

"I'm a capital fellow."

"Yes, yes . . . you are." Aware that his arm still circled her shoulder, she nodded toward the two maids, who were watching with great interest. "I am all right now, you know—and this is unseemly."

Reluctantly he released her and stood. "Is there anything you'd like to have—besides the dress, my dear?"

"No. Go on. I am all right. 'Twas foolish of me."

"Not at all."

"I didn't mean to enact a tragedy for you."

"Annie, after all you have done here, you could throw a tantrum and I would not mind it."

"Yes, well, I am not overgiven to tantrums, sir. Indeed, I rarely cry."

"Even I cry, Annie." He patted her shoulder. "Do not worry over the dress, my dear—ten to one, it will show up somewhere."

After they left, she lay down, staring at the ceiling. She'd made a terrible mull of everything where he was concerned. She ought to have accepted his suit and hoped she could make him love her. But he hadn't actually asked, she reminded herself sadly. He'd merely gone along with her rather bald announcement in Nottingham. But he hadn't had to, she argued. No, but perhaps he wished to save her face ere the story got back to the Haven somehow. Or else 'twas either gratitude or pity that she had nowhere else to go.

Right now, she didn't care. If he'd offer again, she'd take him—or would she? No, she conceded regretfully, she would not. She still wanted someone who loved her. The jest of it all, if there was one, was that she now believed she loved him.

17

The snow finally stopped, but the temperature plummeted, freezing the top of it so that at night the lantern light from the porch made it look like a starry fairyland. By day the sun shone through the ice-draped branches, giving them a barren, crystalline beauty. But as lovely as the scene from the window was, to Anne it was fast becoming nature's prison. Like Dominick Deveraux, she was ready to get on with her life.

"There is no need to stay with me, Miss Morland," Charlotte Deveraux murmured from her chair. "I shall be quite all right, and if I should need anything, I have but to ring for Betty." She lifted her hand and awkwardly slipped the yarn over it. " 'Tis slow, but I shall prevail. Much of what I do, Meg must unravel, but it gets better, don't you think?"

"Yes."

"You must not feel I do not thank you for your stubbornness, you know. You wanted my health more than I did."

"In the beginning, perhaps, but not now. Now I think you will not stop until you walk."

"Well, I have no intention of dying like your Mrs. Cokeham." She looked up slyly. "I have hopes of grandchildren."

"Somehow I do not think Meg shares your hopes, Mrs. Deveraux."

"Not as long as that sapskull is in the house," Dominick's mother conceded. "Though how she can tolerate him above an hour is beyond me."

"You like him also, if you will but admit it."

"In small doses."

"There is no accounting for taste when it comes to one's attachments, I suppose."

"No. No, there is not, is there?" The old woman pulled a noose over her knitting needle. "But I should have thought you would have paid more attention to him. When Haverstoke is gone . . ." She let her voice drop off meaningfully. "And there is no question he has a great deal of affection for you. With your brains, Miss Morland, you could get what you wanted of him."

"I do not love him."

"Love!" she snorted. "A bestial thing at best. At least the fool can be led. My son cannot, you know."

"Mrs. Deveraux—"

"Even if I would, I cannot help you get him, I'm afraid," the old woman continued. "I can only set up his back."

"I cannot think you would wish—"

"A *mésalliance*? I don't."

"Mrs. Deveraux, I have no wish to discuss this," Anne declared firmly. "When the snow melts and the weather warms, I shall be leaving."

"I have hopes of doing better with my grandchildren, provided I am allowed to see them, of course."

"I should think that a matter between you and Mr. Deveraux. Though," she could not help adding, "I do not know what you will do should they resemble your son."

"Dark eyes usually prevail, my dear. And 'twas the eyes that most reminded me of Nicky."

"There you are, Annie!" Meg hurried in, breathless from an unseemly run up the stairs. "Do come! We are going skating on the pond! Your pardon, Aunt Charlotte, but do you mind?"

"Not at all. In fact, I fear Miss Morland would like nothing more than to escape me."

"Meg, I haven't any skates, and I'm afraid I have never skated. I should rather read, I think."

"Pooh. You can borrow Betty's. If they are too large, you have but to stuff the toes with cotton wool. I have procured Wilkins's for Bertie. As for not having skated, neither has he. Mr. Deveraux and I shall teach you."

The thought of looking the fool before him held no appeal to Anne. Shaking her head, she demurred. "I am afraid not. Having no decent wrap, I should freeze."

"Betty will find you my warmest pelisse," Charlotte Deveraux spoke up, cutting off her avenue of retreat. " 'Twill be small, but 'twill keep you as snug as anything. Oh, and tell her you'd have the fur muff also."

"I have never skated in my life," Anne repeated more forcefully.

"You can learn! Mr. Deveraux is quite good at it, you know. But do hurry, though, as he has already gone for the sleigh." With that, Meg was off, rattling something about cutting a fine figure on the ice.

"I cannot say I have ever seen her quite so lively," the old woman murmured. Shuddering visibly, she looked up at Anne. "The children from that union will have no color at all, you know. Let us hope that Haverstoke does not mind having two loobies in the family. Well, what are you standing there for—go on! The air will do you good! Besides, when you are gone from here, you'll not see him again."

"I shall no doubt break my neck," Anne predicted direly. Nonetheless, she started for the door. "And my nose will probably run."

She felt the veriest quiz. Mrs. Deveraux's fur-lined pelisse was too small, its sleeves stopping several inches above her wrists, its frog closures straining across her breasts. To protect her ears, her head was nearly swallowed in a shawl, making her look much like a common village woman. And Betty's skates seemed to wobble beneath her feet whenever she tried to stand. Meg, on the other hand, was smartly attired, her face becomingly flushed from the cold beneath the velvet brim of her bonnet, and her voice was animated and excited. For the first time, Anne felt utterly dowdy beside her.

But the others would not hear of it when she suggested she ought merely to watch. Taking her firmly by one hand, his arm about her waist for support, Dominick Deveraux guided her onto the ice, where she slipped and slid awkwardly, all the while holding on to him shamelessly. If there was any consolation at all, 'twas that Bertie whooped and hollered and clung to Meg with an equally unbecoming clumsiness.

The air was raw and filled with smoke from a pondside fire set to warm cold hands. The wind rattled ice-covered branches above, and the skate blades skimmed the frozen surface, chipping it. Yet as Dominick held her upright, his hand in her hers, Anne found it an exhilarating, heady experience.

"You are doing well, my dear," he murmured, pulling her in a great circle around the pond. "But if you can lean slightly forward, you will have better balance."

"If I lean, I shall fall over," she muttered.

"No, you won't," he promised. "Admit it—you are enjoying this."

"Yes," she answered simply. "But I cannot help being afraid."

"Well, 'tis nice knowing you are not a paragon of everything, you know—that I can show to advantage in something at least."

Before she realized what he meant to do, his arm tightened around her waist, and he turned the both of them into a figure eight. As she came out of it, she twisted her body and, throwing all modesty to the wind, grabbed both of his arms, nearly oversetting him. Their skates collided, and for a moment he lost his balance, then somehow managed to right them.

"I'm sorry, but I cannot seem to get the hang of this, I'm afraid," she mumbled apologetically.

"Practice, Annie—it takes practice. When Cass first brought me out, I nearly broke my leg."

"I'm afraid I'm spoiling your outing."

He looked down at her cold-reddened face, seeing the winter sun in her sparkling dark eyes, and he thought her actually pretty. He grinned. "Not at all. It gives me an excuse to hold you."

"Yes, well . . . perhaps I ought to warm my hands over

the fire. This is quite shameless, you know, and I am beginning to feel like an utter hussy.''

"The Annie Morland I know would like the adventure," he teased. "The Annie Morland I know jumped off a roof."

"You wretch—you pushed me."

"The Annie Morland I know shared an adventure with me," he went on, taking both her hands and pulling her across the ice. "Where is she now, I wonder?"

"That Annie Morland was an aberration, I assure you," she managed through fear-gritted teeth. "I am the real Annie."

"I don't think so. Let yourself go, Annie—feel the freedom of the ice beneath your feet. You need do nothing but let yourself go."

"I don't—"

"Be a sprite. The faster you go, the easier it is to stay up."

To demonstrate, he picked up speed, and she found herself flying across the pond, her skate blades skimming the surface. The wind whipped the ends of her scarf, loosening it, and as they made a turn, it blew off. But she no longer cared. Now she was absorbed in the feel of his hands on hers, the closeness of him, and the utter abandon of skating. It was a wild, exciting feeling.

"Atta girl, Annie! You've got it!"

Suddenly he let her go, and she slid ahead of him. For a moment she panicked, then leaned forward, her face into the wind, and skated. He caught up and reached for her hand, stopping her before she hit the edge. The ice sprayed as he toed down.

"Cold, my dear?"

"No." She rubbed at her raw face unconsciously. "No, I enjoyed it very much, sir."

"Dom."

"Dominick, then."

"You are determined to repel all attempts at familiarity, aren't you?" he murmured.

"I shall be leaving next week," she managed, trying not to meet his eyes. "And you are holding my hands when there is no need. A gentleman—"

"I told you, I'm not a gentleman. Rogues please themselves." She glanced up at that, and the warmth in his eyes
disconcerted her. "Annie," he said softly. "I don't—"

"Watch out!" Bertie yelled, plowing into them. They fell
into a tangled heap, all three of them, with Anne at the
bottom. "Sorry," he mumbled, "but I ain't got this yet."

"Damn," Dominick muttered.

"Clunch—always was. You all right, Annie?"

"If you would get off her, she could tell."

"Oh."

"Are you quite all right, Bertie?" Meg asked anxiously.

"Annie broke m'fall," he admitted sheepishly, struggling
to rise awkwardly on the skates.

Dominick rolled to his knees. "Annie?"

"I am all right—I've twisted my foot, 'tis all," she
managed, chagrined by the stab of pain. Looking up at Bertie,
she shook her head. "You are not the only clunch, you know.
I could not get the hang of it either."

"Nonsense. For a first outing, you did rather well,"
Dominick reassured her. Then, realizing that she winced
when she tried to move her leg, he leaned forward to pull
her skirt out of the way. "Where does it hurt?"

She gritted her teeth. "I am all right. If you will but help
me up, I shall be fine." But he was already feeling along
her ankle. "Really, 'tis unseemly."

Ignoring her protest, he undid the skate and began to
massage her stockinged foot. "Here?"

"No." As his hand moved upward, she paled. "There."

"The ankle?"

"I twisted my foot under when I fell," she gasped.

"I say, Annie, but I am sorry!" Bertie insisted. "Didn't
mean—"

"Of course you didn't!" Meg insisted. " 'Twas an
accident. If any is at fault, 'tis I—I let you go."

"If you would but let me up, I'd walk on it, and
perhaps—"

"No, 'tis swelling already," Dominick told her. "We'll
have to carry you in and send for Dr. Rand."

"Help you carry her," Bertie offered contritely.

"She is not a sack of potatoes," Dominick snapped. "Just get me a blanket."

"Well, I didn't—"

"Of course you did not," Meg soothed him.

"I can walk," Anne said stoutly. "Just help me stand."

Meg shook her head. "What if 'tis broken? Bertie will carry you, won't you?"

The slender young man surveyed Anne doubtfully. "Don't know about that—I mean, dash it, Meg, but she's heavy!"

"I beg your pardon?"

"Didn't mean it precisely like that, Anne, but I ain't exactly Gentleman Jim, you know."

Dominick removed his skates. "Just get out of the way, both of you. Can you help at all, do you think, my dear?"

"Just let me stand."

"You ain't mad at me, are you, Annie? Didn't mean—"

"No, 'twas an accident."

Rising, Dominick leaned to pull her up. For a moment she put her weight on the ankle, and felt sick. "I don't know . . ."

"Buck up, Annie," he murmured, lifting her. "I've got you. But you've got to hang on."

It was all of a piece, she decided wearily. She was an utter wreck—and her nose was running. Sniffing, she threw her arms around his neck and turned her head into his shoulder to hide her mortification.

"I've ruined your mother's pelisse," she told him.

"She's got others."

"Just once I should like to show to advantage, you know."

"Nonsense. You show to advantage every day," Meg said. "Doesn't she, Bertie?"

"Eh? Capital girl!" he declared stoutly. "Ain't another like her."

She felt utterly foolish in Dominick's arms. "I can walk," she said weakly.

"Don't be a martyr, my dear," he retorted. "It ill becomes you."

He was strong, his body solid, and as he carried her, she could not help wishing she'd not been quite so definite about repudiating the sham betrothal. He would not bring it up again, he'd said, and he probably did not want to anyway. But still she regretted it. If only . . . Well, it did not bear thinking about. She was leaving, and she would miss his friendship, she told herself stoutly. That was what he felt for her—friendship and gratitude.

"Nothing's broken," Rand decided. "Soak it in salt water and keep it wrapped until the swelling goes down. No doubt 'twill be weaker than the other now."

As the ankle was now twice the size of the other, Dominick surveyed it skeptically. "Are you quite sure?"

"Don't know why you call me!" the doctor retorted sourly. "Seems to me everybody in this house fancies himself a physician."

"How long until I can leave—walk, that is?"

" 'Twill be sore for quite a while, Miss Morland. And 'twill swell from excessive standing, no doubt, for a month or more. But I'd say the worst will be over within the week. Can ride in a carriage, anyway. Just keep it up, you know. Blood runs down, not up."

Later, standing in the foyer with Dominick, Rand cleared his throat. "Been up to see Mrs. Deveraux, you know."

"What did you think?"

"God's miracle, that's what it is, sir—God's miracle. Woman's in a fair way to making a complete recovery."

"Miss Morland would not let her give up."

"Something to be said for that, I suppose, but I can tell you if the brain'd been as bad as I thought it, your Miss Morland couldn't have done it. You got to see the hand of God in there somewhere. Well, got to go—send you a bill round later."

"Post came while you were out, sir," Wilkins announced when Dominick went back inside. "I put everything in the tray."

Tradesmen's bills and a solicitation for aid to the poor. Dominick sifted through them and was about to push the tray aside when he saw it. The writing was the spidery script of the elderly, but there was no mistaking the franking signature in the corner. "Thos. Morland." Old Morey'd answered back.

He ripped it open and read, and the words he'd thought he wanted to hear for her sake were almost painful. Well, that was that, he supposed. She was going to go. He climbed the stairs slowly.

"Here," he muttered, handing the letter to her.

"What . . .?" She looked down and saw the name. "Oh."

"Read it."

Mystified, she opened the folded paper gingerly and began to read,

My dear Dominick,

Am in receipt of your astonishing letter of Thursday last, and must say the news has gladdened an old man's heart. It has been some time now since I asked my nephew Quentin to initiate a search for my granddaughter, and he had concluded the enterprise fruitless.

You must in all case bring Anne to me, for I long to see Charles's daughter before I die. And, if 'tis as you have written, she must of course make her home here. No Morland of my memory has earned her bread as a menial, and I cannot in conscience condone her doing so. Pray tell her I am ready to put the past where it belongs, and I am most anxious to make her acquaintance.

As for your mother, you must tell Charlotte I welcome the news of her remarkable recovery. I myself, though reasonably well for a man of seventy, suffer from gout greatly, else I should come to see her and collect my grand-daughter myself.

If there is anything I can do for you, my dear Dominick, I shall not hesitate to perform the service. Indeed, if you would have me exert what little influence I can bring to bear on your hearing of the nineteeth, I will be most happy to write to the presiding magistrate for you. He is, after all, an old, albeit irascible friend of mine.

I look forward to seeing Anne Morland on the twelfth, as you indicated in your letter. Until then, I remain

Yr. Obedient, etc.
Thos. Morland

"He asked Quentin to find me?" She reread the letter,

then looked up at Dominick. "Mr. Fordyce did not tell me that."

"Odd, isn't it?"

"I'll say. But my grandfather wants to see me," she said slowly. "I never expected this, you know. I thought I should have to confront him."

"Sometimes age mellows one."

"Even your mother."

"Not my mother."

"She cannot cross the gulf she has wrought, you know—'tis up to you to build the bridge across it."

"I do not think I can."

"If I can go to see my grandfather, you can."

"General Morland did not cause you pain for living," he retorted.

"He denied my very existence." She refolded the letter and handed it to him. "Looking at death can change one also, Dom. I think that though she cannot say it, she wishes you happiness."

He looked down at her for a long moment, then sighed. "You cannot fix everything, Annie."

"I know."

"Has anyone ever told you what an incredibly good person you are?" he asked softly.

"Not since my mother died."

"Well, you are quite the best female of my acquaintance."

"Given your first assessment of females, I shall not refine too much on the compliment, sir—Dominick. Besides, I told you, I am quite ordinary."

"Stuff, Annie." He looked down at the letter in his hand. "I could call you a lot of things, and not one of them would be ordinary." He hesitated. " 'Tis the tenth, Annie."

"Yes."

"If I am to have you there, we will have to leave in the morning. Can you travel, do you think?"

"Yes. If you do not mind it, I shall put my foot on the seat."

" 'Tis nine days until my hearing, else I'd write to your

grandfather and delay. But I might not be coming back for a while."

"Trent—"

"I'd not ask him. Nor your grandfather either. 'Tis time the rogue grew up and became accountable."

"They won't . . . ?"

"Hang me? No. Now that Heflin—my second—has come back, there's no evidence to support that. At worst, I shall be bound over for trial. At best, I shall be acquitted. But more likely than either, I shall either be fined or imprisoned a short time for dueling. I may be deluding myself, but I have hopes of a fine."

"Yes, of course."

"Can you be ready in the morning?"

"Well, I've not much to pack. And the calico is nearly ready, so I shall be able to give most of Meg's gowns back."

"Let me buy them for you." When he saw her shake her head, he reminded her, "I owe you far more than a few dresses, Annie. And you cannot say Meg will miss them."

"Somehow it does not seem quite proper."

"Nonsense." There seemed nothing more to say. He shrugged as though it did not matter, then added casually, "You'd best get some rest. I shall be going into town for a while. If you can think of anything you'd like to have, I'll be happy to procure it."

"No."

After he left her, he made his way down the hall to his mother's room. She was sitting before the fire, her knitting in her lap. When she saw him, she held up the square she'd been working.

"Well?"

"She's leaving in the morning."

"I meant my work," she responded peevishly. "But I shall be sorry to see her go, of course. That leaves only Meg."

"A man on his way to jail doesn't need a ninnyhammer, Mother. Besides, Meg has just about brought Bascombe up to scratch."

"I know. No doubt Haverstoke will not thank us for that."

"I don't know. Apparently he merely wishes to see his heir settled, and Miss Mitford's birth is respectable. It might be the making of both of them."

"It might."

"I am going into town. Do you need anything from Miss Porter's?"

Her eyes narrowed shrewdly. "Miss Porter's?"

"I have an errand there."

"Well, I daresay I could use a bit of black velvet ribbon, of course. I should like to trim my black silk walking dress ere we go to London."

"We?"

" 'Tis the nineteenth, is it not? I had the date of Bascombe, by the by. Much as I hate to admit it, I shall miss him also. One cannot get much out of you."

"Mother, I don't think you can travel."

"Nonsense. Besides, when I am carried into the court, I cannot think they will vote to convict you. I can at least do that for you."

"Why?"

She looked down, her eyes fixed on the fire; then she sighed heavily. "Call it conscience, if you wish. I seem to be developing a surfeit of it since your Miss Morland came."

"She's not my Miss Morland, Mother."

"A pity, don't you think?"

"Mother—"

"Oh, I shan't interfere, of course. You are a man grown, Dominick, and ought to know your own mind. I do hope Morey treats her well."

"He will. He wants her. Black velvet ribbon?"

"Yes."

She waited until he was nearly to the door. "I suppose it is too late for us, isn't it?"

He stopped and swung around. He wanted to shout to her that it was, that he could never forgive her, but he didn't.

18

The carriage swayed as the wheels ground into the rutted ice on the road, but neither passenger seemed to note it. Dominick stared silently out his window, not seeing the barren, ice-covered landscape at all. Beside him, Anne sat, her foot propped on the seat across from them. She too could think of nothing to say as her spirits sank lower and lower.

Finally, unable to stand it any longer, she sighed. "I shall miss them, you know—Meg, Bertie, your mother . . . Betty and Wilkins—all of them."

"How very lowering, Annie."

"And you too, of course—that goes without saying, Dom."

That elicited a mirthless chuckle. "Ah, Annie, now that we are nearly there, you can bring yourself to call me by my name."

"I have called you so before," she reminded him.

"When?"

"On the pond."

"But not often."

"No."

"I will miss you also, my dear. 'Tis a rare adventure we have shared together."

"Yes." She sighed again. "Meg says Bertie is about to offer for her."

"I expect so. He asked me if I thought she would take him. I told him I didn't think she would pass on the chance to become a countess."

"There is more than that, I think—I think she has a very real affection for him."

"He is probably the only person who can make her feel intelligent," he observed dryly. "Though I expect their brats will look positively anemic—there's not an ounce of color between them.''

"Odd—that's what your mother said." It seemed unreal that they could be spending perhaps their last hour together, and yet they sat speaking of the most mundane things. "How much further?" she asked uneasily.

"Not above a couple of miles. Why?"

"I just wondered."

"You ought to be happy, you know. Your grandfather does want to see you."

"I am," she said without enthusiasm.

"Afraid, Annie?" he asked softly.

"No, of course not . . . well, perhaps a bit," she admitted, smiling ruefully. "I mean, he was a general, you know."

"I've met him—he came to Cass's funeral. He's a trifle overbearing, a bit gouty, but on the whole quite decent. If you can charm my mother, you ought not to have any trouble with him."

"I wasn't aware I'd charmed your mother. There were times when I thought she despised me."

"No. She was sorry to see you go."

"Soon you will be alone at the Haven with her."

"I suppose."

"You can deal with her."

"I hope so. If I cannot, I mean to send for you."

Hope flared briefly in her breast, then faded. She was a friend to him, nothing more. "Yes, well, you will do all right," she said lamely.

"Annie?"

"What?"

"You know you are always welcome, don't you?"

"Yes. And I shall always be grateful to you."

For a moment his blue eyes studied her face, sending a thrill through her. "I don't want your gratitude, Annie. If there is any of that, it ought to be on my side."

"I am sorry about that night in the library, Dom," she ventured.

"Which one?"

Somehow she could not bring herself to tell him that she

had been mistaken, that she would take him on any terms. If only he would offer again, but it appeared now he would not. "Both of them," she said finally.

"So am I—particularly the last." He looked out the window again. "I was wrong, my dear."

"About what?" she asked, holding her breath.

"We are arrived."

The house was imposing, a great yellow stone building with a broad Greek porch across the whole front. And at either side of the drive, a row of stone lions stood sentry. Her grandfather must have managed to amass a fortune.

The front door swung open almost before Dominick could lift her from the carriage, and an elderly gentleman hobbled out. "Don't stand there, Deveraux! Present me to the gel!"

"Annie, Thomas Morland—your grandfather." He turned to the old man and managed a smile. "Anne Morland, sir."

Thomas Morland peered at her from beneath heavy brows as he took her hand. "Pretty little gel, ain't you? Must look like her, 'cause my Charles was a big buck. But you got his hair—I can tell that."

"How is that, sir?"

"Never lay down."

She wished she hadn't asked. "Oh, of course—I should have known. Mama's was black, after all."

"Well, ain't no use freezing out here when we can coze by the fire, is there? You got trunks?"

"I have but the clothes on my back, I'm afraid."

"Don't matter—buy you a passel of 'em, if you was to want. Come on in—Billings has got rum punch! Ain't what I'd give you every day, you understand, but dammit, this is different! Billings! Billings! Come meet m'granddaughter, Miss Morland. And fetch Quentin—I got a surprise for him!"

"Quentin is here?"

" 'Course he is! Run off his legs—had to come crawling to me. Put him on an allowance, you know." He looked across to Dominick. "M'sister's boy—couldn't let him starve, after all."

"Oh, dear."

Dominick's arm supported her. "You have nothing to fear

of him. Come on, lean on me. Don't put your weight on the foot.''

"Fear? 'Course she don't—her cousin! Quentin! Quentin, where are you, boy? Come on down!'' he shouted up the stairs. "What's the matter with her foot?''

"She hurt it skating. Just a sprain—that's all.''

"Well, get her in and sit her down. She don't have to do anything around here—got plenty of servants to wait on her. Quentin, where the devil *are* you?''

Quentin Fordyce leaned over the railing above and nearly lost his balance when he saw her. His face paled visibly; then his expression went bland. "Coming, Uncle.''

The general did not let him get down the steps before he said to him, "Knew it wasn't like you said—knew she had not fallen from the face of the earth! Come on—got to meet Anne! Got Quality, I can tell, ain't you, my dear?'' he added to her.

There was a reluctance to Quentin Fordyce's walk as he approached her. Nonetheless, he bowed over her hand. "Er . . . Anne, is it? Charmed, my dear.''

She wanted to snatch it back, but managed to merely murmur, "Mr. Fordyce.''

"Here, now—'tis Quentin, ain't it? Go on—help Deveraux get her to a chair.''

"Yes, sir.'' His sickly smile frozen on his face, her cousin said, "I am glad to discover that you are alive, Coz.''

"I could say the same about you. And I assure you I have quite enough help.''

"Yes, well . . . you two can acquaint yourselves more later. Right now the gel's nigh frozen, and I daresay Deveraux is also. You know Dominick Deveraux, don't you, Quen? Particular friend of Anne's—found her for me.''

"Dominick Deveraux? The . . .'' He caught himself. "Your servant, Deveraux.''

The old man herded them into a large reception room. "Look at the place, my dear,'' he told Annie proudly, "'cause it's going to be yours.''

"Mine? Oh, but I—''

"Told Quen I was wanting to find you—got no heirs, you

know, 'cept him, and he don't count now. Oh, mean to do right by him, but dash it, you are Charles's gel!''

"I see," she said faintly as Dominick eased her into a seat before the fire. He turned to find a stool for her foot.

"If you don't like the place, you can fix it up to your liking, my dear. Since your grandmother died, I ain't done much to it." The general started to putter at the punch bowl. "If 'tis too strong, we can water it down," he said, his back to them.

"Miss Morland," Quentin whispered desperately, "I pray you will forget—"

"Eh, what's that?" the old man asked sharply.

"Nothing, Uncle."

"You viper—you miserable viper," she hissed at him.

"Viper? What's this about vipers?"

"Wipers, Uncle—Miss Morland is wishful for something to wipe her feet on." There was no mistaking the miserable appeal in his face. "Ain't that so, Anne?—Miss Morland, that is."

"Anne. Don't want you two on ceremony." The old man carried a cup of steaming punch to her. "There—just the ticket for the foot—use it for m'gout all the time."

"Thank you."

"Deveraux. You staying to sup, ain't you?"

"Er . . . no. I have to return to the Haven rather quickly. There are matters to be attended ere I go to London."

"Oh, yes—forgot that. Ten to one, it'll blow over. Nasty business, though. Daresay Charlotte ain't too pleased by it."

"No."

"She'll get over it. Women do, you know—soft creatures, all of 'em. Well, don't stand there, Quen—get her something to wipe her feet on!"

As Quentin left, Dominick followed him into the hall. "A word with you, Fordyce."

The young man began to shake. "What?"

"About Miss Morland."

"What about her?" he asked hollowly.

"If you harm one hair on her head, if you so much as think—"

"No . . . no, of course not. Won't do any good now anyway. Don't know what came over me."

"Greed, Fordyce. Greed."

Quentin licked suddenly dry lips. "I wouldn't have hurt her—just wanted to make her marry me."

"Well, don't. For if I hear you have suddenly eloped with her, I swear I will make her a widow—do you understand me, Fordyce?"

"Perfectly. And I assure you, I have not the least intent." As he spoke, his hand crept unconsciously to his temple. "Anne Morland is a virago—I should go to debtors' prison first."

"And if aught unpleasant should befall her, you'll not live to spend the money—do you understand that also? You'll go the way of Beresford and the others."

"Ain't going to touch her—I swear it. You won't tell on me, will you?"

"No. I've a notion the old gent is making you pay already."

"Deveraux! What're you doing out there?"

"Explaining to Fordyce about Miss Morland's foot."

Returning to the room, he approached Anne. "I really have to go, my dear. Suffice it to say, if you ever have need of me, I am but a letter away."

"But . . . 'tis so soon." She cast about for the means to hold him, to make him stay. "I cannot get up the stairs, and—"

"Quen—"

"I'll take her," Dominick offered quickly.

"Billings!" the old man bawled. "Get Mrs. Farrow, will you? Got to get the gel to her room!"

The bedchamber shown them was far more elegant than Mrs. Deveraux's even, with ornately gilded ceiling, thick rug, richly polished dark furniture, and a high poster bed. Anne looked around her, thinking she'd gone from a cubicle in Mrs. Philbrook's attic to this, and she still wanted to cry. Her lower lip trembled as Dominick eased her into a bedside chair.

"God keep you, Annie," he whispered, bending to brush

his lips across her cheek. "For a little while, you brightened my life."

Her throat ached and her eyes were bright with brimming tears. "And you mine, Dom. Ere I met you, nothing exciting ever happened to me."

"Good-bye, Annie."

She wanted to throw her arms around his neck, to hang on to him, to tell him she loved him. But he drew back and smiled crookedly at her. Lifting her chin with his knuckle, he murmured. "I'll write—word of a Deveraux."

It was not until he'd gone, until she heard him talking to her grandfather in the foyer below, that she noticed the box on the bed. "What's that?"

"Mr. Deveraux's coachman carried it up, miss," the housekeeper told her.

"Whatever . . . ?" Anne managed to hobble to the bed. Lifting the lid, she peered into the box, and her heart nearly stopped. "Oh . . . *my!*"

There lay her green silk dress, but there was not so much as a rip or a spot on it. She lifted it out gingerly, admiring it. Every stitch seemed to be in place. A paper fluttered to the floor. The housekeeper bent to retrieve it, handing it to her.

With shaking fingers Anne read the bold, masculine script.

Dearest Annie,

Mrs. Porter could not repair your gown, so I asked her to copy it as best she could. I think you will be pleased with the result. I pray you will wear it in health and think of me.

I'm sorry you chose not to reform this rogue, but I understand. Suffice it to say that I think I have loved you from the first, and that I always will. If you ever have need of anything, you have but to ask it of me.

Ever yours.
Dom

She stared, scarce believing the words on the page, and then the green dress slipped from her nerveless fingers to the rug at her feet. He loved her? He loved her!

"Dom! Dom! Wait!" Hopping on her good foot, she

managed to get into the hall. "Stop him—will somebody *please* stop him? Dom! *Dom!* Wait!"

"Who? Deveraux's gone, Coz," Quentin Fordyce answered her.

Grasping the stair rail, she half-hobbled, half-tripped down the stairs. "You don't understand—he cannot go!"

"What the devil . . . ? Get a hold of yourself, Coz. Here . . . you are going to fall."

"What ails the gel?" the general demanded, coming back into the foyer.

"Hysterics," Quentin muttered.

"Mr. Fordyce, if you stop him, I'll never say a word—I swear it," Anne cried. "Please!"

"Glad to." Thrusting her into her grandfather's arms, he ran onto the porch, yelling, "Deveraux! Deveraux! *Deveraaaaux!* Damn!" He turned back to her. "He cannot hear me, Coz."

"I've got to stop him! You don't understand!" Pushing past both men, she forgot the awful pain in her ankle and ran out into the yard. "Dominick! Dominick! Dom! Wait! Wait for me!" she shouted.

"Gel's ticked in the nob!" her grandfather snorted. "Here now, missy!"

"No!"

She cut across the yard, tripping and falling, as the carriage made the turn. Suddenly it stopped, and the coachman hopped down to confer with his master. The carriage door opened.

"Dominick!" She waved frantically. "Dom! Over here!"

He was running across the snow-covered yard, jumping the drifts. "You little fool!" he shouted when he reached her. "Get off your foot!"

"Oh, thank God you are come back!" She gulped, trying to catch her breath, and threw herself into his arms. "For a moment I thought I should not have a chance to reform a rogue," she gasped.

"What? Annie, what the deuce . . . ?"

"I love you too, you see."

"Oh . . . Annie." His arms closed around her, and he held her tightly. " 'Tis a lifetime task, I fear."

"I shall relish it."

"I don't expect to go to jail, but—"

"If you do, I shall wait for you."

He kissed her thoroughly then, and there was no question she returned the gesture wholeheartedly. They stood locked in each other's arms until the general and her cousin managed to cross the yard to them.

"Damme if I know what to make of this," the old man muttered. "Here, now, gel, enough of this—are you going to live here or not?"

"I shall visit often," she promised.

Dominick lifted her into his arms and started back toward the house. "I suspect Mother will wish to plan the wedding," he told her fondly. "And then I should like to take you to Italy, my love—to Milan."

She turned her head into the soft wool of his coat and snuggled against him. "One of these days, Dominick Deveraux, I am going to show to advantage. My hair will grow, and I will have a gown that is neither dirty nor torn, and—"

"I like the way you look, sweetheart."

"I shall never be a beauty, you know."

"Who wants one? Eliana Antonini's daughter is quite good enough for me." Looking over at the old man who labored to keep up with them, he grinned. "Wish me happy, sir."

"Damme if I don't, sir! Aye, you are a rogue and rascal, but I always did like you. Come on, Quen—got to order up some more punch to celebrate! Ain't every day a man gets a granddaughter and a husband for her all at once, you know. Damme if I won't travel to the Haven for the wedding—be good to see Charlotte, come to think of it."